FRANK BURGESS

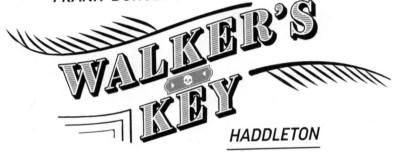

HADDLETON

[signature: Frank B. Haddleton]

ONION RIVER PRESS

Burlington, Vermont

Onion River Press
191 Bank Street
Burlington, VT 05401

Publisher's Cataloging-in-Publication Data
Names: Haddleton, Frank B., author.
Title: Walker's Key / by Frank B. Haddleton.
Description: Burlington, VT: Onion River Press, 2019.
Identifiers: LCCN 2019940332 |
ISBN 978-1-949066-23-4 (pbk.) | 978-1-949066-25-8 (ebook)
Subjects: LCSH Brothers--Fiction. | Family--Fiction. | Fathers and sons--Fiction. | Murder--Fiction. | Gay men--Fiction. | Saint Petersburg (Fla.)--History--Fiction. | Florida--History--Fiction. | Detective and mystery stories. | BISAC FICTION / Mystery & Detective / General | BISAC FICTION / Historical / General
Classification: LCC PS3608.A268 W35 2019 | DDC 813.6--dc23

Author Photograph by Brian C. Jaffarian
Designed by The Image Farm, Middlebury, VT

Printed in the United States of America

Thanks to my grandmother, Constance Flanders Walker, for afflicting me with her passion for family history, for never telling anyone a damn thing about the fate of her husband's father and grandfather at Tampa Bay, and for leaving behind just the right clues to suggest that there was an amazing story which I needed to unearth and turn into a novel. Thanks to my mother, Constance Walker Haddleton, for her unconditional support and for never throwing anything out, including various seemingly worthless treasures most people would have discarded immediately. My eternal gratitude goes to Christian Draz, Ed and Bertha Johnston, Ruth Perry, and Florence Williams, for reasons only they could understand. Thanks to Virginia Wood, for being the earliest and most persistent fan of my writing, beginning all those years ago at Charles River School. Thanks to Greg Thornburg for accompanying me on my visit to Indian Hill, and to Alden Clark for accompanying me on my visit to Egmont Key. And to Norris Brown, for encouraging me in my historical research and writing, "thanks a lot!" Thanks to Freeman Scott for appearing in my consciousness by some mysterious method and telling me his part of the story. Thanks to Willie Docto, Alice Edwards, Dana Isaacson, Sheila Trask, and Richard White for their encouragement and valuable input after the first draft of this novel emerged. Thanks to Jason Wurtsbaugh for his eagle eye. Thanks to Micke Lindström for his perfect image of Walker's Key. Thanks to Rachel Fisher and Matt Heywood for their work in getting this novel into print. Not of least importance, thanks to Brian Jaffarian for everything in my world. Without all of these loving, kind, generous, patient, thoughtful souls, and many others I have omitted by mistake, this book would not exist. (You see, it really isn't my fault.)

For more information about the actual events that inspired this story, please visit **frankhaddleton.com**.

Walker's Key

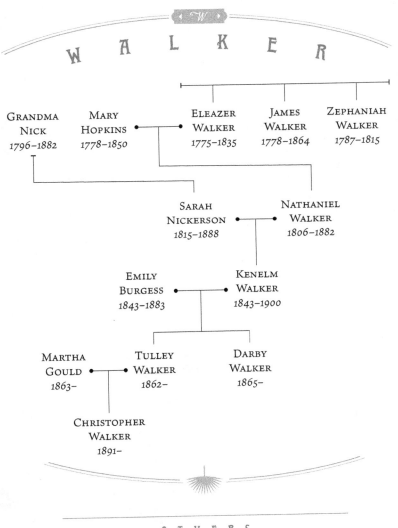

WALKER

| GRANDMA NICK 1796–1882 | MARY HOPKINS 1778–1850 | ELEAZER WALKER 1775–1835 | JAMES WALKER 1778–1864 | ZEPHANIAH WALKER 1787–1815 |

SARAH NICKERSON 1815–1888 — NATHANIEL WALKER 1806–1882

EMILY BURGESS 1843–1883 — KENELM WALKER 1843–1900

MARTHA GOULD 1863– — TULLEY WALKER 1862–   DARBY WALKER 1865–

CHRISTOPHER WALKER 1891–

OTHERS

FREEMAN SCOTT 1787–1881

ANDREW BEAUMONT 1830–

HETTY HOWES 1845–

REV. WILL DYER 1864–

MICHAEL CHAMBERLAIN 1862–

BEN McLAUGHLIN 1846–

JOHN POWELL 1862–

To the Lighthouse

Monday, July 23, 1900

Darby Walker looked up from the deck of the boat just as the first rays of the morning sun brushed the east-facing brick facades of the commercial structures nearest the shoreline. Beads of sweat from physical exertion had just begun to form on his tanned forehead and beneath the sun-bleached hair on his forearms. The realization that he might never return after this morning's trip caused him an almost unbearable sadness. Grandma Nick and Freeman Scott had warned him that something like this would happen eventually. But it didn't matter whether or not he had seen it coming, or what price he now had to pay. Darby had obligations to fulfill.

Dawn was breaking at St. Petersburg, a twelve-year-old town exploding along with the rest of Southwest Florida as the result of the extension of the rail lines, the growth of the citrus and cattle industries, the recent discovery of large quantities of phosphate, and the creation of tourist destinations for wealthy northerners. Two piers extended eastward into Tampa Bay from the shore. On the Atlantic Coast Line Railroad Pier at the foot of First Avenue South, trains could pull right up to the large vessels alongside the pier to load and unload freight in and out of the area. This is where the larger sailing vessels and steamships would dock. Three blocks to the north of the Rail Pier, the Electric Pier, not quite as long, reached out into the water at the foot of Second Avenue North. It served several smaller businesses and vessels.

A small, square shed stood two-thirds of the way out on the Electric Pier. A wooden sign mounted to the side of the shed stated in plain letters "Walker's Ferry Service." Below this sign, a large piece of cardboard announced in hastily painted lettering "Closed this week due to a family emergency. Please come back soon." A few other sheds stood on the pier, and two dozen other vessels of various kinds and sizes floated alongside the pier at different points, including several sailboats associated with a boat livery.

The *Shooting Star*, Darby's forty-foot steam-powered launch, lay impatiently just below the Walker's Ferry Service shed. She was bobbing in the choppy water, a strong southerly wind pushing her against the bumpers hanging down between her port side and the pilings of the pier. The heavy, wooden boat made squeaking and grinding noises as she collided repeatedly into the rubber. Darby, a handsome, lean, bearded man in his mid-thirties, repeatedly bent, lifted, and reached, loading fuel into the *Shooting Star's* firebox.

At this early hour, there was no other living soul on the Electric Pier. But then Darby noticed a man making his way out the pier toward Darby's shed. Even from a distance, Darby spotted the man's generous belly and clerical collar.

Right on time. William Dyer was the perfect person to see him off.

"Darby!" the Reverend shouted, approaching the *Shooting Star*. "Good morning, my friend!"

"Reverend Dyer. Good morning."

After several more paces, Will stood directly above the *Shooting Star*. Close proximity made shouting no longer necessary. "Darby, with all the time we just spent together working on the service, surely we're beyond formalities. Please call me Will. You may call me Reverend Dyer at church services, if you must."

"Okay. Will it is. Of course, that means I will probably never again call you Reverend." Darby smiled up at Will, who smiled back.

"I know. You've made it clear. The god you worship is the sea. I understand that. Your daily swim is more church than many of my parishioners get." Will paused. "But what on earth are you doing out here at this hour, Darby? You're not really thinking of leaving the pier now, are you?"

"Yes, I'm planning to set out as soon as I get the steam up in the boiler."

"Isn't it a bit rough today out on the bay?" asked Will, as he looked out at the dark, menacing waves.

"I know the bay, and I know the weather. We had a trough of low pressure pass through last night, but it's now all but gone. In the time it takes to get the steam up, the wind will be wrapping up, and the waves you see now will begin to die down."

Darby could tell that Will was not convinced that setting out from the pier right now was anything close to a reasonable proposition.

"How long will it take to get the steam up?" Will asked.

"About twenty minutes."

"I see," said Will. "But it's hardly past six o'clock! I don't suppose you have any deliveries or special passengers at this hour. Surely nobody is headed out to Egmont Key yet. Are you going on some sort of adventure?"

"I'm not sure I'd call it an adventure. A misadventure, more likely."

Will stood patiently and watched Darby as he continued to prepare the *Shooting Star* for an outing.

"I would love to go out on a boat ride. May I come with you?" Will finally asked, studying Darby.

Darby knew that going out on a boat under the present conditions would be an entirely unpleasant experience for the minister, and he knew that the minister was well aware of that. "Look, Will, we both know why you've stopped to talk with me. You're worried that I'm overwhelmed. I appreciate your concern and your kindness, but I'm managing well enough. You're more than welcome to come aboard for a few minutes while the steam is building, but I'm afraid that I can't take anyone with me this morning. Regulations for steam-powered vessels require that whenever there are passengers there must also be an engineer aboard. I could lose my captain's license if I were caught violating the regulation. I gave my engineer time off and he's gone out of town."

As he said this, Darby reflected on the dishonesty of his response. He was not representing the regulation in question correctly, omitting an applicable exception, but he imagined that Will would have no idea about such things. More important, Will would be shocked by the emotional struggles Darby had been through in recent days, and even more shocked at what Darby was planning. Darby couldn't possibly discuss any of it with him.

Darby extended his hand to Will, who stepped down the gangplank and onto the gunwale boarding mat. Darby motioned to the bench on the starboard side of the *Shooting Star*, where they both took a seat.

"You know," said Will, "I've always wondered how you happened to decide to run a ferry boat."

Darby was quite sure the good reverend had never, ever wondered that. But Darby knew that Will was a decent fellow who was just trying to make Darby feel comfortable.

"Hmmm," said Darby, "That's a long story, but I'll give you the short version. I've been around boats since I was a kid back at Cape Cod. After I finished high school I worked with Dad on his fishing schooners and, more recently, on the steamboats he captained. Ten years ago, when Dad took the ship pilot position at Egmont Key and my brother became the lighthouse keeper across the bay, it seemed the right time for me to pursue something I've always dreamed of. My mother named me after one of our immigrant ancestors, Darby Field. He had one of the first ferry services in America. Starting in about 1637, he ran a ferry service across a bay near Portsmouth, New Hampshire. I always wanted to follow in my namesake's footsteps, or, more to the point, in his wake."

"That's wonderful. There's something almost poetic in your story. Most people have no idea what their ancestors were doing that long ago."

"I'm sure. My mother's fascination with family history was unusual. She was also a bit superstitious." Darby paused. "You know, my mother would always tell me that she never worried about me being on the water, even though her family had lost an unusually high number of men to the sea. She said that when she was carrying me, a fortune teller advised her that I wasn't going to die at sea. She believed that this fortune teller could see such things. I don't suppose that you put much stock in what fortune tellers say, do you, Will?"

"The Lord works in mysterious ways. I can't claim to understand all of it. However, it would surprise me very much if there was any merit to fortune-telling beyond its entertainment value."

"It would surprise me, too."

A moment passed.

"All right, we both know that nobody needs to be ferried anywhere at this early hour, so where *are* you going?"

Looking at Will, Darby slowly pulled his thumb and forefinger through his neatly trimmed beard. Darby had to be careful how he responded. "Here's the story. It turns out that my brother is taking our loss far harder than I am. As you know, his wife and son went back to New England in June, so he's had to deal with the Egmont Key tragedy all by himself. Tulley has seemed even more depressed every time I've seen him since the tragedy. I'm very worried about what he might do."

"I can understand your concern. Does your brother have any close friends he can turn to right now?"

"What do you think? You met him at the funeral service. I'm sure you observed how he interacted with those who came to pay their respects. What did you see?"

"Okay. I think I know what you're getting at."

"Tulley's always been ill at ease around strangers, and awkward even with people he knows. It's hard to have a normal conversation with him. Unless he's deeply interested in the topic at hand, he doesn't ask any questions and he generally gives only one-word responses."

Darby paused. "He doesn't *intend* to be unfriendly. And he certainly has his strengths. He's surprisingly intelligent. He's the best chess player I've ever known. And in a single day he could take apart the entire engine on this boat, or any engine, and then put it back together so that it works better than it ever had."

"Don't worry. I know you wouldn't bad-mouth your brother. Your description of him doesn't seem unfair or malicious."

"Just before my mother died—I had just finished high school, so this was quite some time ago—she made me promise that I would always watch out for Tulley. She understood that he couldn't completely manage on his own. I promised my mother that I would do my best to make sure Tulley would be all right."

"You're a good brother."

Darby continued. "Thank you. Right now, Tulley is all alone at Walker's Key. On occasion, someone from Gulf City stops in to see him, or somebody who is exploring the coast will happen upon his place and say hello. Tulley regularly sails up to Tampa to pick up supplies or sell oysters he's harvested. Other than that, he's all alone. He's never been a person to reach out to others. After the Egmont Key tragedy, I asked him to come to St. Petersburg and stay with me, but he wouldn't. He said he belonged where he was."

"You're heading across the bay to Walker's Key to check on Tulley right now? Couldn't it wait a couple of hours until the weather's better?"

"No, Will, I'm afraid it can't wait. Tulley's lighthouse went dark last night. In all the years he's been at the island, this has almost never happened. He may be in urgent need of help. I've got to get over there as quickly as I can." Darby looked at the pressure gauge on the *Shooting Star's* boiler, which was getting close to where it needed to be. "I'll be heading out in just another few minutes."

"You really won't let me join you?"

"No, but I appreciate your kind offer."

The attention of the two men was pulled to a woman in her mid-fifties running up First Street toward the pier. Dressed in nothing more than a nightgown covered far less than respectably by a Macintosh, her arms were flailing and her Macintosh flapping. She looked like a total lunatic. She was shouting but too far away for them to make out the words.

Ye gods and little fishes! Darby thought.

He had gone to considerable lengths to avoid this woman. After waking thirty minutes earlier, Darby had carefully arranged the pillows under the quilt on his bed so it would appear that his sleeping body still lay there. "Appearances are often deceiving," Darby had said to himself as he had arranged this illusion, repeating a favorite expression of his father and of his grandfather. The seemingly crazy lady now running toward the pier was none other than Hetty Howes, the owner of the house where Darby was staying, the very woman he'd been trying to dodge. She had obviously not been fooled by a few pillows stuffed under a quilt. Darby had to think fast. "Say, Will, I need you to do something for me," said Darby. "Can you look inside the large box in the wheelhouse and see if you can find my ship's log? I'll look around for it out here. I don't remember where I left it."

"Of course," said Will, and then he got up and went into the wheelhouse.

While Will was engaged in that diversion, Darby rushed to the bow of the *Shooting Star* and untied the bow line. He then darted to the stern and untied the stern line. Though she was rising and falling on the disturbed surface of the water, the *Shooting Star* was nearly pinned against the pier by the southerly wind. She was in no danger of drifting away from her place at the pier, even without being properly secured to it.

Just as Darby finished untying the lines, Will emerged from the wheelhouse.

"Sorry, Darby, it doesn't seem to be here."

"Okay, thanks. I must have left it at home."

Then the crazy lady in the nightgown and Macintosh—a lady Darby knew wasn't really crazy at all—arrived at the shed, breathing hard from running.

"Darby!" she shouted between breaths. "I know where you're going! But you mustn't go!"

"Good morning, Hetty. Are you all right? You're out of breath."

"I'm perfectly fine!" protested Hetty as she stepped from the pier onto the gangplank. "And I'm coming aboard!"

There was no stopping Hetty. Though she looked more like a tugboat, she had the power of a battleship. Darby extended his hand, as he had done for Will, and helped Hetty as she stepped onto the gunwale of the *Shooting Star*.

"I vow and declare, Darby, you are a weaselly little dastard this morning," said Hetty. "You promised me you wouldn't go to Walker's Key, and yet you employed treacherous means—which failed, thankfully—to slink out of my house undetected, and now here you are getting ready to steam across the bay. Don't deny it! But I will not let you go!" At this point, there was as much steam in Hetty as there was in the *Shooting Star*'s boiler.

"No, I must go, Hetty. Tulley's lighthouse went dark and I have to make sure that nothing has happened to him."

"I don't care a hang about Tulley. Nor should you! It's a trap, Darby! Tulley wants you to go to his island so he can kill you!"

"What?" yelled Will, a look of puzzled perturbation on his face. "Hetty, this is the craziest thing I've ever heard you say. Why on earth would Tulley want to harm Darby?"

"Will, there isn't time for me to explain, but we've got to stop Darby from going across the bay! Darby knows why."

Will looked at Darby, who raised his eyebrows and returned the perplexed look.

Darby said, "My dear Hetty, I don't know what's gotten into you this morning, but you should let Will escort you back to the house. And then you should climb back into bed."

Hetty then went right up to Darby, who towered over her, and started pounding her fists into his chest. "NO, NO, NO!" Hetty screamed. "Darby Walker, you promised me that you wouldn't go to Walker's Key! I will not allow it!"

"Hetty, that hurts! Stop hitting me, please!" As he said this, Darby wanted to tell Hetty how much he wished he did not have to go. He wanted to tell her how much he loved her and thank her for everything she had done for his father. He wanted to tell her everything, but he knew he couldn't tell her anything.

Will then put his arms around Hetty, pulling her away from Darby, trying to comfort her.

"Hetty," said Will, "you need to calm down. Let's talk this out. I don't know why you're so upset, but perhaps the three of us can figure out how to fix whatever the problem is." He guided Hetty to a seat on the nearest bench and sat next to her.

Hetty put her face into her hands. Darby could tell that she was afraid she would lose control over the situation, and he was determined that she *would* lose control over it.

"I'm all right, Will. But we can't let Darby go to Walker's Key! There is compelling evidence that Tulley is a murderer. Unless we find out for sure that he isn't, Darby needs to stay away from him!"

Will looked up at Darby. Darby looked back at Will with his lips pursed, his eyes wide open, and his eyebrows raised. Then he rolled his eyes. The effect was a clear suggestion that Hetty had completely lost her mind. Darby hated doing this to Hetty, but he hoped that one day she would understand.

"I don't know what to say, except that it appears that something with our beloved Hetty has gone a little skewangles this morning," Darby said, hoping Will would figure out some way to make his Hetty problem go away. If the minister figured out a way to get Hetty to return home, Darby might have to agree that there's balm in Gilead after all.

Will took Hetty's hands into his. "Tulley isn't a murderer. He's unusual, I grant you that, but he's no murderer. Naturally, Darby is concerned that something has happened to him and wants to check. I think we should let Darby do that, don't you?"

"Absolutely not!" Hetty pulled her hands from Will's, got up from the bench and laid down on the deck. "I'm not getting off this boat! If Darby is going to Walker's Key, I'm going with him!"

"Okay," said Will. "We have a bit of a conflict here, Darby. Why *can't* Hetty and I just go with you? We're not paying passengers, and even if you *are* supposed to have an engineer aboard, nobody's going to be checking for engineers on steam-powered launches at 6 o'clock in the morning on Tampa Bay. Hetty seems determined, and I don't know anybody who has ever gotten their way over Hetty's way, do you? What do you say?"

Darby's right hand instinctively went to his beard as he pondered the question. "You may have a point, but Hetty isn't dressed for a boat ride. You aren't either, for that matter. You really should have another layer on given the wind on the bay. Why don't you both go back to your homes and get properly dressed? I'll wait here and then we'll all go check on Tulley."

Hetty scowled. "Heavens and earth, Darby, you're not going to hoodwink me again! We're not going to a cotillion! Will and I are sufficiently well attired for the purpose at hand, and I'm sure you have a blanket onboard if we get chilled. If you're determined to go to Walker's Key, let's get on with it!"

Darby considered this. "All right, off we go. Hetty, I need you to go up on the pier and untie the bow line from the piling. Will, you can untie the stern line. You are now my first and second mates."

Will helped Hetty up to a standing position, and they set themselves to carrying out Darby's orders, climbing up the gangplank to the pier. Hetty reached the piling where the bow line was tied just as Will reached the piling where the stern line was tied.

In the wheelhouse, Darby thought for a split second about changing his mind. He truly did not want to do this. But he had thought about the situation over and over and from every angle, and there was just no other way, no changing course. He firmly pushed the regulator lever all the way forward. Steam rushed to the engine and jump-started the pistons that started the propeller rotating. The *Shooting Star* thrust forward with tremendous force, instantly generating a massive bubble of churning water at her stern.

Darby made it all happen so fast that Hetty and Will could not possibly recognize what was going on until it was too late to react. Despite her substantial mass, the *Shooting Star* practically jumped away from the pier. The bow and stern lines, Darby having just untied them from the cleats on the *Shooting Star*, dropped limply into the water as the boat shot away from Hetty and Will and out into Tampa Bay.

The strong wind and the whitecaps were starting to diminish and did not represent a danger to an experienced mariner like Darby. However, not everything was favorable to a safe voyage.

The safety valve on the boiler had begun to stick the prior week. The pressure in the boiler was, as a result, unusually erratic, climbing more than it should before the valve would grudgingly open and restore the pressure to 60 pounds per square inch, at which the boiler was designed to operate.

Darby had been aboard a steam-powered vessel years earlier when one of its boilers exploded. The sound of the boiler deforming just before it blew up was seared into his memory. The vessel had been large, and though the explosion had caused a tremendous amount of damage, the ship had remained afloat and, rather miraculously, nobody had been killed. Darby understood as well as any steamboat owner the necessity of addressing any pressure valve issues.

To avoid an explosion, Darby would have to watch the pressure gauge more carefully than he ordinarily did. He could release pressure from the boiler manually if it came down to it, and prevent an explosion. The proper thing to do was to replace the safety valve, and he wouldn't be taking any passengers on board until he had made the fix.

Darby had sailed to Tampa on the Steamship *H.B. Plant* the day after the valve on the *Shooting Star*'s boiler had started misbehaving. In Tampa, Darby had made several stops in search of a replacement safety valve. He explained what he was looking for to as many people as he could, and in the end he was directed to a company that built and serviced boilers of various kinds. Finally, people who could help. He would have saved himself a lot of time if he had visited them first. At this last stop, he was able to procure a safety valve nearly identical to the safety valve on the *Shooting Star*'s boiler, surely close enough that he could swap it in and make it work. He paid for the valve and brought it back home with him.

Darby knew that he should have installed the new valve by now, but he had not. He'd had plenty of time in the last several days to take care of it, but hadn't done it. Walker's Ferry Service was closed for the time being anyway. As the *Shooting Star* churned away from the Electric Pier, the valve for which Darby had searched so widely on his Tampa trip remained inside a pint-sized cardboard box on his desk in his bedroom in his home back at 141 Second Avenue North in St. Petersburg.

Nevertheless, everything was working within normal parameters at the moment. Darby only had to make it six miles across the bay. He looked at the pressure gauge and it indicated an ideal 60 pounds per square inch of pressure inside the boiler. The wind was still strong, but declining. The waves on the bay, still higher than usual, were breaking forcefully across the bow of the *Shooting Star*, soaking the deck with spray. There were no passengers aboard to complain about the rough ride or about getting wet, and a little salt water on the boat didn't concern Darby in the slightest.

After a few minutes, Darby scanned the horizon and saw the Walker's Key lighthouse rising up above the water. The lighthouse was on the highest ground in all of Hillsborough County, and it was the first thing that came into view when approaching the eastern shore of Tampa Bay.

The *Shooting Star* continued pushing across Tampa Bay. At that early hour, there were no other vessels, other than a lone steamer that had started south from Tampa on its way to the Gulf of Mexico, bound for Key West or New Orleans. It was probably a couple of miles distant.

Ordinarily, Darby would have thoroughly delighted in the wild ride. He would have smiled at the wind-driven spray of the water splashing up and over the bow of the *Shooting Star* as she collided into and climbed over the waves in her path. He would have marveled at the prospect of the huge body of water spread out before him and the complete freedom to go in any direction he pleased. But today he was completely lost in thoughts about his family, about everything that had happened in the last couple of weeks, and about what lay ahead.

Several minutes passed. When the world came back into focus, the *Shooting Star* was within a hundred yards of the eastern shore of the bay. Darby was heading for the Walker's Key channel, a natural channel between two low-lying barrier islands. He pulled back on the *Shooting Star's* throttle, slowing the vessel down. The wind and the water at this far corner of the bay were now fairly calm.

At that moment, a disconcerting sound of metal deforming under excessive stress emanated from the depths of the *Shooting Star's* boiler. Darby had heard this awful sound before. He looked at the pressure gauge, now showing over 200 pounds per square inch of pressure.

Darting from the wheelhouse to the starboard side of the boat, Darby lunged over the rail without a fraction of a moment's delay.

As he plunged into the water, there was a tremendously forceful and breathtakingly loud explosion onboard the *Shooting Star*. The explosion was heard all the way back across the bay in St. Petersburg, all the way up the bay in Tampa, all the way down the bay on the Manatee River, even all the way out at Egmont Key, where the bay met the Gulf of Mexico.

Fragments of steel, chunks of burning wood, and all manner of broken boat parts flew in all directions as scalding steam enveloped the disintegrating vessel. Flames broke out, rapidly advancing across the jagged remains of the *Shooting Star*. Smoke billowed into the sky. Darby disappeared under the water as heavy boat fragments crashed down with more than enough force to kill.

A Murder is Announced

Hetty and Will stared in disbelief as the *Shooting Star* sped away from the pier.

"We've been overreached!" said Will.

"Yes, we have," said Hetty. "This is not the Darby we have come to know. And we may never see him again." Hetty began thinking about the scene that might unfold at Walker's Key. Perhaps Darby would be able to defend himself from Tulley, but perhaps not. Hetty couldn't understand why Darby was so determined to go the island, especially now that he had been warned that Tulley could be their father's killer. It just didn't make sense.

"I'm sure that's not the case, Hetty. Tulley isn't the sort of person to physically harm anyone, especially his own little brother."

"I hope you're right. Anyway, I guess there's nothing we can do about it now."

"No, there *is* something we can do. We can pray for Tulley and for Darby."

"Oh, sure."

Will and Hetty watched the *Shooting Star* shrink into the distance.

"Will, I suppose I should start my day. It's still early, but I won't be able to sleep now."

"All right. I was just on my way out to the end of the pier for my morning ritual."

"You come out here every morning? What do you do?"

"Weather permitting, I sit at the end of the pier at sunrise and take time for quiet reflection. Perhaps you should try it. You're welcome to join me."

"No, thank you. Perhaps another morning. Enjoy your ritual."

"I shall. Good day."

Will turned and headed to the end of the pier. Hetty buttoned up her Macintosh and majestically swept off the pier.

There really was nothing Hetty could do about Darby's departure. He would arrive at Walker's Key in less than half an hour. There were no steamboats at the pier, and even if there were, nobody would agree with Hetty that Darby was in danger, let alone offer to take her across the bay in this wind.

Hetty made her way back to her house where she got properly dressed and had a quick breakfast. Then she walked to the office of the *St. Petersburg Post*, which consisted of one large room on the second floor of the two-story brick building at the northeast corner of the intersection of Central Avenue and Second Street North, a block from the waterfront. The twice-weekly printing of the paper, published on Sundays and Wednesdays, was done by a printer down the street.

The *St. Petersburg Post* was Hetty's creation. Ten years earlier, at the age of forty-five, for a princely sum she had sold a newspaper business in Burlington, Vermont. She had inherited that business when her mother had died, and then she had managed it herself for several years. Hetty had grown tired of winter and tired, she thought at the time, of running a business. She moved to St. Petersburg and built one of the city's grandest homes on one of its most coveted lots. From this beautiful home, she could gaze unimpeded across constantly changing Tampa Bay. It was a view of which she could never grow weary.

It took Hetty less than a year to realize that retirement was boring her to death. But otherwise she loved living in St. Petersburg. There being no newspaper at that time, she established the *St. Petersburg Post*, a small business consisting of herself and three part-time employees, all of whom had also been formerly associated with larger papers in the north.

Hetty entered the newspaper office and went straight to a wooden file cabinet at the back wall, from which she pulled out the Sunday, July 8, 1900 issue of the *St. Petersburg Post*. She brought it to her large desk, spread it out in front of her, and sat down to read, for only the tenth time, a front-page article, an article she had herself researched and written. She was still searching for clues, still trying to make sense out of events that made no sense at all.

◁‖ ST. PETERSBURG POST ‖▷
St. Petersburg, Florida
PILOT WALKER FOUND DEAD
Found In His Room By Anxious Friends
The Popular Captain Apparently Shot
Himself Through The Head With A Pistol
No Known Reason

EGMONT KEY, FLA. Well-endowed with this world's goods, popular with all who knew him, and having loving children and a grandchild nearby, Captain Kenelm Walker, one of the best known pilots on the Gulf coast, sometimes called the "star pilot of Port Tampa," apparently shot himself through the head on Egmont Key sometime late Friday or early Saturday. Captain Walker was 57 years of age.

When some of Captain Walker's associates at the Key noted, Saturday around noon, that he had not left his room all morning, they forced an entrance and found the captain lying on the floor in a pool of blood. A revolver was found on the floor near the body. The bullet had entered the head under the chin and had ranged upward to the brain. Death must have been instantaneous.

The sheriff of Hillsborough County, Charles Kimball, was summoned from Tampa to Egmont Key after the discovery. According to Sheriff Kimball, the death was a suicide. Captain Walker shared his home on Egmont Key with a servant and three lodgers, none of whom had any motive for harming him. His bedroom was locked when he was found, nobody other than Captain Walker possessed a key to it, and there was no evidence of any alternative entry or exit. Walker's key was found inside his jacket pocket. No items in the room or elsewhere in the house were disturbed or missing. No strangers were seen in the vicinity.

There is no known motive for the suicide, if suicide it was. No suicide note was found. Captain Walker derived a handsome revenue from his work as a Tampa Bay pilot, and he also occasionally worked for the Plant System, guiding tourist excursions to the fishing grounds out in the Gulf. He was the soul of affability wherever he went, and his friends and acquaintances, old and new, always enjoyed Captain Walker's colorful stories of his adventures on the seas. He had many friends here in St. Petersburg and in Tampa, in both places being highly esteemed.

Captain Walker was originally from Harwich Port, Massachusetts. A mariner from the age of 17, Captain Walker worked as a young sailor in the coastal trade before acquiring his first fishing schooner, from which for some time he fished off New England during the summer and off the Gulf Coast here in Florida during the winter. Later, for several years, he was a steamship captain for the Tampa-based Miller & Henderson Steamship Line, commanding ships on the Gulf Coast between New Orleans and Cuba. Nearly ten years ago, Captain Walker became one of the first pilots to guide large vessels on Tampa Bay, building his own residence five years ago on Egmont Key, where the Tampa Bay pilots are based.

Captain Walker was widowed many years ago. He leaves behind his son, Tulley, the lighthouse keeper on Walker's Key, across the bay from St. Petersburg, and Tulley's wife and young son. He also leaves behind his son, Darby, of St. Petersburg, the proprietor of Walker's Ferry Service, based at the Electric Pier.

Funeral arrangements have not been finalized at this time.

Every acquaintance of the genial pilot, and he had legions of them, will be shocked to learn of his apparently self-inflicted death. All of his friends are at a loss to account for it.

⌐

Hetty's last discussion with Sheriff Kimball about the captain's death had become heated when she had said: "This conclusion that Captain Walker took his own life is pure horseshit. Captain Walker was murdered." Hetty had been certain from the start that it had been murder, but Sheriff Kimball wouldn't investigate, certainly not without any objective reason to doubt the suicide and when the family wasn't pushing for an investigation.

Hetty was focused on getting to the truth behind Captain Walker's death. If Sheriff Kimball wasn't going to investigate, then, Hetty decided, the job fell to her.

A suicide could have been staged. There were any number of suspects. The captain was a fairly wealthy man. Wasn't it possible that in his room he kept cash or other valuables which someone found out about and tried to steal?

Nobody would think the Walker children were capable of murder, but from her years of newspaper work, Hetty recognized something most people failed to see: people act out of character *all the time*. One of the sons could have murdered their father. And as the primary legatees under the captain's will, the captain's sons had a clear motive: money.

Hetty considered Captain Walker's two sons. Could Tulley have murdered the captain? Of course he could have. Tulley might be capable of anything. Tulley was impenetrable, inscrutable. Nobody knew what went on behind his dark eyes.

Hetty felt sure that Darby didn't have murder in him, but couldn't even Darby act out of character? And what about Darby's regular trips to New York City, the trips about which Darby never said a word? Hetty had once asked Captain Walker what Darby did when he was in New York, and the captain had replied, "If Darby wanted us to know what he did in New York, I'm sure he'd tell us." Hetty never asked again.

If Captain Walker was really murdered, however, by one of his sons or by anyone else, there was from the start the problem of entry into and exit from the captain's locked room. If anybody did have a key, or access to a key, they weren't exactly stepping forward to admit it to the sheriff. Hetty knew that at least one individual other than the captain possessed a key to the captain's room, but she wondered how many others might also have one.

While Hetty reflected upon these and other problems, Attorney Andrew Beaumont entered his law office downstairs. He strolled from the reception area adjacent to the front door into his large, comfortable office, where he removed his jacket and hung it on the back of his chair behind his huge partner's desk. He was alone. Neither his associate nor his two assistants would arrive at the office for another couple of hours.

Andrew, a strong, tall man in his late sixties or early seventies, owned the building that housed his law firm and the St. Petersburg Post. The diplomas hanging behind his desk indicated to all who had occasion to sit in his office that he was a graduate of Haverford College and Harvard Law School. His story, when he was asked, was that he had been born and raised in Philadelphia, but this was not true. He had been born on a prosperous Southern plantation. The plantation, owned at the time of his birth by Richard Beaumont, had made the Beaumont family wealthy. Cotton, peanuts, and a seemingly endless supply of virgin yellow pine were harvested there and shipped up the East Coast to growing cities and towns. Boat-loads of cash made the return trip.

The thick, curly hair on Andrew's head was as white as the cotton Andrew picked during his youth on the plantation owned by the Beaumonts. His skin was as dark as rich Southern soil. Andrew, a very private person, had decided many years earlier that his unspeakably horrible youth as a slave was nobody's business but his own and did not need to be relived or recounted.

As he did every working morning, Andrew reviewed his work calendar to see what lay ahead of him. It was the sixteenth day after the death of his client, Captain Kenelm Walker. According to the captain's last will, which Andrew had drafted years earlier, any beneficiary who failed to survive the captain by at least fifteen days would be treated as if he or she had died before the captain and would inherit nothing. In the unlikely event that only one of his two sons survived the captain by at least fifteen days, that son would inherit the entire estate. The survivorship provision was there to prevent assets from passing through an estate of a son if, for example, both father and son received fatal injuries in the same incident. The delay and expense relating to that son's estate could thereby be avoided.

The will had not been revised since it had been executed those many years earlier, despite Andrew's advice that it should have been adjusted to reflect changes in the Walker family, particularly the birth of Tulley's son. The captain had always said that he was in no hurry about taking care of this detail, claiming he knew that Darby, if Darby was the only surviving son, would do right by Tulley's family.

This day, sixteen days after Captain Walker's demise, should have been the day that Andrew, as the estate's executor, would contact Tulley and Darby Walker to arrange a formal meeting in his office, beginning the process of settling their father's estate.

As Andrew glanced at the notation in his calendar, however, he already knew this meeting would not take place. Settling Captain Walker's estate would be delayed for some time, and would involve more complications than anyone anticipated.

Andrew knew many things nobody else knew. For example, he knew what Darby did on his New York trips. A private detective he'd hired had given him a full report. Andrew read the report, committed certain details of it to memory, and then burned it. Andrew also knew that within the next couple of days it would be reported that one of Captain Walker's sons was, like Captain Walker, dead. Andrew was not the only person who knew this.

Shell Game

At about the same time Darby Walker tiptoed out of Hetty's house, Ben McLaughlin lay in his bed in the home he and his wife owned in Gulf City, the tiny and deceptively named village across Tampa Bay from St. Petersburg. Ben served as the deputy sheriff for eastern Hillsborough County and also owned a sardine canning factory that employed many village residents. The lighthouse at Walker's Key, three miles to the south, had gone dark during the night. This troubled Ben deeply. All night long, the wind had been strong and unusually erratic. Ben had slept poorly.

Ben and his wife, Annie, had already been established in Gulf City in 1890, the year the work crew showed up and constructed the lighthouse at Walker's Key. Since that time, Ben could remember only two occasions when the lighthouse had gone dark. The first time, nine years earlier, coincided with the birth of the Walkers' only child, Christopher. The light had run through its eight-day supply of fuel on the day that the

Walkers' child came into the world, and with all the excitement of the birth of his child, Tulley had forgotten to refuel it until late that night. The residents of Gulf City had noticed that the light had been out that night, but nobody thought much of it.

More recently, Tulley and his family had taken a trip down Tampa Bay to Egmont Key to visit Captain Walker for a few days. Tulley thought he'd refueled the light before leaving, but he hadn't. The night before the Walkers returned, the lighthouse had been dark.

After that second slip-up, Tulley had been worried news of his error would reach the headquarters of the U.S. Lighthouse Board, the federal agency managing lighthouses. Tulley had told Ben that he feared that there would be a reprimand, but either nobody reported the outage to the Board, or the Board hadn't considered it a matter worth addressing.

Ben knew Tulley's wife and son were away in New England. Supposedly they were visiting relatives, but they had been away since the beginning of June, and some Gulf City residents were speculating there was more to that story, and that perhaps Tulley's wife and son were not planning to come back at all.

Something was wrong. Tulley needed help.

There was still little activity in the village as Ben rose and got dressed. The sun had barely risen above the tree line across the river. Thankfully, last night's storminess had just about died away.

"I believe I need to go check on Walker," he told Annie, as he walked into the kitchen and found her setting their breakfast of coffee and eggs on the dining table.

"I agree. I am worried. The poor man just lost his father, and that's on top of his wife leaving him and taking their son with her. All of that would be enough to sink anyone. If he hasn't gotten really sick — or worse — it would be a miracle."

"Annie, you don't know for sure that Martha and Christopher have left for good."

"Of course they have. They must have heard about the captain, but did they come back for his service? No. If Martha were planning to return to Tulley, she certainly would have done so upon hearing about his father's death."

"But what if Martha or Christopher has been in some accident or has developed some illness?"

"Not impossible, I suppose, but there hasn't even been any correspondence between Martha and Tulley since Martha left." Annie would know. She was the postmistress at Gulf City. "An accident or illness would have been reported to Tulley."

"Don't forget that Darby comes over here now and then. How do you know that Tulley hasn't been giving Darby his correspondence addressed to Martha, or that Martha hasn't been sending her correspondence through Darby?"

"Because Tulley doesn't like Darby. He wouldn't want Darby to know if he was sending a letter to Martha, and he'd probably worry that Darby would open the envelope and read the letter. Darby would never do such a thing, of course. But it's the sort of thing Tulley might do, and so, naturally, he would think others capable of it."

"Oh, Annie. How you can say Tulley doesn't like Darby? Everyone likes Darby."

"Perhaps everyone else, but not Tulley."

"Annie, really. How could you possibly know such a thing?"

"I've watched them together. Tulley intensely dislikes his brother. You need to be more observant."

"Now you're just disagreeing with me for your own amusement."

"Sometimes I do enjoy disagreeing with you, but not this time: Tulley truly dislikes his brother. Why is that? If I had to guess, I'd say it's rooted in envy. Darby is always happy. He always has a smile and a kind word to offer. Tulley, on the other hand, always has a black cloud hanging over his head. He never knows what to say, nor even how to have an ordinary conversation. Honestly, I can't understand how you—the leading citizen of this town, a man who is aware of most everything that goes on around here—could have missed this. Tulley may also be envious of his brother's appearance. Tulley is just a bit too tall and thin, while Darby is splendidly proportioned."

Ben's furrowed brow suggested displeasure with the "splendidly proportioned" comment, but he let it go, realizing that Darby could never threaten their marriage. "But Annie, you're not also suggesting that Darby dislikes Tulley, are you? And besides, how can you claim to know any of these things?"

"I don't think Darby hates anybody. Unless I'm mistaken, Darby doesn't even dislike his brother. I think he doesn't quite *trust* Tulley. As for how I know these things, women can see things in people that men can never see. It's just the way it is."

Ben thought about this, but let it pass unchallenged, just as he always did.

After a few moments, Ben finally said, "I still say that we don't know that Martha has left Tulley for good."

"I agree. *We* don't know that. *I* know that, but *you* don't know that." Annie smiled at her husband, who smiled back.

After the couple finished their breakfast, Ben kissed Annie and set off to round up a search party to join him on his trip to Walker's Key. If Tulley was ill, Ben was going to need help getting him back to Gulf City, and if a doctor was needed, he would need someone to go to Tampa and fetch one.

Ben assembled a volunteer team of himself and five village neighbors. The party of six pushed off in two large canoes from the Gulf City pier. The tide was mostly out but was still retreating, so there was a good current pulling them toward the mouth of the Little Manatee River and away from their village.

Sand Key was the island at the mouth of the Little Manatee River, on the southern side. The two canoes were about to round Sand Key when the men heard an enormous explosion.

"What on God's earth was that?" yelled one of them. They stopped paddling and turned toward the south. But Sand Key and the row of barrier islands to the south stood between them and the point of the explosion.

"It's a Spanish warship!" cried another man. "And it's firing on Gulf City!"

"Don't be an idiot," said the first man. "The war has been over for two years."

"Then what was it?"

"It could have been a meteor crashing into Tampa Bay."

Another volunteer said, with apparent authority, "A meteor is just a shooting star. You meant to say *meteorite*, which is a meteor that doesn't burn up in the atmosphere and instead makes it all the way to the earth."

"All right then. Meteorite. Same idea. That's what it must have been," said the man who had suggested the meteor possibility.

Ben said, "Boys, it's not a warship and it's not a meteorite. Whatever it was, it's now on fire." Sure enough, they saw black smoke rising from the direction of the explosion, somewhere on the bay on the other side of Sand Key. "We need to get out there right away." With that, the six men dug their paddles into the water, and the canoes all but lifted out of the water.

With an increased sense of urgency, the men quickly put the river behind them and passed beyond Sand Key into Tampa Bay. Now the source of the explosion was in plain view, though still at some distance from them.

"Dear God!" one of the men exclaimed.

"It's a steamboat!" another called out.

Ben could tell which steamboat it was, its lines familiar to him even with much of its superstructure blown away. The volunteer who had suggested that a meteor was responsible for the explosion had been correct, in a sense — the explosion had been a shooting star, Darby Walker's *Shooting Star* to be exact.

"Come on, there must be men overboard!" shouted Ben. "Paddle!"

Within a few minutes, the two canoes drew up to the burning remains of the steamboat. The men sat there in their canoes, stunned by the scene of destruction. They scanned the surface of the water, looking for any sign of life, but they found none. Several large chunks of what had been the *Shooting Star* bobbed in the waves, fragments of the wooden hull in random sizes and configurations. The men carefully searched among the wreckage but found no survivors.

Darby had to have been aboard. The *Shooting Star* never left the pier without Darby at the helm. Everyone in the party quickly concluded that Darby must have been fatally injured in the explosion or had drowned shortly thereafter.

After the men expressed their agreement that nobody, including Darby Walker, could have survived the accident, and that no bodies were visible in the area, Ben announced to the group that they would continue on to Walker's Key to carry out their original mission, checking on Tulley. A stony silence prevailed among the shocked men as the two canoes headed east toward Walker's Key. By this time, the fire aboard the *Shooting Star* had consumed nearly all of the flammable material above the waterline of the vessel. The flames had all but died out.

On the remaining portion of their trip to Walker's Key, the six Gulf City residents continuously scanned the surface of the bay and the shores of the barrier islands, hoping against all reason for any sign that Darby had survived the blast. However, nobody was swimming to the shore and nobody was on shore beckoning for help.

The men finished their trip to Walker's Key without any further discussion. All six of them were bracing for what they might discover at Tulley Walker's home. After several minutes, the two canoes drew up to the small island.

A series of heavy planks supported by two lines of piles served as the boat landing at Walker's Key. The boat landing extended several yards out from the shore into deep water. Without it, arriving at Walker's Key would have been a messy and unpleasant affair at all times other than high tide. At anything less than high tide, the shoreline consisted of a sticky muck that could easily pull a man's boots right off his feet. The firm beach, comprised mostly of white shells, only began higher up, right by the high tide line.

The men secured their canoes at the end of the boat landing, and then, one by one, made their way across the planks of the boat landing to the beach. From the beach they looked up at the Walker house, standing atop a thirty-foot hill, the highest point of land in Hillsborough County except for the slightly higher hill a very short distance to the southeast. Ben had been to Walker's Key countless times before, and nothing appeared to be different this time. Tulley's boat was secured in its usual place at the boat landing.

Ben surveyed the scene. The Walker house, with its west-facing front door, was plain and unimposing, only a story and a half in height and having a limited footprint. Ben had been inside the house many times. He knew that behind the front porch, in the main part of the house, a parlor was on the left, and Tulley and Martha's bedroom was on the right. Above these rooms and under the roof, accessed by a steep and narrow set of stairs just across from the front door, was a broad, low room which served as Christopher's bedroom. An ell behind the parlor contained the kitchen and dining area. Tucked next to the ell sat a large cistern that stored rainwater directed into it from gutters on the roof.

Ben also knew, as was apparent to any knowledgeable person setting foot on the shore, that Walker's Key was actually an ancient Indian shell mound. The mound was composed of shells, mostly the shells of oysters but from clams and conchs as well. The mound also contained large quantities of bones from fish, shark, rabbit, and deer. These shells and bones had been discarded at the site over centuries, along with fragments of tools and pottery. For nearly a thousand years, the island had been a gathering place for Native Americans who held feasts and took meals there.

Other early Florida settlers had built their homes on Indian shell mounds, these being the highest and driest spots along the coast. Over the years, Ben had visited several such homes on Florida's west coast, including the Webb home at Spanish Point, the old Tom Weeks place on Crawford's Key, and the Watson place way down on the Chatham River.

The lighthouse, forty feet in height, stood a short distance behind the house on the highest part of the island. The steel tower was painted white, except for the very top and a section near the middle, which were painted red. Tulley had given Ben a tour of the lighthouse just after it had been constructed, and Ben had climbed up its circular staircase to see the breathtaking view from the top on countless occasions since. The light came from a burner housed inside a salvaged sixth-order Fresnel lens that had been built into the small glassed-in chamber in the room at the top of the tower.

The light from the lighthouse was, of course, visible in nearby Gulf City, and it was also visible six miles across the bay in St. Petersburg. It could be seen from the highest stories of the taller buildings in Tampa, twelve miles up the bay. The light was even visible at Egmont Key, sixteen miles to the southwest at the mouth of Tampa Bay, but only from the top of the eighty-seven-foot tall lighthouse there, a structure dating from 1858.

Walker's Key, not more than an acre in size, had been cleared of trees the year the Walkers moved there, except for nine or ten palm trees. None of these trees was big enough to block the beams of light from the lighthouse.

Ben and his party walked up the hill to the front porch of the house. The bad feeling Ben had initially felt turned into an absolute foreboding as he and his search party approached the structure. There was no movement or noise from within the house, and no sign of any recent activity on the porch.

Ben knocked on the door.

"Tulley!"

The men waited. No response.

Ben tried the door and found it locked. "See if any of the windows are open," he commanded. Two of his men investigated the windows facing onto the porch, while the other three left the porch to check around the house.

Someone was watching Ben and his volunteers as they approached Walker's Key in their canoes and walked up to the house. This person, fully concealed in the lush vegetation of a nearby barrier island, studied their movement through an old spyglass on which was painted "N W." The person continued watching as the search party finally gained entry into the house.

They That Go Down
to the Sea in Ships

The old family cradle of Thomas Burgess was rocked near the sea-side. The bay was spread out in full view, and the roar of the surf was heard in every tempest. His athletic sons, early accustomed to adventure in the fisheries, and poorly rewarded by a sterile soil for work on the land, were often allured to seek their fortune on the treacherous ocean. Many of them have been ordinary mariners, and not a few the brave commanders of ships. No pen has noted down the number of the lost, and no monumental stones indicate their resting place. In some instances, father and son, or two brothers, have fallen victims in the same disaster. Death has followed hardship and danger. In vain, anxious hearts have throbbed, and tears have freely flowed. The husband, the brother, the son, did not return. Where are so many wives made widows, and so many children fatherless, as along our maritime borders? How marvelous is the Christian doctrine, so contrary to our natural sense, "The sea shall give up the dead that are in it." The ocean cemetery has no inclosing wall, and no names are inscribed on its rocks. Every descendant of Thomas may know that many of his kindred sleep in tombs invisible and unvisited, around which the waves and storms chant a requiem. *Burgess, Rev. Ebenezer (1865).* Memorial of the Family of Thomas and Dorothy Burgess, who were settled at Sandwich in the Plymouth Colony in 1637. *Boston, MA: T.R. Marvin & Son.*

35 years earlier.
Tuesday, July 4, 1865

Before the birth of Darby Walker, Captain Kenelm Walker, wife Emily Burgess Walker, and their three-year-old son Tulley lived in a modest home on Main Street, at the eastern end of the village of Harwich Port.

Next door was the home of Kenelm's parents. Nathaniel and Sarah lived in the old Walker homestead, a full Cape Cod house dating from the 1770s, where they had raised Kenelm and his siblings. As a wedding gift, Nathaniel and Sarah had given Kenelm and Emily the home they now occupied. It had been a general store operated by the captain's grandfather, Eleazer Walker. The captain and Emily had remodeled the building, carving out a bedroom from the large open space at the front and adding a kitchen and two bedrooms of modest size onto the back.

The sandy road to Chatham lay directly in front of the house. Across the road and down a gentle slope was Salt Water Pond, a small, round kettle pond connected to Nantucket Sound by a tidal creek. Beyond that stretched Nantucket Sound, the broad body of water between Cape Cod and the island of Nantucket thirty miles to the south. The view from the Walker homestead caused all passersby, even those who had seen it all their lives, to turn their heads in admiration. From the front yard and through the front windows, one could see vessels lying at anchor and vessels sailing, salt works and mills pumping water into them, and the round Salt Water Pond in the foreground. The vessels in the offing appeared small enough to be scooped up in one's hands.

At the time of Eleazer Walker's death in 1835, he had owned 130 acres, extending south from the Walker homestead all the way to the shore on the east side of Salt Water Pond, east to the Andrews River, and north for quite a distance back into the forest behind the house. By 1865, the land had been carved up into parcels. Nathaniel's siblings, their children, and Nathaniel's two eldest children had earlier been given pieces of the property on which to build their own homes. Most of these relatives now lived within view of the old homestead with their families. It was a place where children grew up surrounded by their aunts, uncles, and cousins.

Emily had grown up less than a half a mile away in a modest farmhouse on the road up to Harwich Center, the house in which Emily's mother and sister still lived. Emily's father, Albert Burgess, a sea captain just like Emily's young husband, had been lost in a gale off Nova Scotia the year before Emily married Kenelm. Her two brothers had been lost in the Pacific on a whaling voyage three years before that.

The Civil War had ended, and soldiers were returning to their homes in Harwich. Fishing schooners that had lain idle on ship cradles by the shore for the duration of the war were being restored so these men could return to their livelihoods on the sea. Normalcy was returning to the seaside town, and a mood of great optimism prevailed.

On this warm, bright, Saturday morning, Emily was three and a half months into her pregnancy with her second child. The townspeople had decided to have a day-long Independence Day festival in Harwich Center to celebrate both Independence Day and the end of the war. Emily and the captain were offered a ride to the center by the captain's older brother, whose wife and children rode with them in the carriage.

Arriving at the festival, Emily and the captain joined most of the residents of the town who were circulating in the main street. All the shops in the center were open, as were the Congregational Church and Pine Grove Seminary. People were filing into and out of these places, reconnecting with friends and neighbors.

Vendors of all kinds had set up booths to display their goods both in the street and inside the Exchange Building. At various points in the center, musicians were playing patriotic tunes on their instruments. All sorts of games and contests had been arranged, both indoors and out. A photographer had set up his camera and for a reasonable price was offering photographs of the revelers. The scene felt to those present much like the annual county fair in Barnstable, the only difference being that the annual harvest was months away.

Emily noticed that a fortune teller had set up shop along the edge of the main street. A small, makeshift tent created out of poles and bed sheets was fronted with a sign: "Madam Inez, Fortune Teller." A line of people stood outside the tent, where an assistant collected entrance fees.

"Ken," said Emily, "I'd like to see the fortune teller. Let's get in line."

"All right, dear," said the captain, "but you know that fortune telling is just bunkum and balderdash."

"Perhaps you're right, but I think it would be fun!"

"Then to the fortune teller we go!"

The captain escorted his beautiful wife across the road, and they joined the line to meet with the fortune teller. The captain and Emily knew all the others waiting in line and chatted with them until it was their turn to go inside the tent.

Madame Inez had a dark complexion and long, dark hair that flowed out from underneath a bright scarf worn tightly around her head. She wore heavy makeup, lots of jewelry, and an unusually colorful outfit suggestive of Gypsy origins.

"Welcome," Madame Inez said to the Walkers as her assistant directed them in. "Please make yourselves comfortable."

The Walkers seated themselves in the chairs directly in front of the table, draped with a colorful silk cloth. In the center of the table was a large crystal ball.

"Who wishes to know their future?" asked Madame Inez.

"I do, Madame Inez," said Emily.

"Then let us begin."

After a few moments of gazing into the crystal ball, the fortune teller said, "You were born in 1843."

"That's right!" Emily exclaimed.

"You recently lost a close family member ... no, three family members."

Emily nodded, impressed with the accuracy. She thought about the tragic deaths of her brothers and father.

"You are happy in your marriage, and have a child."

"Yes," Emily said. "Yes to both."

"You have a warm and open heart and a firmness of character. You have tremendous insight."

"Go on," said Emily. "Please tell me what you see about my future."

The fortune teller continued. "You will travel to warm and sunny places, but your home will always be here. You will be with your husband for the rest of your life."

Emily smiled upon hearing this information, not considering what it implied about the timing of her death. "What else do you see, Madame Inez?"

"You will bear a second child at the end of the year."

"Yes, Madame Inez, I shall. Will it be a boy or a girl?" Emily asked.

The fortune teller continued gazing into the crystal ball.

"I cannot tell whether it will be a boy or girl. Something is preventing me from seeing that."

This unexpected answer didn't bother Emily. A daughter or a second son would be equally loved. At the time of their marriage, the captain had said to her that Emily would get to choose the given names of all their children. He said that this was only fair since the children would be getting his family name.

Emily had already settled on a boy's name and on a girl's name, as would be appropriate, for her second child. The captain had asked her what names she had come up with, but Emily wasn't revealing anything yet.

"Will the child be healthy?" Emily asked.

"Very healthy."

"Will the child be happy?"

"Very happy."

"What else can you tell me about the child?"

Madame Inez continued to gaze into the crystal ball. "Your child will be kind, gentle, and unusually intuitive. Your child will be well-liked."

Emily smiled.

Madame Inez resumed her forecasting. "Your child will be sensitive, easily wounded by rougher souls, and slow to learn the art of self-defense."

Emily wasn't thrilled to hear this, but, she reasoned, sensitivity could be a good thing.

Madame Inez looked up at Emily. "I believe that you have a specific question for me."

"Yes, Madame Inez, I do." Emily was a bit reluctant to ask it, but after a short reflection she decided that she wanted to hear what the fortune teller would say. "Will my child die on the land or on the water?"

Madame Inez's gaze was unwavering. "Are you sure that you wish to know?"

Emily had to think again about whether or not she really wanted this information. She was from a Cape Cod family that had been devastated by maritime disasters. In addition to losing her father and her brothers to the sea in the past few years, she had earlier lost two of her four uncles to the sea. The list of Burgess family members who had been lost in maritime disasters was long. Surely no Cape Cod family had lost more men to the sea than had the Burgesses. No Cape Cod family had erected more memorial stones that overlooked empty graves.

Emily knew from the captain that, unlike her own family, the Walkers had, incredibly, never lost a single soul to the sea. This was despite the fact that the proportion of men who had been mariners was no less in the Walker family than in her own. Emily felt that if her child inherited its luck from her family, the child would be in great danger of dying on the sea, but that if her child inherited its luck from her husband's family, the child would have nothing to fear about maritime engagements. Emily had once explained these thoughts to the captain, who had responded by saying: "I love you Emily more than any other husband loves his wife, but this is rubbish."

"Yes, I would like to know," Emily said to Madame Inez.

Madame Inez gazed into her crystal ball once again. After a moment she said, "Your baby will be a true child of Neptune. Your child will never be in any danger on the water and will die on land. This I can see with complete clarity."

Emily was pleased, thanking Madame Inez profusely. Madame Inez's body relaxed, and her attention now seemed focused entirely on the present. Emily and the captain were about to stand and leave the makeshift tent when Madame Inez motioned with her hand that they should not leave yet.

"One last thing I must tell you," said Madame Inez. She looked this time at the captain. "Be careful with your first-born child. If you don't, you could be in serious danger." Madame Inez stood and said, without a hint of emotion, "Thank you and good day to you both."

Emily and the captain stood. As they made their way out into the brightness of the midday sun, Emily turned to the captain, her raised eyebrows indicating concern about what she had just heard.

The captain waved his hand in the air in a dismissal of the whole consultation. Walking away from the fortune teller's tent, he took Emily's hand in his, squeezing it with great affection.

"Ken, what do you think Madame Inez meant by that last comment?" Emily asked.

"The whole thing is stuff and rubbish! Your cousin and his wife were just ahead of us in line. He winked at me as they left the tent. I'm sure he told Madame Inez the facts she recited back to you. The rest of it she just created out of whole cloth."

"Oh, Ken," said Emily. "Why do you always have to be so skeptical? You need to admit that there is a lot about this life we will never understand and never know. Anything is possible."

"Am I too skeptical or are you too credulous?"

Emily glared at him.

"All right, Emily. You're right. Anything is possible, or almost anything. It's also true, as my father always said, that appearances are often deceiving."

"Well, there may be something to Madame Inez's ability to see the future, and I'm certainly happy that our baby will not die on the sea."

"Fine, but then what about her last comment about Tulley being a danger?"

"Bunkum and balderdash!" responded Emily, though she only said this to make her husband happy.

The captain and Emily smiled at each other, then went to get ice cream.

The following Sunday proudly presented itself as another sunny and pleasant day. After church, Emily suggested that she and the captain go for a row around Salt Water Pond. The captain thought this a fine idea. The Walkers kept a rowboat and a little sailboat at the shore of the pond.

Emily sat in the stern of the rowboat facing forward as the captain, seated in the middle of the boat and facing Emily, rowed them around the pond. A pleasant breeze turned up the leaves on the silver leaf poplars on the eastern edge of the pond, causing their silver-white undersides to flash. Seagulls wheeled high above the shore.

Suddenly, the rowboat shuddered as it banged into a hard object. The captain, facing to the rear, hadn't seen anything in their path. Nor had Emily, who had been lost in pleasant thoughts as the boat pushed across the water.

The rowboat was not large, and Emily had not yet adjusted to her larger than normal belly, which was increasing in size every day. When both the captain and Emily stood up from their seats at the same moment to find out what they had bumped into, the boat listed to the starboard. Emily lost her balance and tumbled into the middle of Salt Water Pond.

Emily found herself in a different world. She was upside down at the bottom of the pond. She opened her eyes. She was looking out from the edge of a bed of eelgrass. She saw several fish swimming by, and a tiny crab ambling sideways along the bottom of the pond. Time slowed to a crawl. Was Emily dying? What about the child inside her? Hadn't the fortune teller told her that her child would die at an old age and on the land?

But here she was at the bottom of Salt Water Pond. Perhaps the captain had been right. Perhaps the fortune teller was just a fraud.

Then, just as suddenly as Emily had reached the bottom of the pond, she was looking out over the surface of the water, fresh air filling her lungs. She had no idea how she had risen so quickly. It felt as if her body had been magically transformed into a giant bubble of air that had raced to the surface and popped out of the water.

The captain had jumped into the water as soon as he had realized that Emily had tumbled out of the boat. Just as he began searching for her, he saw her pop out of the water ten feet away. She was already swimming to the boat. The captain closed the distance between them in a couple of strokes and reached out.

"Are you all right, Emily?"

Easily treading the water and keeping herself upright, Emily began laughing. "I'm … fine … Ken! The baby's … fine!" Amid laughter, Emily's words came out in fits and starts.

Both the captain and Emily were strong swimmers, and the salt in the water added to their buoyancy. They were in no danger, and the shore was just a few easy strokes and kicks away.

"Why are you laughing?" asked the captain.

"Don't you see? The fortune teller was right! When it comes to the water, our second child is a Walker, not a Burgess!"

"Emily, my sweet Emily. That's just silly."

The captain kissed Emily and then they both laughed.

The object which the rowboat had banged into was just a log floating on the surface of the pond.

The unborn baby inside Emily's womb experienced Emily's near-drowning in its own mysterious fashion. Darby, whose tiny heart was already beating strongly, and whose cells were dividing and multiplying at a furious pace, somehow sensed that the watery sphere in which he lived was turning and twisting in a much larger body of water. Something about this felt right. He sensed that the larger body of water would welcome him.

Heart of Darkness

Thursday, June 27, 1867

Tulley was sure it had been the worst day ever. That was the day eighteen months earlier, the day his mother exploded and the thing came into their lives.

Tulley's mother, who had been sick for many weeks with tummy problems, screamed for a long time that day. Mrs. Merrick from North Harwich came to the house to help. Dr. Sturgis also came to the house to do whatever he could do. Tulley was not allowed to go into his parents' room to see his mother. After his mother finally stopped screaming, there was lots of crying. From the thing. The thing that had come into their lives.

The thing was hideous, the scariest, ugliest, most disturbing object Tulley had ever seen. It was squishy looking, and red, and sort of shapeless. It randomly moved its useless, puffy little parts. It smelled bad. It made noises of various descriptions, all of them too loud and all of them horrible. All the time.

Since that day, Tulley's life had never been the same. Mother, and Dad when Dad was at home, focused all their attention on the thing, as awful and disgusting as it was. The thing was constantly wetting and soiling itself. It was unable to take care of itself or do anything useful.

Mother was constantly feeding and washing it, changing the clothes it had soaked and fouled. The house, which had always been clean and sweet-smelling, now stunk of the fluids and substances that sprang forth from the thing often and without warning, and of the stinky clothing and blankets that had been used to cover the thing up.

Bewildered, Tulley had no idea why his parents wanted to keep the thing. From day one of the thing, Tulley just wanted it to die, and for some time after the thing came along, he was hopeful that it would expire quite naturally and of its own accord. Certainly, it would do just that if it could understand what would be best for Tulley and his parents. The thing needed so much, it was so utterly helpless and weak, and it constantly wore his mother out.

Tulley had to do what his parents told him to do, and they told him the thing was his baby brother and had a name, "Darby." Tulley was ordered to call the thing "Darby," and not "the thing." When his parents were present, Tulley complied, but when his parents were not around, he called it "the thing," or just "Thing" if he was addressing it directly.

Tulley's mother told him he had been just like the thing when he was little, but Tulley dismissed this idea. Tulley could never have been so vile and so wretched. He had no recollection of being in that miserable condition.

From the beginning, Tulley had shown himself to be an unusual little boy. Sadly, he had no friends, despite his parents' best efforts. There were several boys in town who were around his age, and over the years Tulley's parents had brought him to various community and private events where he was given the opportunity to interact with his peers. However, while the other boys had begun to reach out to and build friendships with each other, Tulley apparently preferred being by himself.

On the occasions when another boy approached him, Tulley invariably said or did something sufficiently strange or mean to put the other boy off. He wouldn't look anyone in the eyes. He wouldn't share his toys. He wasn't interested in the games the other boys played.

Tulley's parents believed that when he started at the village school he would come out of his shell. That would prove to be wishful thinking. Actually, Tulley wanted to be friends with the boys he met, but all of his efforts toward that end failed miserably. Tulley never understood why that was or what to do about it, and nobody could figure out how to help him, in part because Tulley never gave any indication that he wanted things to be any different.

From an early age and long before the arrival of the thing, Tulley loved playing in the sand at the beach. In the spring of 1865, the captain had hauled up several loads of sand from the beach and smoothed them out in a hollow at the back of the house. There, Tulley could play on his very own beach while still under the watchful eye of Emily. The family called this play area "the sand garden."

A shovel, old tools, and various random pieces of wood which Tulley had requisitioned from here and there could be found in the sand garden. Tulley used these tools and materials to create entire villages and then, when they were fully completed, wipe them out and begin again. He buried various objects in his sand garden, including a frog he'd killed—an unintentional killing, Tulley would have explained, had he been asked—and a hairbrush stolen from his mother. Tulley liked to bury things.

Tulley's father was away for several days in charge of a ship hauling lumber from Maine to New York City. It was a pleasant, partly sunny day and, for most of the morning, while his mother was tending to the thing and to her usual housework, Tulley was outside reordering the universe in his sand garden.

Around noon, Tulley's mother opened the back door and told him it was time to come in for lunch and then a nap. Tulley had just finished stomping out a section of a sand village where Portuguese people had somehow managed to move in, and so the timing was good. He went inside with his mother.

While his mother spoon-fed the thing, Tulley consumed the lunch his mother had prepared. Then his mother, who was exhausted from a busy morning, took the thing into his parents' bedroom at the front of the house for a nap, telling Tulley he was to go to his room, which was at the back of the house next to the kitchen. In another hour, she told him, she'd come find him and then they would all read together. As if the thing could understand words.

Tulley went to his room and lay down on his bed. A gentle breeze blew from the east, fluttering the curtain in the window. Tulley wasn't sleepy. He stayed still for a few minutes, then sprang up and tiptoed out into the kitchen, and then continued to his parents' bedroom at the front of the house. When he peered in, the thing was in its cage, staring up at the ceiling like an idiot, which it was. His mother was asleep on her bed, on the far side of the thing's cage.

Tulley walked quietly over to the thing's cage. After checking to see that there was no danger of his mother waking up — poor, exhausted Mother — he reached into the cage and slowly and quietly pulled the thing out despite the unpleasantness of having to touch it.

The thing stared at Tulley with its gray-green eyes. It smiled and gurgled as Tulley strained to pull the thing over the cage's low wall. The thing was getting heavier by the week, Tulley realized, but he could make the thing go places with him if he led it by the hand and made sure it didn't tip over. For a moment he considered what would happen if bad stuff came out of the thing's business end, but he concluded that the clothing in which the thing had been carefully wrapped by his mother would hold back the bad stuff for as long as he needed.

Tulley, with the thing in tow, quietly backed out of his parents' room and turned around to walk through the kitchen and out the back door. All the while, the thing emitted soft animal noises and drooled its slime onto Tulley and elsewhere.

Tulley wondered briefly if he was making a mistake, but decided he could endure a little slime to do what was necessary.

Tulley's idea was to feed the thing to the family's horse, Lorenzo. He led the thing out to the horse's pasture, just on the other side of the barn. Tulley opened the nearest gate and let the thing crumple to the ground. Lorenzo, who had been standing under a nearby tree, swatting flies with its tail, saw Tulley and the thing and sauntered over.

"Here, Lorenzo," Tulley said. "I brought you the thing, for you to eat. I'm sure you're hungry."

Lorenzo snorted. The thing, which was sitting where Tulley had set him down, looked up at the horse and at Tulley and smiled, making more idiotic, unintelligible noises.

"Come on, Lorenzo, it's all yours." Tulley waited, but it soon became clear that Lorenzo was not interested.

"Wait a second. I'll be right back." Tulley dashed off to the kitchen garden which was in front of the pasture. He rooted around under some green stalks and came back with a carrot.

"Here Lorenzo, now you'll like the thing." Tulley brushed the dirt off the carrot, broke it into a couple of pieces, and placed the pieces in the thing's lap. Lorenzo bent his long neck down. The thing laughed contentedly as Lorenzo's huge head dipped past its own. Lorenzo's wet lips softly brushed the thing's lap. Then Lorenzo's head moved away, having gently licked the pieces of carrot from the thing's lap.

This wasn't working. Time for a new plan.

"Well, all right, Lorenzo. I don't blame you. Thanks, anyway." Tulley pulled the thing to its feet as it babbled nonsensically. He left the pasture with the thing in tow, carefully closing the gate behind them.

"Thing, let's find out if you can fly," Tulley said. He led the thing to the large oak tree that stood between the barn and the sand garden. The prior summer Tulley's father had made a swing for Tulley out of a sturdy crate, cutting out holes for Tulley's legs and suspending it from a substantial tree branch. Tulley plopped the thing into the crate, which was large enough to accommodate all of the thing's body without even making use of the leg holes. The thing smiled and cooed.

"Here we go, Thing." Tulley stood behind the crate and gave it a push. The crate swung back at Tulley and then he pushed it away with greater force. In no time, the crate, with the thing in it, was swinging in a large arc beneath the branch of the oak tree. The thing was laughing happily, to Tulley's great disappointment.

"You're not scared?" Tulley asked the thing on his next contact with the crate. From the thing there came no clear statement in response, although it was burbling in a way suggestive of pure enjoyment.

"All right then. We'll see what else we can do with you," said Tulley, as he slowly arrested the crate's swinging. He plucked the thing out of the crate and set it on the ground.

This was not going as Tulley had imagined.

He got another idea. "I know," Tulley said to the thing. "We'll bury you in the sand garden and see what happens." Tulley stood the thing up and led it to his sand garden.

Tulley set the thing down in the middle of the sand garden, found his shovel, which wasn't far away, and then started digging a hole to put the thing in. All the while, the thing regarded Tulley with a smile, making noises and waving its little arms in the air as if wanting to help.

Just as soon as Tulley had started digging the hole, the first raindrop of a rapidly approaching rainstorm landed on his hand. Tulley looked up and saw a line of dark clouds he had earlier failed to notice. He dropped the shovel and stood the thing up on its pathetic little leg parts. Then he brushed the sand off the thing and took its slimy hand in his. "I don't want to get wet," Tulley said to the thing, "so I guess we have to go back indoors."

Tulley led the thing back into the house, and through the kitchen, and into his parents' bedroom where his mother was still sound asleep. He maneuvered the thing into its cage as quietly as he could, then turned and left the room.

Once Darby was standing in his crib, he turned and saw his mother sleeping on her bed. "Mama!" Darby yelled as loudly as his little lungs would allow.

His mother's eyes fluttered. "My little angel!" Darby's mother exclaimed as she swung her legs off her bed and went to embrace him. "From sweet dreams back into Mother's arms," she said, picking Darby up and wrapping her arms around him.

Tulley, meanwhile, was laying on his bed listening to the rain fall on the roof above his room as his mother, who had obviously lost her mind, exchanged stupidities with his idiot baby brother.

Tulley was determined even from this early age that one day he would find a way to show his parents just how awful Darby really was, and that by doing so he would restore himself to the position he had formerly held in his parents' hearts.

What Ever Happened
to Baby Darby?

Friday, July 12, 1872

Emily stood in front of the kitchen table chopping up vegetables for a stew. The captain had been away a few days but was due to return later in the day.

The weather could not have been more pleasant that afternoon, mostly sunny and neither too warm nor too cool. Outside the kitchen window, a light breeze played through the treetops. Puffy white clouds drifted lazily across the sky.

Tulley, ten years old, and Darby, six-and-a-half, were playing in the sand garden, although not together. Darby was building tiny buildings and tiny villages in one end of the sand garden while, in the other end, Tulley was slaughtering toy soldiers in a bloody war, then burying them.

Five years had passed since Tulley had tried to get Lorenzo to eat Darby. During that time, Darby had grown into a sturdy little boy and Tulley had seemed to accept his little brother as a permanent fixture in the Walker household.

Tulley turned to Darby and said "Hey, Darby, do you want to go out in the sailboat?"

Darby always agreed to do anything his brother suggested. He was desperate to be Tulley's friend. "Uh-huh, let's!"

The boys went into the kitchen where their mother was at work.

"Mother," said Tulley, "can Darby and I go out in the sailboat?"

Emily looked out the window. The breeze appeared to be gentle and there wasn't the slightest threat of storms.

Until recently, there had always been at least one adult on the sailboat with the Walker children at all times, but on a couple of occasions earlier this summer the boys had been allowed to take the boat out unsupervised. The captain had suggested that Darby was still a little too young to be out on the boat with just Tulley and no adult, but Emily had reminded him of what the fortune teller had predicted for Darby, and of the miraculous incident in the pond during Emily's pregnancy. The captain had laughed and had said, in response, that he "wasn't even going to try to argue with any of that."

Emily said "Tulley, I'm sure you *can* go out in the boat, but you're not asking me the question you should be asking."

"Oh, Mother. *May* Darby and I go out in the sailboat?" Tulley asked, this time getting the question right.

"Okay, boys, you may go out in the sailboat, but remember the rules. You must both wear life jackets. You must stay inside

Salt Water Pond, even if there's enough water in the creek to get the boat out into the Sound. Tulley must be the only one at the tiller, and Tulley, you must not tip the boat at all. Do you understand?"

"Yes, Mother," said Tulley.

"Yes, Mother," said Darby.

The boys ran out the kitchen door. Emily watched as they went into the barn at the back of the property and came out a moment later with their life jackets. Then they disappeared around the house on their way down to Salt Water Pond.

Like all the Walkers before them, both boys had been taught how to swim at an early age. Grandfather Walker had taught Tulley how to sail, and Tulley was already a competent sailor. Darby would soon get his own sailing lessons from Grandfather Walker.

The boys ran all the way down to Salt Water Pond, where the Walkers' sailboat lay waiting, pulled up on the shore of the pond beyond the reach of the tides. The boat was only ten feet long and had only a mainsail, not a jib. Grandfather Walker had built the simplest sailboat one could build, perfect for kids to sail on in a small pond.

Because they had been using it regularly during the summer, the boat was always left so that almost no preparation was needed to take it out. The sail was left in place, furled and tied around the boom. All the boys had to do was attach the rudder to the stern, drop the center board into its slot, unfurl the sail and hoist it up the mast.

Within a couple of minutes, the boys were sailing around Salt Water Pond. The boat tacked back and forth. Darby was smiling broadly, happy to be riding with his big brother as the gulls wheeled in the sky above. For Darby, the world was a perfect place.

Emily left the kitchen periodically to go to one of the front windows of the house and look out at Salt Water Pond where she could see the boys out on the little sailboat.

After some time tacking back and forth across Salt Water Pond, Tulley said "This is boring. Let's go out into the Sound."

"No! That's against the rules!"

"Rules are meant to be broken. Besides, Mother is in the kitchen. She'll never know."

Darby stared at his brother in disbelief as Tulley sailed the boat to the narrow creek that connected the pond to the ocean at its south. As it was high tide, the water was deep enough to let the sailboat through.

"Tulley, turn the boat around! We can't go out of Salt Water Pond! You know the rules!"

"Rules are for babies," Tulley responded. "We can go out into the Sound. Don't worry. It's okay."

"No, Tulley, it isn't. Stop! We're not supposed to do this! It's not safe!"

"Oh, shut up. I'm in charge," said Tulley.

By then the sailboat was already nearing the southern end of the creek, on its way into Nantucket Sound. Terror darkened Darby's face.

At times the conditions on Salt Water Pond were quite different from those just a hundred yards to the south on the Sound. Sometimes the pond could be flat and the winds soft while the waves in the Sound were larger and the wind stronger and more irregular. This day was one of those days when the conditions on the pond were significantly calmer than those on the ocean to its south. As the Walkers' sailboat dropped out of the creek and into Nantucket Sound, this was immediately apparent. The boat began bucking as it encountered the large waves rolling into the shoreline. It started tipping as stronger winds pushed against the sail.

Darby began crying. "Tulley, turn back! Please! I'm scared!"

Tulley laughed. "Don't be a baby, Darby. This will be fun!"

Darby began to wail, and Darby's wailing just made Tulley laugh louder. The boat continued south, away from the beach.

In 1872, there weren't yet crowds of tourists on the beaches. There were hardly any pleasure boats in the area. Everyone there was there to work. Fishing schooners passed by further out on the water, and along the shore a few people attended to various tasks, but nobody had their eyes on the little sailboat with the boys in it.

The further out the Walker sailboat went, the larger the waves got. The wind was much more irregular and unpredictable than Tulley had imagined. Darby cried and screamed. Tulley continued to sneer and laugh at Darby, whose little face was soaked with tears.

At one point, between his screams and wails, Darby looked through tear-streaked eyes and said to Tulley, "You're trying to drown me!"

Tulley laughed even louder.

After a short time on the Sound, Tulley turned the tiller to bring the boat around and head along the shore rather than away from it. At that moment, a larger than usual wave and a sudden gust simultaneously struck the sailboat. Tulley was not a sufficiently skilled sailor to deal with this dual assault. The boat rolled onto its side. The mast and the sail dipped to the surface of the water as the boys were dumped into the sea.

Darby hit his head on the boom as he fell out of the boat and was knocked unconscious. Tulley dropped harmlessly into the warm Nantucket Sound water, barely getting his hair wet.

Tulley assessed the situation as soon as he was in the water. He saw Darby floating limply, his head held barely above the water by the life jacket. He paddled over to him, but he couldn't get him to respond.

Tulley did not panic. Instead he swam to the shore, which wasn't as far away as he had thought it was. He went up the beach. He saw a fisherman a couple of hundred yards to the east. The fisherman was walking toward the east, away from the creek to Salt Water Pond and away from his own little boat which he kept on the shore near the creek. He was carrying fishing gear and a bucket of fish. The fisherman had not seen the sailboat capsize. Tulley tore off his life jacket and ran as fast as his legs would carry him toward the fisherman, yelling, "Help, help!"

Soon the fisherman was racing back to where Tulley had swum ashore. The fisherman pulled off his shoes, stripped down to his undershorts, and ran into the water. He swam out to the capsized boat and the unconscious Darby. He grabbed Darby and pulled him back to the beach.

By this time another man, having heard the shouting, appeared on the scene. Together, the two men tended to Darby. They made sure his mouth was fully open, they pressed down repeatedly on his chest, and they blew forcefully into his mouth. Before long, Darby was no longer unconscious and was coughing up sea water and sucking in air.

The memory of his near-drowning would be cemented into Darby's memory just like this for the next twenty-eight years.

The Branded Hand

Saturday, August 12, 1876

Darby, ten years old, had invited his friends, Manuel Silva and Joe Pina, over to the Walker house to play. Manuel and Joe were always fun to be around. Their fathers were sailors. Their families had come to Harwich from the Azores several years earlier. Like Darby, they had expansive imaginations and knew how to create their own games that could keep them happily engaged all day long. Also, like Darby, they loved baseball.

Manuel and Joe arrived together at mid-morning. Tulley was sitting in the kitchen reading a newspaper and Darby was in his bedroom, adjacent to the kitchen. When Manuel knocked at the back door, Darby called through his bedroom window that they should let themselves in. Manuel and Joe entered the kitchen.

"Hi, Tulley," said Manuel.

"Hello, Tulley," said Joe, following right behind. "How're you?"

Just as Darby was entering the kitchen from his bedroom, Tulley looked up at Manuel and Joe briefly, then looked away. He did not acknowledge them. Instead, he folded the newspaper he'd been reading, stood up, and left the house.

"I'm really sorry," Darby said to his friends. "My brother can be a wretch."

"It's all right, Darby," said Manuel. "We're used to this stuff."

"I don't know what's bothering him today," Darby said. "He isn't usually quite so rude."

"Forget it. We're here to have fun," said Joe.

"Right," said Darby. "Let's go."

The three boys left the house and walked down to the beach, where they spent a couple of hours tossing around a ball and playing along the shore. Around one o'clock, they came back to the house, where Emily served them lunch. By then, the sky had begun to darken and there was a cool wind. They decided to play inside the barn.

In the barn they found Darby's grandfather, Nathaniel, grooming Lorenzo.

"Hi Grandpa," said Darby. "These are my friends, Manuel and Joe."

Nathaniel stood back from Lorenzo and smiled at Darby and his friends.

"Nathaniel Walker," said Nathaniel, shaking hands with Darby's friends. "It's an honor to meet you both. What are you boys doing today?"

"Well," said Darby, "it looks like it might rain, so we thought we would find something to do here in the barn."

"Fine, Darby. Would you like me to find some work you can all do?"

"Thanks Grandpa, but I don't think so."

Nathaniel chuckled. "Don't worry, I wasn't going to press you into service today."

"Mr. Walker, may I ask you a question?" asked Manuel.

"Sure."

"It looks like you have something burned into the palm of your right hand. What is that?"

Nathaniel turned his palm up and appeared to study it. "Well, son, the story of the mark on my hand is a rather long one." Nathaniel looked at Darby. "I'm not sure you'd want to sit long enough for me to tell it to you."

"No, Grandpa, I think you should tell it. We're not doing anything anyway. Manuel, Joe, this is a good story. Do you want to sit with Grandpa for a while and hear his story?" Darby knew that his friends would be fascinated.

"Yes," said Joe.

"Yes, please," said Manuel.

"All right then," said Nathaniel. "Come sit down, and I'll tell you all about my branded hand." He led the boys to a row of old wooden chairs that must have been retired from service in a kitchen or on a porch decades earlier. When everyone was seated, Nathaniel began.

"When I was a young man, I decided that I needed to get away from home and have an adventure, so I boarded a vessel bound for Pensacola ..."

"Did Mrs. Walker go with you?" asked Manuel.

"No, I hadn't yet met Darby's grandmother. If I had, I would never have left."

"What year was this?" asked Joe.

"Oh, let's see. It must have been almost forty years ago now. 1837. Or was it 1838? No, it was 1837 when I went. Anyway, I sailed to Pensacola. When I arrived in the South, I liked everything about it except one thing: the institution of slavery. I have always considered that slavery was among the most evil of evils, subjecting the slave to the deepest of misery and the master to dissipation in this life and eternal suffering in the next. I considered all enslaved men and women as my brothers and sisters, and 'brothers and sisters' I always called them. However, I have never borne hostility toward any of my fellow men, including slaveholders."

"Mr. Walker," asked Manuel, "if you were so much against slavery, how could you stand slaveholders?"

"Well, Manuel, I pitied the slaveholders for their blindness to their sins and for their utter, soul-destroying depravity. It's hard to feel hostility toward someone you pity." Nathaniel looked at Manuel, who seemed satisfied with that answer.

"Shortly after I arrived in Pensacola, I secured a position working as a shipwright. I enjoyed the work and the people I was working for. During my own time, I built an open sailboat of twenty feet in length. I used it for fishing and exploring on days when I wasn't beholden to my employers.

"White folks in the South did not associate with colored folks, but I could not adhere to that custom. Instead, I be-

friended whites and coloreds alike as I went about my business. I never hid the fact that I opposed slavery.

"Of course it quickly became known that I was on good
terms with colored folks, and on several occasions I was
warned in no uncertain terms by the local authorities that they
wouldn't be able to protect me from violence directed at me for
this friendliness and for my opposition to slavery. Fortunately,
no violence came my way during my time in Pensacola."

"Mr. Walker," asked Manuel, "was Florida even a
state when you were there? How many people were living
there back then?"

"No, Florida was still a territory of the U.S. It didn't become a state until about 1845, I believe. It had only been acquired from Spain in 1821. Outside of a few small towns along
the coasts, some military outposts and plantations, most of
Florida was undeveloped. At that time, you could sail an entire day along much of either coast without seeing any human
activity, not a single settlement or another vessel. The three
largest towns in the territory were Pensacola in the west, St.
Augustine in the east, and, of course, Key West at the southernmost extremity."

Manuel seemed happy with that answer.

"Anyway, after nearly two years in Pensacola I decided
that it was time to come back home. Shortly before I was set
to leave Pensacola, I met some colored folks, four young men
and two boys. One of the boys was about your age, or perhaps
a year or two younger. They were slaves on a large plantation,
and told me that they wished to leave the place. I didn't answer

them right away. I knew that helping them was a crime and that I would be severely punished if caught. But after a day or two of thinking about it, I realized that it was my duty to assist them, and so I told them to meet me about an hour after sunset the next evening and we'd set sail for the Bahama Islands. This gave me an entire day to collect supplies for the trip.

"How would it help the slaves to sail to the Bahama Islands?" Joe asked.

"The Bahama Islands are under British control, Joe. The British Empire abolished slavery about 1834, if I remember right. But even before 1820, they had decreed that any slave brought to the Bahama Islands would become a free person."

"Mr. Walker," asked Manuel, "how could you sail to the Bahama Islands in your little boat? Aren't the Bahama Islands a long way out in the Atlantic?"

"No, Manuel. The closest parts of the Bahama Islands are only about fifty miles east of the Florida coast. With good weather, it was a trip that could be made from that coast in less than a day, even in a boat as small as mine. Many slaves achieved their freedom this way. Plenty of Seminole Indians also fled to the Bahama Islands rather than be forced into the reservations west of the Mississippi. When I was in Florida, our contemptible government was at war with the Seminoles as the result of the government's reprehensible decision to force them out of their territory."

"Okay, I see," said Manuel, "but wouldn't the plantation owner try to get the slaves back?"

"Yes, Manuel. That's a smart question, and that's exactly what happened. The plantation owner offered a substantial bounty for capturing my brothers and myself, and bounty hunters set out after us as soon as they figured out that the slaves must have sailed off with me. Fortunately, that didn't happen right away, so we had a bit of a lead.

"That first night we headed east along the coast all night. When the sun rose the next day, my first priority was to teach my brothers how to sail the boat. I did this by putting each of them in succession at the tiller and guiding them as they experimented with adjusting the boat's direction and speed.

"By the end of the day, they had all mastered the basics, including how to avoid capsizing, which meant I could sleep as needed. I insisted that one of my brothers stay at the helm at all times, while I sat in close proximity for guidance, except when there was a risk of us being seen. Then I'd take the tiller and my brothers would hide under a spare canvas.

"The first several days of our trip were uneventful, except for rain, and some perilous passages around the capes, where the currents and waves were unusually strong. We encountered vessels here and there, but on each such occasion we were able to hide my brothers beneath the canvas before we were close enough to any vessel for them to be spotted.

"Around the end of the first week we were just north of the bay called Bahia Espiritu Santo—or Bay of the Holy Spirit. The Bay was named by Hernando de Soto, the sixteenth-century Spanish explorer."

"That's Tampa Bay!" said Manuel. "That's where Tampa is."

"Right again, Manuel. Tampa didn't exist when I was there, but there was an American military post, Fort Brooke, where Tampa is now.

"On the eighth day I started to become ill, feeling feverish and exhausted, and the illness only got worse. It was also on that day that a sloop much faster than my boat appeared from the north, and I suspected this was a boat from Pensacola coming to apprehend us. We turned toward an opening between two barrier islands, and my suspicion was confirmed when, instead of continuing south, the sloop came about and made directly toward us.

"It was only because we were in a small boat that we were able to escape our pursuers that day. The sloop drew too much water to follow us into the channels between the barrier islands and the mainland. The bounty hunters lowered a rowboat in hopes of pursuing us, but the rowboat, though able to go where we had gone in the shallow channels, could not keep up with us.

"Toward the end of the day, I figured the bounty hunters would just wait off the coast for us to emerge from the barrier islands. We continued south a little ways and found that we were at the end of the Pinellas peninsula. On my old chart it was called 'Punta Piñal,' Spanish for 'Piney Point.'

"After the sun went down, we slipped through a cluster of tiny islands and sailed east across the lower section of the Bahia Espiritu Santo. I knew that we couldn't outrun the bounty hunters, so I was looking for a place where we could hide out for a while. My hope was that we could make the bounty hunters think, at least temporarily, that we had gotten away from them to the south.

"The moon was bright, and we sailed east toward the far side of the bay, which was low and uninviting except for a solitary hill that rose up above the shoreline. When we reached the eastern shore, we found the hill was an island. It was behind a string of tiny barrier islands and near the mouth of a small bay. We entered a narrow, natural channel between the barrier islands and went to the back of the island with the hill on it. We unloaded our gear, hid the boat on the far side of a mangrove island in the bay, and spent that night on the backside of the hill.

"In the morning we discovered that the island with the hill on it was actually an ancient Indian shell mound."

"What's an Indian shell mound?" asked Joe.

"It's a huge pile of shells, sometimes ten or twenty or thirty feet high, and sometimes higher. The shells are mostly oyster shells and conch shells, shells which the Indians discarded at meals. In many cases, the piles of shells became actual hills because these were feasting places for the Indians over many centuries. They don't exist here in New England, but there are a great many of them in Florida."

"Gosh," said Joe. "I've never heard of Indian shell mounds."

"Someday, Joe, you should go and see them. They are rather amazing."

"Could you take us to the shell mound someday?"

This question took Nathaniel by surprise, and he stopped to consider it.

"I'm sure I *could* take you there," Nathaniel finally said. "This shell mound wouldn't be hard to find, since it was the only shell mound right on the eastern edge of the bay. But my days of adventure are over. Here in Harwich Port is where I belong. Now back to my story ...

"We set up a makeshift camp on the back side of the island. The mainland was only fifty yards to the east of the island, across a shallow channel. Two of my brothers explored and eventually found, about a mile distant, a freshwater spring that enabled us to replenish our supply of water.

"My other brothers took turns hiding in the vegetation at the top of the shell mound and keeping a lookout across the bay. We saw the bounty hunters sail up the bay that afternoon, but they didn't discover our hiding place. From a distance there was no way to tell that the hill was an island with a body of water behind it. Before sunset, the bounty hunters sailed out of the bay.

"That night, a fierce storm blew in. I was glad to be high and dry and not out on the water, where my sailboat would have gone down and taken us all with it. That shell mound saved our lives in more ways than one. Hiding out apparently worked because when we left the next morning we had no sight of the bounty hunters' schooner.

"For three more days we were unmolested and were able to round Cape Sable and begin our easterly course toward the keys that make up the eastern edge of Florida Bay, beyond which lies the Atlantic. I feared that it was only a matter of time before the bounty hunters would find us. We were again running low on water, and I was getting gravely ill.

"Sailing east that day we came across a sad sight, a capsized sailboat drifting toward the shore. We sailed up right next to it, hoping to find a survivor or survivors clinging to the overturned hull, but there were none."

"Was it a big boat?" Joe asked.

"No, Joe, it was a boat that was similar in size to my own and only slightly different in design. Well, we secured a line to the capsized boat and towed it to one of the low islands that dot the southern edge of the Florida peninsula. We pulled it as close to the shore as we possibly could. At that point, one of my brothers put his head under the water and looked up under the hull to see if there might be a survivor or a dead sailor there, but there was none.

"There was a line tied to the stern of the boat, and when we got to the beach and pulled that line in, we found the dead body of a sailor. He must have decided to tie himself to his boat so that he could pull himself back to it if he fell overboard. Sadly, he fell overboard and drowned."

"Who was the dead man?" Joe asked.

"I don't know, Joe. There was no way to tell who it was and nobody to ask. He could have been a local fisherman. He could have been a traveler, perhaps someone running from the law.

"Anyway, that's when I got an idea. Appearances are often deceiving, and a deception might be just what we needed at that moment. We were unable to help this poor soul who had perished during the storm. His boat could no longer be sailed because the mast and rigging were destroyed, and there was nothing to do about that either. But though it was older, his boat looked a lot like my boat.

"I told my brothers that we would bury the dead sailor, and that I would stay at this place with the wrecked boat while they sailed onto the Bahama Islands. I would report to my captors, who would surely soon be upon us, that my boat, which I would say was the wrecked boat, had capsized and that my brothers had drowned or run off into the Everglades. I was far too sick to continue the trip. I felt that I was probably going to die.

"My brothers talked among themselves while I lay on the beach near the two boats. They returned shortly and then the eldest one of them said that they could not accept the proposal as I had offered it. He said that if I were captured without them I would be held responsible for their escape and would surely be put to death. Instead, he proposed the three oldest of their group stay with me to be taken by the bounty hunters while the three youngest would sail to the Bahama Islands, if they could get there.

"He further proposed that I and the three left behind would all report that we knew nothing of the fate of the other three slaves and that they had run off on their own at Pensacola and had never been with us on my boat. He told me they had been observed having a fight among themselves the day before they'd run away, so it wouldn't be hard to convince anyone that they had broken into two groups.

"I didn't want to let even three of my brothers be taken by the bounty hunters and returned to their lives as slaves, but they insisted, pointing out that there wasn't enough food or water to sustain all six of them to the Bahama Islands, a point which I felt certain was true."

"Mr. Walker," Joe asked, "are you saying that you and the slaves decided to lie to the bounty hunters about all of these things?"

"Yes, Joe. I'm a firm believer in telling the truth. However, duplicity is sometimes the only thing that will save you from death or serious injury at the hands of evil forces. When the truth won't save you from dangerous and dishonest people, it's perfectly okay to employ dishonesty to save yourself. Never forget that. In this case, our lies were necessary to get three souls to freedom."

Nathaniel looked at Joe and Manuel, who nodded their understanding. Then he resumed his story. "I was too weak to undertake any labors, so my brothers, following my suggestions, carried the dead sailor through the shallow water up a creek that snaked from behind the beach and buried him in the sand at the back of the beach, careful not to leave tracks. I said a prayer for the unknown sailor, and thanked God for the opportunity to salvage something good out of the circumstances of his tragic death.

"We sent the three youngest of my brothers off in my boat. They had one jug of rainwater and just enough food to sustain them. I told them to follow the southern edge of the peninsula east until they reached the Atlantic, which they would know by the larger waves crashing on the far side of the barrier islands they would run directly into.

"I gave them the compass heading they would need to follow after leaving the Florida coast in order to put them right in the middle of the archipelago of the Bahama Islands, a target a hundred miles wide which, even allowing for the currents, would be hard to miss if they followed my instructions.

"Not ten minutes after the three youngest of my brothers and my boat disappeared out of our view to the east, the sails of the bounty hunters' sloop appeared to our west. My three remaining brothers and I were soon captured and taken aboard the sloop. We were taken to Key West. From there, we were sent by steamer back to Pensacola. At that time, I still thought I was going to die, but over the next two weeks my body slowly returned to health.

"The bounty hunters had no reason to doubt that the wrecked sailboat with which we were found was my boat. Our deception worked.

"The story of my trial and brutal incarceration is too long and too unpleasant to recount now for you boys, but, as you can see, as part of my punishment, they used a hot iron to brand 'SS' into my hand." Nathaniel raised his right palm and showed the boys.

"Oh my gosh," said Joe. "That must have really hurt!"

"Yes, Joe, I was in severe pain when they did it, and the pain didn't go away for several days."

"But what were the letters for?" asked Manuel. "Why two S's?"

"They chose S.S. to indicate that I was a slave stealer."

"Then what happened?" Joe asked.

"I was in jail at Pensacola for a year. My fellow abolition-ists back here in Harwich came up with the money to pay the fine imposed upon me for my efforts to save my brothers from the unjust cruelty imposed upon them. I can only imagine how much worse I would have been treated if it had been discov-ered that three of my brothers had escaped on my sailboat.

"As for my three brothers who were apprehended with me, they were returned to the plantation owner. According to the charges filed against me, they each had a value of a mere six hundred dollars. While I was in jail, I heard that each of them was beaten to the point of unconsciousness for trying to escape. I imagine that each of them continued on in that evil system until their deaths. The pain and suffering I endured as a consequence of my efforts in trying to secure their freedom was nothing compared to theirs."

Nathaniel stopped talking, and after a moment it was clear to the boys that Nathaniel believed he had reached the end of the story.

"Mr. Walker," asked Manuel, "what about the slaves who sailed away in your boat? Did they make it to the Ba-hama Islands?"

"Very good question, Manuel. For many years I didn't know whether or not they made it to the islands. I didn't know if they'd lived or drowned. Then, at the end of 1865, on the same day Darby was born, and only a few months after the abomi-nable practice of slavery was finally ended in this country, one of the brothers who had sailed off in my boat, the youngest one, now grown into a fine man, showed up at our front door. He was called "Dee," but I never knew his real name.

"It turned out that they had indeed made it to the Bahama Islands. Dee had attended school and had worked hard and put enough money aside to pay for passage to Boston and take his life in a new direction. The first thing he did when he arrived was to come down to the Cape and see the man who had helped him escape slavery. It made my heart sing to see him.

"Darby won't remember this of course, but while Dee was here, we went next door. Dee took Darby into his arms. Unfortunately, Darby's father had gone away on a voyage and didn't get the chance to meet him. Anyway, Dee told me that he hoped that at a future time he could be of help to Darby as a way to thank me for my role in securing his freedom. I said that I was grateful for the sentiment but that Dee's survival and success were more than sufficient thanks for me only discharging my duty.

"I was sorry to see Dee go at the end of the day, but he said he had just wanted to see me again and couldn't stay."

Now they really were at the end of Nathaniel Walker's story. Manuel and Joe thanked him for telling it.

That evening, after Manuel and Joe had gone home, Tulley, who had poked his head into the barn when Nathaniel was halfway through his story, said to Darby: "I've heard Grandpa's stupid story a dozen times, and you probably have too. I don't know how you could stand to hear it again. I bet it isn't even true."

"But what about the letters burned into his hand?" Darby asked.

"Grandpa probably once worked for a farmer somewhere who had the initials SS, Sam Smith or something, and he probably burned his own hand by accident when branding the owner's cows."

Darby was angry and offended. How could Tulley be so disrespectful? Darby knew in his heart that Grandfather Walker's story was true.

The Purloined Paper

Monday, June 7, 1880

The end of Darby's first year of high school was approaching. Miss Kinsman had directed her students to write a ten-page paper on any event or period in American history. For a solid month, Darby had spent several hours each weekday in the Broadbrooks Free Library up in Harwich Center researching the Civil War. Never being a person who did things by halves, Darby assembled more than enough notes to write a paper fifty pages long. He set to work composing a paper that was far beyond the skill level of anyone else in his class.

Darby took great care not to let anyone see his work before it was finished. He didn't even tell his family what he was working on. He didn't want anyone to give him any assistance or influence his work. Instead, he wanted people to be impressed and surprised with what he was able to do on his own. A full week before it was due, Darby read his paper from start to finish for the first time. He knew it was good. It was better than anyone could have possibly expected of him, and he was pretty sure it was at least as good as any of the older students at Harwich High School would have been able to write. After reading it a second time, he placed it in the drawer of the desk next to his bed.

The next day, when Darby came home from school, he opened his desk drawer to pull out the paper and read it again. The paper wasn't there. Darby panicked. He searched his room frantically, turning the space into a dizzying vortex.

A few minutes into this search, Emily came to the door of the bedroom and looked in.

"Darby, dear, are you okay? Your room looks like a tornado just passed through it!"

Darby ran his right hand through his hair, a look of torment on his face. "Mother, I've spent all my free time lately working on a paper for Miss Kinsman. She gave us the assignment a month ago. It's due next week. I finished it yesterday. I left it in my desk drawer, and now I can't find it!"

"So that's what you've been working on lately. I knew you were doing something important. What's the assignment, exactly?"

"We were told to prepare a ten-page report on any event or period in U.S. history. I chose the Civil War. That's why I've been up at the library most afternoons for the last month. I read parts of all their books on the Civil War and a bunch of old newspaper articles. I've been working really hard on this. Now it's gone! You haven't been in my room, have you?"

"Oh, Darby, I'm so sorry! No, I haven't been in your room. I'm sure you'll find it, though. Papers don't just disappear."

"Mother, I've looked everywhere! It's gone!"

Emily put her hand on Darby's shoulder. "We'll find it, sweetheart."

Tulley walked into the kitchen. He saw Emily and Darby talking in Darby's room.

Emily stepped out of Darby's room and into the kitchen. "Hello, Tulley. How was school?"

"Okay."

"Tulley, Darby can't find a report he's been working on for the last few weeks. You haven't seen it sitting around anywhere, have you?"

"Nope, sorry."

"Okay. Well if you do see it, please bring it to Darby right away."

"Sure, Mother."

Emily went back into Darby's room, where Darby sat on his bed, his face registering complete despair.

"Tulley hasn't seen the paper."

"Yes, I heard. Mother, I put my heart and soul into this paper. I know it was really good. Now it's gone. What am I going to do?"

"You've really looked everywhere?"

"Yes. Everywhere."

"And it's not in your book bag?"

"No." Darby lifted the empty canvas bag from his bed, turned it upside down and shook it.

"Is there any chance you left it somewhere else?"

"No, Mother. I haven't left it anywhere else. It's gone!"

Emily took Darby's hand in hers. "I'm so sorry, sweetheart. I'm sure you're right about how good your paper is. If you're absolutely sure it's gone, you're just going to have to rewrite it. The good news is that it won't be nearly as much work as it was to write it in the first place."

"I don't know. It's going to be a lot of work. My notes are gone too."

"Oh, sweetheart, I'm so sorry."

Darby contemplated the tragic situation. "I guess I'll go up to the library and start right now," he said finally.

"Darby, it's not going to be as bad as you think, I promise. Go get a good start on the rewrite. While you're at the library, I'm going to bake a chocolate cake. When you come home, you'll be well on your way to completing your work and will feel better. We'll have the cake for dessert tonight."

Devastated by his loss, Darby threw a notebook into his book bag and headed to the library. Darby decided to dramatically narrow the paper's focus in order to make writing the paper again an easier task. He abandoned his goal of turning in the best paper in the class and now only wanted to do what was necessary to get a passing mark. He was so disheartened that he decided that this was all he was capable of.

The following week, Darby gave Miss Kinsman the second version of his paper, but it wasn't the masterpiece he had produced the first time.

Tulley, in his final year at Harwich High School, was about
to turn in his best work ever. The prior day, while Darby was
visiting their grandparents next door, Tulley had opened the
drawer of Darby's desk and found Darby's paper. His own
teacher had also assigned a final report, and no boundaries of
any significance had been set on its subject matter. Tulley had
been unable to come up with a worthwhile subject on his own,
so he started working on a subject his teacher had suggested
for him: Peter Cooper and the Baltimore & Ohio Railroad, the
country's first public railway. Though Tulley was interested in
this topic and knew a fair amount about it already, the problem
was that Tulley didn't feel like writing anything. And even if
he could have mustered the motivation, he would never have
produced much more than the minimum needed to receive a
passing grade.

As soon as he began reading Darby's paper, Tulley knew
that his ordinarily pathetic brother had produced something
truly outstanding. So good, Tulley thought, that he would just
take it and claim the work as his own.

He spent a long time carefully copying the paper in his
own handwriting, and then he ripped up Darby's paper, along
with the notes, and placed the shredded paper into the wood-
stove in the kitchen. With a smile, Tulley watched until the
flames obliterated any remaining trace of Darby's work.

While Darby's final paper received no special recognition,
Tulley's paper was hailed by his teacher as a truly brilliant effort from a student who had outdone himself and all his classmates. She was only disappointed that Tulley had waited so

long to reveal his formidable talent as a writer, and she wanted to have a discussion with Tulley about considering a career in which he could employ this talent. Tulley was not interested in having any such discussion and declined the offer as politely as he could. A couple of days later, the captain and Emily received a note from Tulley's teacher praising the report that their literary son had produced. Captain Walker had just returned home from weeks on the sea, and there was discussion that evening at supper about Tulley's impressive and surprising achievement.

"Tell us about your wonderful paper, Tulley," said the captain.

"Actually, Dad, it wasn't as good as Miss Harris says it was. I don't know why she even bothered to mention it."

"Tulley, there is no need for modesty. You have distinguished yourself just as you are finishing your studies. By my reckoning, you should be proud. Tell us about the paper. What was it about?"

"Thanks, Dad, but the paper isn't worth any further thought. Honestly."

"Now, now, Tulley, Miss Harris's note says that the paper was about the Civil War. Is that right?"

Darby looked up from his plate. Tulley squirmed in his chair. Tulley was only then realizing that he had not fully considered the consequences of submitting Darby's work as his own, including the possibility that his family would hear from his teacher, and the possibility, now unfolding suddenly, that Darby would discover what had actually happened to his paper.

"Well, sort of. Not really," said Tulley. "It was more about things that happened as a result of the Civil War but weren't really part of the war itself."

Tulley's mind was racing, trying to find ways to break the connection between "his paper" for which he was receiving so much praise and the paper Darby had written, both of which were, of course, the same thing.

"I'm not sure I know what you mean, Tulley," said the captain.

"My paper ... is really ... mostly ... about ... how the Civil War ... affected trade," said Tulley haltingly.

"Well, that's fine, Tulley. Fine. Why don't you get the paper now and you can read us part of it as we finish our supper?"

"Yes," said Darby, gazing intently at his brother, "it would be great to hear you read from the paper."

"I would like nothing more than to read it to you," Tulley responded, "but I left it with Miss Harris. She wanted to show it to some of the other teachers."

Darby frowned.

"Well that's fine, Tulley, fine," said the captain. "You let Miss Harris know that your parents are anxious to see your wonderful paper just as soon as she gets it back."

"Of course, sir, I'll do that," said Tulley.

Darby had no doubt that Tulley had stolen his paper, and he was certain that Tulley would make sure that nobody ever saw the paper again. He was certain of this as soon as the topic of Tulley's fantastic paper about the Civil War had come up. But what could he do about it? Darby realized there was no proof that Tulley had stolen the paper.

When supper was finishing up, Darby asked his parents for permission to go visit his father's grandmother Nickerson. Everyone in the Walker household called her "Grandma Nick," which is what the captain and his siblings had always called her. Grandma Nick lived in South Harwich, nearly a mile east from the Walkers. Though in her 80s, she was still strong and independent. The captain and Emily gave Darby their permission.

"What happened, Darby?" said Grandma Nick when Darby stepped into her kitchen. She pulled her youngest great-grandchild into her arms. "You look sorer than a blister!"

Darby hesitated. At first, he wasn't quite sure he should say anything about the stolen paper. But then he reviewed in his mind all the occasions on which he had discussed his problems in this old kitchen with his old great-grandmother, and he realized that in every case she had given him sound advice on how to handle them. As far as he knew, nothing he had ever said in confidence to Grandma Nick had been repeated outside her kitchen.

Darby told Grandma Nick the story of his Civil War paper. He told her about all the effort he had put into researching and writing it, and how Tulley stole it, submitted it as his own, and received glowing praise for the stolen work.

He told his great-grandmother how he had gone back to the library and rewritten the paper and that the rewrite had failed to come close to the quality of the original on account of the lack of remaining time and the fact that Darby's heart was no longer in the project.

Grandma Nick listened attentively, not interrupting Darby's sad story. When Darby was finished, she said "Lord in Heaven! That brother of yours is going to get himself into serious trouble one day. I'm sorry this happened to you, Darby."

"I just don't understand it, Grandma Nick. Since I was a little kid, all I ever wanted was to be friends with Tulley. I've always treated him right. I've tried to include him in whatever my friends and I were up to, since he never has his own friends. He's never shown any gratitude. Instead, he repays me by being mean to me, and now stealing my work. I'm going to kill him!"

"Now hold your horses, Darby," said Grandma Nick. "You are just as upset as you should be, given what has happened. Your brother can be extremely provoking, and this time he seems to have outdone himself. I understand that. But killing your brother isn't the solution. It would only destroy lives, including yours. People who dance have to pay the fiddler."

"You may be right, Grandma Nick, but if you're telling me I need to just get over what Tulley has done to me, then all I can say is 'I can't.'"

"Darby, I've told you this before. You must never say that you CAN'T do something. Before you ever say 'I CAN'T', you must add the letters 'R' and 'Y' on the end. Then you have 'I CAN TRY.'"

"Grandma Nick, I can't even try. How would you react if you had a diabolical brother like mine whose primary aim was to ruin your life?"

Grandma Nick paused for a moment before responding. "Darby, you need to step back and get the broader view. It is not your brother's objective to ruin your life. Your brother, though he doesn't know it, is in your life to make you a stronger person."

"That's a crazy idea."

"No, listen to me. You are a capable young man. If you set out to do it, you are going to write more brilliant papers. You can do anything you put your mind to doing."

Grandma Nick looked intently into Darby's eyes. "What is the real consequence to you of the theft of this paper? Is it going to prevent you from doing anything you want to do?"

Darby nodded his understanding, then Grandma Nick continued. "Of course it isn't. Next year it won't matter at all, not to you and not to anyone else. You see, Darby, time is just an illusion, but in a strange way it's an illusion that makes us see things clearly."

Darby had no idea at all what Grandma Nick's last statement meant, but he could imagine that there would come a day when he wouldn't care about the stolen paper. "Maybe you're right, but having my paper stolen doesn't make me stronger."

"Darby, you are wrong about that. The things that challenge us in life are the things that make us stronger, smarter, and wiser. When you write your next paper, are you going to do anything differently?"

"Well, I'm certainly not going to leave it sitting around for my brother, or anyone else, to steal."

"Good. It's best to have an anchor to windward. Nobody is ever again going to steal a paper from you. Have you learned anything else? Would you want to trade places with your brother?"

Darby thought hard about this question. "No, I suppose I wouldn't."

"Why not, Darby? He got the credit for the paper, didn't he?"

"Yes, he did ..." Darby paused.

"Do you think a person who feels confident about his own ability goes around claiming credit for other people's work? Isn't that a pretty desperate thing to do?"

"I guess I see your point," Darby conceded, but the dark scowl on his face made it clear that he was not anywhere near ready to surrender his anger.

"You see, Darby, Tulley may be older than you, but you're much more capable than he is, in many ways. When you're angry at someone because of something he did, ask yourself if what this other person did makes him happier, and if you would stand in his shoes if you could. You wouldn't want to be your brother, would you?"

This sounded a lot like what Grandfather Walker had said about his feelings for the slave owners, but Darby wasn't ready to go along with it yet. "No, I wouldn't want to be my brother, and I don't want *him* to be my brother either. It would be much better if he were dead."

"Oh, Darby. You don't mean that. Perhaps you can't see this right now, but you really wouldn't want that. Tulley is your teacher. Not in the same way Miss Kinsman is your teacher, but you are going to learn from him much more than you ever will from your schoolteachers. Tulley is not going to be the last difficult person in your life, and he won't even be the *most* difficult person in your life. As you learn how to deal with him, you will prepare yourself to deal with the other difficult people you are going to encounter, of which there will be many. In addition, you will find that Tulley is going to need you a lot more than you will ever need him. By figuring out how to help Tulley, you are going to figure out how to help other people, even people who don't know they need your help."

"Do you really think Tulley is going to ever see that he needs me more than I need him?"

"It doesn't matter whether or not he sees it. It's the way it is. You've already saved his life once, as you know."

"What do you mean?"

"I'm talking about the time Tulley took you sailing and he would have drowned if you had not gone for help."

"But I'm the one who nearly drowned! I didn't save anyone's life."

"Of course you did, dear. You were our little hero that day."

Darby frowned, but didn't say anything more about this. It was upsetting to realize that Grandma Nick's memory was starting to fail.

Darby knew Grandma Nick was wrong about Tulley ever needing him. There was nothing he would ever be able to do to help his brother. Darby decided right then and there that from that point on he would be no more than civil to Tulley. He was finished trying to become closer to Tulley. Darby's only objective now was to avoid being seriously harmed by his older brother. Fortunately, Tulley was finishing school and would soon be away from home most of the time.

Darby was glad to have spoken with Grandma Nick, but he still wanted to kill Tulley.

The Old Man by the Sea

Saturday, June 19, 1880

Captain Walker was away on a fishing trip in the Gulf of Maine for a couple of weeks. Emily was visiting her sister and mother around the corner at the Burgess home. Nobody knew where Tulley was, though nobody was actually considering the question.

Darby had finished his chores on this ordinary summer day and decided to take a walk up Main Street through Harwich Port. He had no particular destination in mind. It seemed likely that he'd run into a friend or two and find something fun to do. That's what ordinarily happened. The matter of the stolen paper was still near the top of his thoughts.

The sun was bright and there was a light breeze. Carriages and carts were passing in the street. People were out taking care of errands at the village shops, or sitting on their porches, or working in their gardens. Here and there, neighbors stopped to converse at the edge of the road. Several people smiled and said hello to Darby as he passed by, and he replied in kind.

Darby walked past Sea View House Hotel, the large, recently built, three-story tourist hotel on the shore of Salt Water Pond. Just beyond the hotel, he passed the road that went along the western edge of Salt Water Pond to the shore and Long Wharf. He passed in front of the homes of the Smalls, the Nickersons, the Doanes, the Jenkinses, the Snows, the Bakers, the Smiths, the Youngs, the Kellys, the Coles, and the Eldredges. Darby knew all these families, and they all knew his family. All the houses Darby passed were simple, one- or two-story structures with weathered shingles. Nothing fancy.

Darby passed the road that went to Union Wharf. He passed the shoe store of Ethan Eldredge, the dry goods store of Simeon Sears, the clothing store of Lovell Burgess, the blacksmith shop of William Cole, the art gallery of Hepsibeth Nickerson, and the sail loft of Gilbert Smith. He passed the Harwich Port school buildings on the north side of the street and the dry goods store of Shubael Kelley on the south side of the street, the largest store in the village and home to the Harwich Port post office. As he went by these business establishments, Darby mused that with only a couple of exceptions the structures housing the businesses in the village were nearly indistinguishable from the residences. Only the signage differentiated them. Darby understood that most of the businesses had been inserted into what had originally been people's homes and in many cases still were.

Darby turned and looked south, down the road that went by the lumberyard and onto the wharf of Henry Kelly & Co. To the west was the white spire of Pilgrim Congregational Church, set off against the nearly cloudless blue sky. The Walkers, when they went to church, always went to the Methodist Episcopal Church in South Harwich. Darby and his family never spent any time at Pilgrim Congregational.

Darby looked across to the other side of Main Street. Almost across the road from Pilgrim Congregational Church stood the home of old Freeman Scott. The Scott house loomed over the village from its lot just next door to Elvira Cahoon's boarding house. The Scott house was two stories high with a steeply pitched roof over the attic. All the windows were tall and narrow, with pointy arches at their tops rather than rectangular frames. There was an abundance of ornate woodwork under the gables and eaves, and fancy railings stood out above the large first-floor porch and on the widow's walk at the top, though it appeared all the railings were rotting and in need of replacement. The clapboards were a buttery yellow and the trim was a dark green, but the paint was flaking off. Several shingles were missing from the roof. Darby figured that because the roof was so steeply pitched it probably hadn't begun to leak. The Gothic Revival house was unusual for Harwich Port, and though he had never been inside it or spoken with its owner, the house had been Darby's favorite in the village from the time he was old enough to be aware of his surroundings.

Darby had heard the basic story about the Scott house and its owner. The house had been built by Freeman Scott's father, a ship captain, sometime in the late eighteenth century. Freeman was the only child of Captain Scott, who was descended from a long line of Cape Codders, and his wife, Ruth, who was from Bar Harbor, Maine. Freeman had grown up in the house and now lived there alone. His father had been lost at sea when Freeman was in his last year at Williams College, leaving behind what was rumored at the time to be enough money to support Ruth comfortably for the rest of her life, but not much more than that. Ruth had died several decades after Captain Scott, and, if what Darby heard was correct, the Scott financial well must now be getting pretty dry. The peeling paint on the exterior of the Scott house was confirmation. It was said around town that Freeman would surely have starved by now but for the fact that he was extremely frugal.

Freeman was known to be a soft-spoken man, happy in his own company. Some of the townspeople considered him eccentric. After his father died, Freeman finished his college studies and returned home to his mother in Harwich Port. He never applied his college education to any lucrative purpose, and after his father's death he never left the Cape. Instead, he was content to remain in Harwich Port, where he walked the beach, read books, kept a journal, painted, and watched the world go by as he rocked contentedly on the front porch of the Scott house. Freeman became his own mother's personal nurse in her final years, taking care of her every need.

Freeman had taken up painting while at Williams and was talented, but he never sold any of his work. When asked, he always said that assigning a monetary value to his artwork would demean and diminish it. Instead, he gave away paintings to friends and neighbors who admired them. Over the years a large number of his paintings, the ones Freeman didn't give away, found their home in the attic of the Scott house.

Nobody had ever told Darby how old Freeman was, because nobody in town really knew. They only knew that he was very, very old. Freeman never married, and all his former classmates and contemporaries were long gone. These days he ventured out of the house only when necessary to pick up provisions, periodicals, and books, or to vote or attend to some other civic duty.

This morning, as Darby continued west on Main Street towards the Scott House, Freeman sat in his rocking chair on his front porch, reading a newspaper. Though slow-moving and impossibly old, he was still tall and straight, and his face looked surprisingly youthful. He had a full head of white hair and a full, white, well-kept beard.

"Freeman Scott is crazy," Tulley had told Darby on a couple of prior occasions. "If you see him rocking on his porch, steer clear of him."

"Is he dangerous?" Darby had asked.

"I can't say for sure," Tulley had answered, "but I wouldn't take any chances."

Darby stopped a short distance in front of the Scott house when he saw Freeman rocking on the porch. He didn't see how a lonely old man like Freeman Scott could be dangerous. Freeman certainly didn't *look* dangerous. He didn't particularly look crazy, either, Darby thought, though he supposed that one couldn't always tell if someone was crazy just by their appearance. Appearances are often deceiving, after all.

As Darby was studying Freeman and the Scott house and pondering these issues, Freeman lowered the newspaper so that his face was no longer hidden from Darby's view. Freeman wore glasses, but only to read. His clear blue eyes, looking out above the rims of the glasses, stared right into Darby's hazel eyes.

"Well, hello there, young man," Freeman said. "What is a fine squire like yourself up to on this exquisite morning?"

Darby had never before heard Freeman speak. He didn't think Freeman *sounded* crazy or dangerous, although his speech contained traces of his mother's Maine accent.

"Nothin' much," Darby answered. "Just seeing what's going on around town."

"Ayuh. It's very important to know what's going on. When I was your age, I used to walk all over Harwich just to see what was going on." Freeman folded his newspaper and placed it on a little table next to his rocker.

"How old are you?" Darby asked without thinking, immediately regretting it because he knew perfectly well that it wasn't polite to ask someone's age.

"I'm old, son. Unbearably, unbelievably, undeniably, and unfathomably old. Weather-beaten, wizened, wound down, and worn out. I'm the oldest person in town. In fact, I'm probably the oldest person you'll ever meet."

Freeman smiled broadly, exposing a full set of straight, white teeth. *Not dangerous*, thought Darby.

"Oh, dear! I'm sorry for asking! I didn't mean to be rude." Darby paused. "I guess I should introduce myself, sir. I'm Darby. Darby Walker."

"I know who you are, Darby. I know the Walkers. I knew your great-grandfather, Eleazer Walker. His youngest brother and I were in the same class and were close friends. I'm guessing that you already know that I'm Freeman Scott, but don't call me Mr. Scott. Call me Freeman."

"Okay, Freeman."

"Why don't you come up and rest your feet awhile? Perhaps you can tell me what you've discovered so far this morning."

Darby went up the porch steps and took a seat in the rocking chair next to Freeman's. He passed the next hour with Freeman on the porch of the Scott house. Darby answered many thoughtful, thought-provoking questions put to him by Freeman. Darby asked for, and received, a general outline of Freeman's life story along with Freeman's observations on the origins of the Scott house.

"May I see the inside of the house?" Darby asked after Freeman finished outlining its history.

"I don't let people go inside the house unless they have business to attend to inside," Freeman answered.

"I understand. Forgive me for asking."

"No, you can go in. Tour the whole place, if you want. But first, promise me one thing."

"Sure. What's that?"

"You must not tell a living soul that you were inside the house."

"Okay. I promise."

"Good. If you even think of telling anyone, I will have to dispatch my henchmen to silence you." Freeman laughed. "One other thing, you must not go up attic. The ghosts up there are not known to be particularly sociable. The ghosts down cellar are the friendly ones." Darby was about to laugh, but then realized that Freeman wasn't kidding. He would not be going up attic.

Exploring the Scott house was the most exciting thing Darby had done in months. Darby loved old houses and the old things inside them. The contents of the Scott house were unusually old and interesting. It appeared to Darby that that none of the furnishings in the house were from the current century. Darby was surprised to find that the interior of the house, as old as it was, was shipshape and perfectly clean.

An unusually large ship model stood on top of a sea chest on the landing at the second floor. Darby found it fascinating. The model, nearly four feet long, was an intricately detailed replica of a late eighteenth century schooner, complete with the correct rigging fashioned out of string and sails made of cloth. Affixed to the transom was a sternboard on which was painted "Lone Star" and just below that "Harwich Port." A quarterboard on the starboard side near the bow also bore the ship's name.

Back out on the porch, Darby asked about the ship model.

"The *Lone Star* was my father's schooner," Freeman answered. "Dad commissioned a professional ship modeler in Boston to make the model of it. I believe he did a superb job."

"He sure did. What happened to the real *Lone Star*?"

"Caught in a gale on her way to New York in the fall of 1804. She went down off Long Island. Miraculously, all the men aboard made it to shore, except my father and his first mate. The body of the first mate was recovered the next day, but my father's body was never found."

"I'm sorry, Freeman. What a tragedy."

"Ayuh."

"Say, Freeman, I'm sorry I never came up to talk with you before today. My brother always told me you were crazy, and I was dumb enough to believe him. I hope that doesn't upset you."

"Oh, good Lord! Why should it matter to me if someone says I'm crazy? I'm going to tell you something, Darby. Life itself is crazy. Every person on this planet is crazy. But everyone has their own kind of craziness. The only thing that should matter to you is whether someone else's craziness combines well with your own craziness. If it doesn't, you have to figure out how to deal with the conflict or get away from it entirely. You may not understand what I mean right now, but one day you will."

Darby listened carefully to Freeman's words. He thought he understood.

There was an amused glint in Freeman's eye. "Do you want me to tell you why your brother thinks I'm crazy?"

"Yes, please do."

"It's a delectable story, and I mean that in multiple ways. I remember this like it was yesterday, but it must have happened at least five years ago. I was sitting here on my porch, just like

I am now. It was early on a Sunday afternoon. One of the ladies from Pilgrim Congregational Church across the street had brought me a couple of doughnuts left over from the social hour, and the doughnuts were sitting on a plate right here on this table. I didn't get to be as old as I am by eating doughnuts. I don't eat doughnuts and never have. Sugar and fried foods are bad for you, Darby. Remember that if you remember nothing else I say.

"Well, this kind lady needed to do good works every Sunday. I suppose that bringing doughnuts to an old man who lives alone qualifies, at least in Harwich Port. I've never turned down her kindness, and after she heads home I usually find a taker for the doughnuts, or the cookies, or the muffins, or whatever she brought me. People are always coming to talk with me when I'm out here on my front porch.

"Anyway, these two doughnuts were resting on the table. I was sitting here in this rocking chair with only one eye partially open, pretending to be asleep. I do that sometimes when I feel like just watching the world go by without getting drawn into it. Well, I saw your brother, Tulley, walking up the road. I could tell that he was looking up at me and, much more intently, at the doughnuts. He came up to the foot of the porch steps and was salivating over the doughnuts while I continued to pretend I was asleep. I jolly well knew what he was after. At that point, I altered my breathing to really make it seem I was sleeping soundly.

"I probably shouldn't have done what I did. I probably should have greeted him politely and invited him up on the porch to get the doughnuts, which I was going to be giving away anyway, but I didn't. I felt like having some fun. If it was anybody other than Tulley, I probably would have behaved more like an adult, but I know a few things about Tulley. Well, after a moment, he tiptoed up the porch steps. When he was just in front of the table, and after convincing himself that I was still sound asleep—a couple of sluggish snorts from me sealed the deal—he reached down and gently liberated the doughnuts from their place of rest. Just as he did that, I opened my eyes wide, thrust my arms out at him, and in a loud voice screamed, 'AAARRRRGGGHHH!'"

Freeman and Darby laughed. Through the laughter, Freeman continued. "You should have seen it. Your brother was scared to death! He dropped the doughnuts like they were burning coals, turned around, and damn near fell down the porch steps. He couldn't get away fast enough! I bet he didn't stop running until he got back to your house!"

When the laughter subsided, Freeman studied Darby's face. "Say, Darby, what sort of a person do you suppose would steal doughnuts from an old man sleeping on his front porch?"

"That's a good question."

"Perhaps it was out of character for your brother to steal anything."

"No, I wouldn't say that."

"Really? Why not?"

"I'm not sure I should tell you this ..." Darby hesitated.

"You can tell me, Darby. Your secrets are safe with me."

"Okay. As a matter of fact, my brother just stole something important from me."

"What was it? And how did he execute his crime?"

After Darby told Freeman about Tulley's theft, the old man said, "That's despicable! I'm sorry to hear it. This must be demoralizing for you."

"It is."

"Did you turn Tulley in?"

"No."

"Why not?"

"I have no proof that he did it. My paper is gone. He took my notes as well. If I accused him of stealing my work, he would just deny it, and I might even get in trouble for making the accusation."

"Ayuh. Did you tell Tulley that you know that he did it?"

"I decided it might be better if he didn't know I knew. That way I'm more likely to catch him off guard in the future."

"There's sense in that, I suppose. Now how do you feel about your brother after all this?"

"I despise him."

"I don't blame you."

"I want to kill him."

"Perhaps you should."

"What!?"

"Perhaps you should kill him."

"I heard you the first time, Freeman, but you must be kidding. I can't kill my brother!"

"Why not? He deserves it, doesn't he?"

"Oh, I'm not sure he deserves to *die* exactly."

"But you just said you wanted to kill him."

"I guess I have to think about it some more."

"Ayuh. It's rarely wise to act precipitously."

"What would you do about it if you were me, Freeman?"

"I suppose one thing I would do is make sure that I never let anything like it happen again. If he stole from you once, he is likely to strike again."

"Yes, I thought of that."

"I don't know, Darby. A kid who would steal a paper from his own brother must have pretty big problems. I think I'd feel sorry for him, actually, even though I was the victim of the crime, not him."

"I felt sorry for him up until this latest cruelty. I'm through feeling sorry for him."

"I can understand that. But if I were you, I probably wouldn't kill him. Not yet anyway. Wait until he does something even worse, which he probably will, eventually."

Freeman smiled, and then Darby smiled, reluctantly.

"Darby, it seems to me that your brother is going to need you a lot more than you will ever need him."

"That's strange ..."

"What?"

"That's exactly what Grandma Nick said to me."

"Is that your father's grandmother Nickerson?"

"Yes."

"A very intelligent woman. I knew her cousin Thomas pretty well. Thomas's son, Thomas, Jr., was a cabin boy on the *Essex*, the whaling ship out of Nantucket which was sunk by a whale and became an inspiration for Herman Melville's *Moby Dick*."

"Grandma Nick told me about that. It's a small world."

"Ayuh. You can't possibly know just how small."

Darby was disappointed that Freeman was as mistaken about the situation as Grandma Nick had been. The idea of his brother ever needing Darby's help, or ever accepting it, was crazy.

It was time for Darby to return home for lunch.

"Freeman, I should be heading home. I've enjoyed this visit."

"As have I. Come back any time. Oh, but not the first and third Wednesdays of the month. That's when my cousin comes down on the train from Provincetown to visit for the day. She helps me with the cleaning."

"Okay." Darby stood and turned toward the steps of the front porch. "I like you, Freeman."

"I like you too, Darby. Now remember, don't tell anyone that you went inside my house. And please don't tell your brother that I'm *not* crazy. It's just as well that he thinks I'm crazy."

Darby and Freeman laughed.

"One other thing Darby. Something to remember. Love many, trust few, and always paddle your own canoe."

Darby thought about this. "That's good. Did you come up with it?"

"No, it's just something my mother said. I'm not sure where she got it."

Darby walked the down the steps, then turned and waved at Freeman as he started down Main Street toward home.

Later that day, when Darby saw Grandfather Walker, Darby told him that he had spent part of the morning with Freeman Scott on Freeman's front porch.

"Darby," Nathaniel said in response, "Freeman Scott is one of the finest people on the planet. You are fortunate to have him as a friend."

All's Well that Ends Well

Saturday, June 26, 1880

A week later, Darby returned to Freeman's house. Freeman was delighted. They sat on Freeman's front porch and watched the townspeople pass by.

"Freeman, last week you told me that you knew my great-grandfather, Eleazer Walker."

"Ayuh. I knew him well."

"What was he like?"

Freeman thought for a while before responding. "Have you asked your Grandfather Walker what Eleazer was like?"

"Yes."

"What did your grandfather have to say?"

"He said that he and his father were not close. He didn't seem to want to tell me much."

"Ayuh. I'm not surprised."

"What can *you* tell me about him?"

"Well, do you want me to say something kind about your great-grandfather, or do you want me to tell you the truth?"

"I want the truth, of course!"

"Eleazer Walker was a fiend. A monster. A knave. One of the most pestilent agents of Satan I ever encountered. A son of a bitch, if you'll forgive my language. He was dishonest, and a bully. He didn't care a whit about other people. All he cared about was himself, and good luck to you if you got in his way."

Darby was taken aback by Freeman's candor. It took him a moment to fully react. "He sounds a lot like my brother."

"No, Darby, Eleazer was far worse. Eleazer knew what he was doing. He knew how to intimidate and manipulate people, and he *did* intimidate and manipulate them. Did anyone ever tell you how he died?"

"Yes, he fell down an old well."

"Ayuh. That's the story all right. But he didn't really fall down an old well. He was *pushed* down an old well."

"You mean he was murdered? Who did it?"

"You're going to have to promise not to tell anyone that I told you. In fact, you better not even tell anyone any part of what I'm about to tell you."

"I promise."

"I'm probably the only living person who knows the whole truth."

"I promise I won't tell."

"It's a long story but I'll try and keep it short. As you probably know, your great-grandfather, Eleazer, had two younger brothers. The youngest brother, Zephaniah, was my friend. He was so much younger than the other two brothers that he didn't spend much of his childhood under the same roof as Eleazer, but the middle brother, James, was only three years younger than Eleazer. James and Eleazer hated each other from the start."

"Why?"

"Eleazer bullied James constantly. That's just the way Eleazer was, miserable and mean-spirited. He had no empathy for anyone. No compassion. Naturally, James didn't like the way Eleazer treated him."

"Naturally."

"Anyway, it was what happened in 1814 that drove these brothers apart for the rest of their lives. During the War of 1812, there were British warships in the waters off Cape Cod, and, on occasion, one of these ships would capture one of our merchant ships and claim it for England as a spoil of war."

"We studied the War of 1812 with Miss Kinsman this year. We learned that this kind of stuff went on."

"Ayuh. Well, in 1814, this happened to a merchant vessel out of Boston named, as I recall it, the *Dove*, which was on its way past Monomoy, transporting a load of corn. A British man-of-war stopped her and forced the crew off. Shortly thereafter the wind shifted and a cool, thick fog blew in, as it so often does around our corner of the Cape. Of course the British crew commanding the *Dove* had no idea about the locations of the hazards in our local waters. Lost in the fog, the crew managed to run her aground just off Monomoy Point. The next morning, the *Dove*, grounded helplessly on the shoals, was visible from Harwich Port. James rounded up a crew of several of his friends and they sailed a sloop out to the stranded ship. The British crew surrendered without too much persuasion, knowing that they were in a hopeless situation and in hostile waters. James and his crew unloaded enough of the corn from the *Dove* so that at the afternoon's high tide she floated off the shoals. They proceeded to sail her to Harwich Port, taking the British sailors as prisoners."

"Gosh. Nobody ever told me this story!"

"Ayuh. That doesn't surprise me, given how it reflects on Eleazer. Well, meanwhile, though he was well aware of what James was engaged in doing, Eleazer rode to the Customs House in Barnstable and secured a prize commission, a document granting him legal authority to recapture the *Dove* from the British and have all of the rights of handling that recapture. Then, Eleazer, with a couple of his friends, rowed out in a whaleboat to the *Dove* just as she was on her way into port under James's command.

"Eleazer boarded the *Dove*, showed his prize commission to James, and told James that for his role in the recapture, he would give him ten percent of whatever bounty Eleazer could negotiate with the owner of the *Dove*. Eleazer made James believe that the prize commission gave Eleazer full authority over the *Dove*, but this was a lie, and Eleazer knew it. James had *already completed* the recapture by taking control of the *Dove*, meaning that when the *Dove* was on her way into Harwich Port, the prize commission was a worthless piece of paper. Eleazer bullied James and lied to him, and James felt that he had no choice but to turn the *Dove* over to Eleazer. A few weeks later, long after the matter of the *Dove* was fully concluded, James found out that Eleazer had lied to him, and he vowed that he would never speak to Eleazer again."

"You're right, Freeman. Eleazer was a son of a bitch."

"Ayuh. But that's not the end of the story. I'm sure you heard about Eleazer's plan to convert Salt Water Pond into a harbor."

"Yes. He was going to make a lot of money creating the first harbor in town, but his partner in the venture was lost at sea before they started the work."

"That's right, Darby, but that's only part of the story. It was in 1835, as I remember. Eleazer had acquired, at a steep price for the time, all the land around the east side of Salt Water Pond. I guess your family still owns most of that land, though it's been carved up for them. Anyway, Captain Small, who owned the land around the south and west side of the pond, wouldn't sell any of it to Eleazer but he agreed to be a partner with him in the conversion of the pond into a harbor. Eleazer and Captain Small got a corporate charter from the state legislature, and hired an engineer to come up with the plans for dredging a canal and building a breakwater, wharves, and various other structures you'd find at a harbor. Then, as you know, before the plan was executed, Captain Small was lost at sea on a voyage to Russia. He harpooned a small whale, got tangled in the line, and was pulled overboard. Not a pleasant way to die. But that's not what killed the harbor project."

"I have wondered about that. Captain Small drowned, but why wouldn't his widow just agree to let the plan go forward?"

"You're a shrewd observer, Darby. That's the right question. The answer is that soon after Captain Small was lost at sea, James Walker married Widow Small, and he convinced her that it would be a huge mistake to go into business with his brother, Eleazer."

"I never heard that part of the story!"

"Ayuh. The part I'm now telling you is not a part of any story that would be proudly passed down in your family. Well, anyway, you can imagine how upsetting this was to Eleazer. He had used his life savings to acquire the land around the east side of the pond and pay the lawyers and the engineer, and he couldn't sell the land for anything near what he had paid for it. Nobody was particularly interested in land in Harwich Port in 1835. Eleazer was all but ruined as a result of James's intervention."

"That's quite a story, but what does it have to do with the death of Eleazer?"

"Well, you see, Darby, Eleazer was so mad at James for putting a stop to the harbor conversion that he said he was going to kill James as soon as he had the chance. It's hard to say if he really meant it. In any case, shortly thereafter James came across Eleazer on the road to Chatham, right by an abandoned farmhouse on the south side of the road just before the town line. I think a branch of the Gorham family had once lived there. Anyway, Eleazer and James got into a fight. James managed to knock Eleazer down, and then he pushed him down the old well that had served the farmhouse. Eleazer died in the fall."

Darby was taken aback. "I can't believe that James killed his own brother!"

"Oh, he killed him all right. You know, fratricide isn't something new or unusual. Think of Cain and Abel, or Romulus and Remus."

"But those are made-up stories."

"Ayuh. I suppose they are. But most murder victims know their murderers, and in most of these cases, the murderers are family members. Familiarity breeds contempt, as they say. If you spend all your time with someone, you come to know all their flaws. In the case of brothers, there is always a sort of competition anyway. First, for their parents' approval and love, then for social recognition, then for property and power. When things go off the rails, it's not surprising that a man would kill his brother."

"But, Freeman, how could you really know that James killed his brother?"

"I was there when it happened. James and I had been riding together on our way to Chatham when we ran into Eleazer coming back to Harwich."

"You mean you watched as James pushed Eleazer down the well?"

"Ayuh. And I would have *helped* James push Eleazer down the well if he had asked."

"But isn't it wrong to kill a person? Did Eleazer really deserve to die?"

Freeman thought for a moment before responding. "Ayuh. Of course, it's wrong to kill another person. Generally. But when that other person is someone who causes the death of others, someone who has no concern about the fatal consequences of his actions, then exceptions creep into the picture. It is sometimes necessary to kill in order to stop evil in its tracks. Of course, you have to be ready to face the consequences of taking action. Anyway, Eleazer had done something even worse than I've already related. Eleazer was responsible for the death of their youngest brother." Freeman stopped suddenly and coughed. His eyes became watery.

"How? What did Eleazer do?"

Again, Freeman took time to gather his thoughts. Darby could see a tremendous sadness in Freeman's old, blue eyes. It wasn't clear to Darby if Freeman was going to answer his question, but after a long pause, Freeman cleared his throat and began speaking again.

"Eleazer's youngest brother had a secret he didn't want revealed. Well, Eleazer discovered this secret and threatened to reveal it. His brother couldn't bear the thought of his secret being known and took his own life. He hung himself from a beam in the barn behind your house. Eleazer either knew or should have known that this would be the result of his threat, but he didn't care."

"Holy Mackerel! I had no idea! That's horrible! But what was the secret?"

"I'm sorry, Darby. I can't tell you that right now. Ask me in a few years."

"Are you the only one who knows what the secret was?"

Freeman studied Darby's face. "At this point, I might be the only person who knows. Look, Darby, I know what you're thinking. In case anything happens to me, I'll be sure to leave you enough information so that you can figure out what it was all about."

Darby knew it wouldn't be right to push Freeman about this, and that pushing Freeman wouldn't yield any further information. "Okay, Freeman. But back to James. Why didn't James get into trouble for killing Eleazer?"

"James was never charged. There was never any investigation of the incident. James claimed that after he and Eleazer met in the road, Eleazer tried to kill him, and that while James was defending himself, Eleazer fell into the well by accident."

"Did people believe that story?"

"No, I don't think anybody in town really believed it, although nobody, other than James and I, of course, could be sure what had actually happened. James told everyone I was still in the road and hadn't been looking when Eleazer went down the well. I never felt the need to undeceive anyone on that point."

"But if nobody believed James's story, then why didn't James get into trouble? Why wasn't there a formal investigation?"

"Nobody was unhappy that Eleazer was dead. That's how hated Eleazer was. But, at least for the record, the townsfolk saw no reason to question the story James told. All's well that ends well, or that ends *in* the well, I suppose you could say. Of course if there had been an investigation, James would have claimed he was acting in self-defense. Given what Eleazer had told others about wanting to kill James, James probably would have been acquitted on that basis anyway."

"Okay." Darby thought a moment. "Did James regret what he did?"

"Not for a single solitary second."

"You know, Freeman, several times I've thought about killing Tulley. I almost tried to kill him one day a while back. I got a cranberry scoop from the barn and I was going to jam it through his neck as he was lying in his bed, but I didn't do it. I doubt I could ever actually kill anybody."

"Ayuh. You could be right. Or you could be wrong. Sometimes, when you have no choice, you find that you are able to do things you never thought possible. In any event, it's probably best that you didn't kill Tulley with the cranberry scoop."

Freeman paused and looked at Darby, who was waiting for him to finish the thought. "Believe it or not, Darby, some people don't like blood in their cranberry sauce." Freeman smiled at Darby, and Darby smiled back.

Freeman's Valentine

1881

Darby got into the habit of visiting Freeman regularly, first once a week, then almost every day. Eventually, it became clear that Freeman's body was failing at an increasing rate. Darby started helping Freeman out however he could. He delivered wood for Freeman's wood stove, got him supplies at the market, and picked up and returned library books. Freeman's cousin from Provincetown, whom Darby finally met, continued to clean the house and do Freeman's laundry. She was in her seventies and said that she was only sorry that she didn't have the energy she once had.

When Darby suggested that Freeman should move his bed from the second floor down to a back room off the kitchen so that he wouldn't have to go up and down stairs, Freeman embraced the idea. Freeman watched as Darby took the bed apart, brought it downstairs, and reassembled it in Freeman's new bedroom. Darby also carried down smaller pieces of furniture from the bedroom, including a chair and a side table, and the clothes Freeman usually wore. Darby was impressed that Freeman put up no argument about moving downstairs and seemed not to mind the change. When Freeman offered to pay Darby for his help, Darby said he didn't want any money and that he was happy to help. "I know you'd do the same for me if our roles were reversed," Darby said.

A few weeks later, when Darby realized that Freeman was no longer eating as well as he should, Darby asked Freeman about it and Freeman said it had become too difficult to pre-pare meals. Darby went next door to Elvira Cahoon's boarding house and spoke with Mrs. Cahoon, who happened to be a second cousin of his mother. He asked if she could bring a prepared meal to her next-door neighbor once a day, and she said that she'd be happy to. Freeman accepted the idea but in-sisted upon paying her for the service even though everyone understood that his funds were nearly exhausted.

On St. Valentine's Day, 1881, Darby stopped by Freeman's house on his way home from school.

"Freeman, did you ever fall in love?"

Freeman waited an unusually long time before respond-ing. "Ayuh. I did fall in love with someone once," he said wist-fully. "Very much in love."

"What happened? Why didn't you get married?"

Freeman hesitated. "We couldn't get married. Our re-lationship was not countenanced. At that point in my life, I wasn't strong enough to fight for what I knew was right, and then the person I loved died tragically."

"Oh, Freeman. I'm sorry. I shouldn't have asked about this."

"No, Darby, I'm glad you did. There's an important lesson here. Don't do what I did. When you fall in love with someone, pay no heed to what other people say or think. When you find the right person, be with that person. You never know when a chance at happiness will be snatched away."

Darby sat and listened.

"You know, Darby, life goes by in a flash. Pursue your dreams. Don't waste time doing things you know you're not meant to be doing."

It seemed to Darby that Freeman had always lived by that advice. It also seemed that Freeman knew that the end of his life was almost upon him.

Paintings in the Attic

Monday, May 15, 1881

On a cool spring morning, nearly a year after Darby met Free-man, Darby headed over to Freeman's house to check on him before going to school. By this point, Darby was checking on Freeman twice each day.

Darby knocked on the front door as usual, expecting that Freeman would be in the front parlor with a hot cup of tea and would yell "come in," as always. But on this morning, there was no response. Darby knocked again. Darby stepped around to one of the windows looking onto the porch. Peering into the front parlor, he saw nothing out of the ordinary. And nobody. Freeman wasn't in the parlor.

Darby returned to the front door, turned the knob, and let himself in.

"Freeman?" Darby called out.

Darby rushed through the parlor and dining room and into the kitchen. He found Freeman on the floor.

"Freeman!" Darby screamed. He knelt on the floor by his dear friend. Freeman was not dead. His breathing was very shallow, his eyes wide open. He looked at Darby plaintively, his face contorted. There was a cut on his head and some blood on the floor.

"Freeman, what happened?" Darby took Freeman's hand, his eyes welling up. Freeman's hand felt like ice.

Freeman opened his mouth and made a sound, but it was nothing intelligible. And it wasn't loud.

"Freeman! I'm going to run and get Dr. Sturgis. Oh, hang on. You must be cold."

Darby dashed into the back room off the kitchen, tore a blanket off Freeman's bed, brought it into the kitchen, and draped it over Freeman's crumpled body. Then he retrieved a pillow and placed it gently under his old friend's head. He didn't dare try to move Freeman.

"I'll be back with the doctor in just a minute." Darby sprinted out of the house and up Main Street to Dr. Sturgis's house. Thankfully, this house was only six houses west of the Scott house.

When Dr. Sturgis arrived at Freeman's house a few minutes later, making a diagnosis was not difficult for him. Freeman had suffered a major stroke. Elvira Cahoon from next door was on the scene immediately along with two boarders, having seen Darby run out and return with Dr. Sturgis. With the doctor supervising, Darby, Dr. Sturgis, and the boarders carefully lifted Freeman and carried him the few steps back into the room off the kitchen, placing him as gently as possible onto his bed.

Darby did not go to school that day. Darby did not go to school all that week. Instead, he was by Freeman's side nearly the whole time, having brought another mattress down from an upstairs bedroom. A nurse engaged by Dr. Sturgis stopped by several times each day to attend to Freeman's personal care, but she was not available for much more. The only thing anyone could really do for Freeman was to keep him comfortable and try to get fluids into him.

Dr. Sturgis was also at the house several times each day. He hadn't expected Freeman to survive the day Darby found him on the floor, and had said as much. Then he doubted that Freeman would survive the week.

But Freeman made it through the week, and slowly, almost imperceptibly, his ancient body recovered to a limited extent from the damage done by the stroke. The right side of Freeman's body was paralyzed and would never return to normal. His speech remained unintelligible. The doctor indicated that it was probably only a matter of time before Freeman would have another stroke that would end his days on earth.

At the end of that first week, Captain Walker came to the Scott house, accompanied by Mrs. Merrick, the woman who had attended Emily during Darby's birth. He took Darby aside.

"Darby, by my reckoning it's time for you to come home now. I am prouder of you than words can express for being so attentive to your friend, but you have your own life to live and you can't miss any more school."

Darby didn't argue with the captain.

"Dad, what's going to happen to Freeman?"

"Well, son, Eldon Doane, Freeman's lawyer, went to the Probate Court in Barnstable. The Probate Court has made Eldon Freeman's guardian. He's in charge of Freeman's affairs now. Unfortunately, as you know, Freeman has almost no money, and as long as he lives he's going to require full-time care. There's a county home for the aged where Freeman can get the care he needs. There is no alternative. Eldon has made the arrangements for Freeman to be transported there as soon as Dr. Sturgis thinks he can be moved. Mrs. Merrick will stay with Freeman until that happens."

"But Dad, that's not what Freeman wants! It will kill him to be moved out of his house. He spoke to me about the possibility of something like this and he insisted he wanted to die in his own home!"

"I understand, Darby, and I know how hard this must be for you, but Freeman needs care on a full-time basis. Getting that care in his own home would cost a great deal of money, money Freeman doesn't have."

Darby was devastated. He knew, however, that his father was right.

After several moments, he said, "All right, Dad. Let me spend a few more minutes with Freeman, and then I'll be home."

"I'm so proud of you, son. If even half the population were half as compassionate as you are, the world would be a much better place."

After the captain left the Scott house, Darby went in and sat in the chair that had been pulled up along the side of Freeman's bed. Mrs. Merrick left the room. Freeman lay in bed looking up at Darby.

Darby didn't know how to say what was on his mind. He started to open his mouth but Freeman slowly reached out and squeezed Darby's hand, which had been resting on the arm of the chair. Then Freeman removed his hand from Darby's, put his thumb and forefinger together and made slow circular movements in the air.

"What are you trying to tell me, Freeman?"

Darby watched Freeman as he continued to move his left hand in a circular motion, pressing his thumb against his forefinger. Suddenly he realized what Freeman meant.

"Oh, I see. I'll be right back."

Darby returned a moment later with a slate and a piece of chalk he had found in Freeman's bedroom upstairs. He positioned the slate under Freeman's left arm and put the chalk in his left hand, helping Freeman to manipulate it. Freeman was right-handed, so what he wrote on the slate was very messy, but it was legible. He wrote: "MONEY UNDER BEDROOM FLOORBOARD."

Darby read the message and looked at Freeman. "You have money under a floorboard in your bedroom?

Freeman nodded.

"Do you want me to go find it and bring it down to you?"

Freeman nodded again.

Darby went upstairs to Freeman's bedroom. The floor-boards were nearly a foot wide. He walked around the room tapping the floor with his right foot in search of a loose board. Soon he found one directly underneath where Freeman's bed had stood before Darby had moved it downstairs. He placed his fingertips at the end of the board a few feet in from the wall, and was able to lift the board up. In the space between two joists was a narrow metal box. Darby removed the box and carried it downstairs to Freeman.

"Is this what you wanted?"

Freeman indicated "yes."

"Would you like me to open it?"

Again, "yes."

Inside the box were two stacks of ten-dollar bills, and in each stack were one hundred bills, for a total of two thousand dollars. Darby was astounded.

"Freeman! This is a lot of money!" Darby looked up at Freeman and smiled. "Now you can stay at home!"

Freeman looked at Darby and turned his head slowly from side to side. He opened his mouth and with great effort and deliberation forced out two noises that sounded like "OAR OOH." Then he motioned for Darby to help him again with the slate and the chalk. On the slate he wrote, "FOR YOU."

"Oh, no, Freeman! I can't take your money! Please, we've got to use this for your care here in your home. You're getting stronger every day, and summer is coming."

Freeman just stared at Darby.

"Please, Freeman. Thank you, but I can't take your money."

Finally, Freeman moved his left arm toward Darby and squeezed Darby's hand, indicating that he wasn't going to fight Darby about it.

When Darby left the house, he went straight to Eldon Doane's house with Freeman's metal box full of cash. Eldon was as surprised by the discovery of the cash as Darby had been, but agreed that the money was sufficient to keep Freeman in his own home, at least for now. Darby was elated. It took Eldon only a couple of days to engage full-time care for Freeman on a long term basis, enabling Mrs. Merrick to return home.

When another three weeks passed and Freeman's condition continued to improve, though not tremendously, Eldon sent a message to the Walker home asking Darby to come and speak with him again. Darby went to see Eldon promptly.

"Darby, as Freeman's guardian I have to act conservatively, meaning I have to plan ahead. The money you found isn't going to last forever, and I'm going to have to choose a date when Freeman will have to go to the county home. We can't just wait until the money runs out."

"I understand, Mr. Doane. I have been thinking about the situation, and have a proposal. Mrs. Cahoon's boarding house is next door to the Scott house. Freeman has five empty bedrooms on the second floor. The summer season is just about to begin. I spoke with Mrs. Cahoon about this, and she says that she thinks she can fill all of those bedrooms for the whole summer, as a sort of annex to her boarding house."

Eldon thought about this briefly. "I'm impressed with your thinking, I must say, Darby. But how will Freeman feel about five strangers in his house?"

"I've already talked about it with him. He thinks it's a great idea."

"Well, Darby, this is very good, but I'm not sure that the income from the five bedrooms is going to cover the cost of full-time care, and even if it does, what happens when the summer ends?"

"I've thought about that too. I imagine that you know that Freeman painted pictures for several decades."

"Sure. He gave me a particularly good one of the twin lights at Chatham."

"Okay. Well did you know that there are nearly two hundred of his paintings up in his attic?"

"Two hundred paintings? I was under the impression that Freeman had given all of his artwork away."

"No, Mr. Doane, when I was at Freeman's house the other day I went up attic and I counted just under two hundred. I think they're very good. Freeman never wanted to sell them. He always felt that it would somehow spoil his art to put a dollar value on it. Anyway, I asked him if he would reconsider the idea of selling the paintings if it meant that he could stay at home, and he said yes."

"My goodness, I'm impressed. All right. Since you've already thought about this, how do you propose to sell the paintings?"

"I've spoken with three different art dealers, one in Chatham, one in Wellfleet, and of course the Nickerson Gallery here in Harwich Port. They all want as many paintings as we can give them, and will sell them on consignment."

Eldon considered everything Darby had said. "Okay, Darby. You've come up with an excellent proposal. Let's give it a try and see how it goes!"

With the blessing of Eldon and, of course, Freeman, Darby implemented his plan.

Mrs. Cahoon was able to fill the five bedrooms almost right away, and the income began flowing in. When she first entered the house to have a look at the rooms with Darby, she had said, "Darby, I can hardly believe how well maintained the interior of this house is! I was sure that the inside of the house would be a total wreck by now. I was told that Freeman ran out of money ages ago. How did Freeman manage to take such good care of the place?"

"Freeman's cousin, a nice lady from Provincetown, cleans the house on her visits."

"Well, that's sweet. I never even knew that Freeman had a cousin from Provincetown."

Darby enlisted the help of his friends Manuel Silva and Joe Pina, whom he had already introduced to Freeman. The three of them carried Freeman's paintings down from the attic. With great pleasure, Freeman reviewed them one at a time, then they divided the paintings into three lots and distributed them among the art galleries.

First, though, Freeman insisted that Darby choose one for himself. He picked a warm, colorful painting of Salt Water Pond in front of the Walker homestead which Freeman had painted fifty years earlier. Grandfather Walker later told Darby that he remembered the day Freeman had come to the house to paint that picture. He had had tried to give it to Nathaniel when it was finished, but Nathaniel had thought the offer too generous, and Freeman refused to accept any money for the painting.

The paintings were received with great enthusiasm in the art galleries, and more money began flowing in. Financially, Freeman was now on sufficiently firm ground.

Freeman had a good summer and early fall. He had excellent care. He was never alone. He spent warm afternoons on his front porch, almost the same way he always had. Darby was at the house for part of every day. Freeman developed close ties to his nurses and to Mrs. Cahoon, who was also at the house for part of each day. Freeman's cousin still visited, but now her visits were strictly social. Mrs. Cahoon and her staff had taken over the cleaning and the laundry. Freeman enjoyed meeting all the guests who stayed in the upstairs bedrooms and became friends with some of them. Freeman's old body was broken, and he struggled with the loss of function, but he knew he was being cared for by people who loved him.

Everyone knew, however, that eventually Freeman's time would be up. The fatal stroke came one evening near the end of November. Suddenly, Freeman was gone.

Dr. Sturgis delivered the news to Darby at the Walker home. Darby was beside himself with grief. It was the first time he had lost a friend as dear to him as Freeman had become. After Dr. Sturgis left, Darby went to his room and cried his eyes out.

The memorial service for ninety-four-year-old Freeman Scott was held at Pilgrim Congregational Church just across the street from the Scott house. Everyone in town knew Freeman to some degree or another and all the pews were full. The minister gave a eulogy in which, after praising Freeman for his unique contributions to the town and the world, he commended Darby for befriending Freeman and making sure that his last six months were spent at home, where he'd wanted to be. "We are blessed to have in our village a young man of such compassion," said the minister, looking directly at Darby Walker. The attention made Darby uncomfortable, and he looked away. Darby noticed the grimace on Tulley's face as the minister praised Darby.

Two days after the memorial service, Eldon Doane showed up at the Walker house shortly before suppertime. Darby was summoned by his parents to the front parlor.

"Darby," said Eldon, "I've come to read the will of your friend, Freeman."

"All right, but what has that to do with me?"

"Darby, Freeman treasured you. He summoned me a few weeks before his first stroke and had me draw up a new will. His new will gives you a quarter of his estate."

"Heavens to Betsy! I never wanted anything from Freeman!"

"I know that, Darby."

"What about Freeman's cousin from Provincetown? She came down on the train every two weeks and helped Freeman clean his house. I hope that Freeman left her something."

"Freeman didn't have a cousin. The woman from Provincetown was his cleaning woman. Freeman let her go several years ago when he knew that his funds were running low, but she wouldn't agree to be let go. Instead, she kept coming every two weeks and doing the cleaning for free—that is, up until the time Freeman had his stroke and you got Mrs. Cahoon involved."

Darby nodded.

"Anyway, Freeman left the cleaning woman a quarter of his estate, the same as he left you. The other half of his estate goes to a couple of organizations that help homeless young people."

"Good. I'm glad to hear that."

"As for what you'll actually end up with, it's too soon for me to say, exactly. It'll take up to a year to get everything settled. The house will have to be sold, and there are still unsold paintings. My best guess is that you'll end up with two or three thousand dollars. Freeman would be happy about that."

Darby was taken by surprise. "Holy Mackerel! I don't know what to say. That's a lot of money! I never expected anything!"

"There is one other thing, Darby. Freeman gave me this box to give you. I don't know what's inside it, but it's yours." Eldon handed Darby a sealed, rectangular wooden box.

"Should I open it now?" Darby asked as he received it.

"You don't have to open it now, but if you want to, I'd love to see what's in it. I have wondered about it since Freeman entrusted it to me."

"Okay. Let's find out what it is." Darby went and got a screwdriver out of the junk drawer in the kitchen and carefully pried open one end of the box. When it was open, Darby set it on the floor in front of him and pulled out a framed painting about fifteen inches tall by twelve inches wide. There were protective blocks on the corners of the painting, which Darby removed.

It was a portrait of an unusually handsome, serious looking young man in his twenties. The portrait was signed by Freeman Scott in the bottom right corner, just like all of Freeman's paintings were, but the quality of this one was a notch above his other paintings. The colors were richer and the details sharper, and Freeman had succeeded brilliantly in capturing the spirit of his subject. The young man's eyes looked directly at the observer, and the image was so lifelike that it almost seemed the young man's lips would open, and he would start speaking. Darby was sure this was the best painting Freeman had ever done.

When Darby turned the portrait around for all to see, everyone in the parlor marveled at it. Then, on the back of the painting, Darby saw some printing, "Zephaniah—June, 1814."

"I wonder who this Zephaniah was," Darby said.

"Zephaniah was your great-grandfather's youngest brother," Captain Walker answered in an even tone.

"Oh, yes, I can see the family resemblance," said Darby. "He's definitely got the Walker nose! Freeman told me that he and Zephaniah had been in the same class at school. What a beautiful legacy this is!"

For a moment it appeared to Darby that Captain Walker was going to say something more, perhaps something of great significance, but after some hesitation, he only said, "Yes, Darby. It certainly is."

Nearly everyone in the Walker house was delighted by the news of Darby's inheritance, though for Darby the inheritance came at a price too dear. He would rather have had Freeman back.

One person in the Walker house did not appear to Darby to be at all delighted, however. Tulley Walker looked unhappy. Very unhappy.

The Wateska

Wednesday, January 3, 1883

Under full sail, the *Wateska*, Captain Walker's forty-four-foot fishing schooner, traversed the gentle ocean swells about thirty miles southwest of Tampa Bay. Captain Walker, Tulley, and four other crew members from the Cape had sailed the *Wateska* down to Florida in October for a few months of fishing. They were not planning to return to the Cape until April.

Darby, on a long winter break from his final year at Harwich High School, had arrived in Tampa just before Christmas, along with his mother and his friend, Manuel Silva. Darby and Manuel were filling in for two crew members who had returned to the Cape for a few weeks. Captain Walker and Emily were enjoying a vacation. Captain Walker had put Tulley in command of the *Wateska*, so Darby and Manuel and two of the regular crew members—one from Chatham and one from Truro—were serving as the crew under Tulley.

The *Wateska* had been out on the present fishing trip southwest of Tampa Bay for a week. Nearly 8000 pounds of red snapper lay in the hold, each fish having been filleted and salted by the crew before being stored. This had been a successful trip and the hold was full. It was time to return home. Tulley was at the helm on this warm, sunny morning. The two regular crew members were below decks catching up on sleep. Darby and Manuel were sitting up at the bow, where the noise of the water against the hull prevented anyone from overhearing their conversation.

"Darby," said Manuel, "I've been thinking. I don't mean any offense by this, but I don't think Tulley has the skills to captain a ship. He's a tolerably good fisherman, but he's not a good captain. Why did your father put him in charge of the *Wateska*?"

"I'm not offended. You're right about Tulley. I think Dad knows that Tulley isn't really cut out to be a captain, but he also knows Tulley would be hurt if he had offered the command of the *Wateska* to anybody else, and I think he's hoping that Tulley will grow into the job."

"But Tulley doesn't seem to be able to read the sea. He knows where the wind is coming from, all right, and can navigate well enough to get by, but it seems like he doesn't really follow the currents or the tides. Your father is lucky the crew members know what they're doing."

"I agree. Dad may have been too optimistic when he gave command of the *Wateska* to Tulley, but it's not my place to say that to him."

"I guess that's true."

After a few hours of sailing, Darby began to see the vertical line of the Egmont Key lighthouse coming into view, the first indication that they were approaching Tampa Bay. At first, it was nothing more than a ghostly hint of a structure sticking above the water, but it gradually became more real. Darby pointed it out to Manuel. Tulley noticed it a few moments later, and soon the horizontal line of Egmont Key itself came into view. They were on course. Darby was still at the bow of the *Wateska* with Manuel.

"I'm anxious to see whether or not my brother follows Dad's orders about going to the north of Egmont Key on our way into Tampa Bay."

"Why do we need to go north of Egmont Key? That sounds like a longer route."

"The mouth of Tampa Bay is full of treacherous and shifting shoals, and really bad ones are south of Egmont Key. Dad says that they are even more dangerous this year than they usually are. The safest way into Tampa Bay from the Gulf of Mexico is to stay to the north of Egmont Key and continue east just below Mullet Key at the northern edge of the mouth of the bay."

"Are you sure Tulley knows about the shoals?"

"I was there when Dad asked him to promise that he would not try to return on the south side of Egmont. Dad made it clear that the risk of grounding isn't worth the time that might be saved."

"What did Tulley say?"

"He said he'd do as Dad said, but I'm not sure he understood how important it was." Darby thought for a moment. "You know, I should probably go back and speak with Tulley about this."

"Better safe than sorry," said Manuel.

Darby stood and made his way back to the stern, taking a seat near his brother, who was at the wheel. "Tulley, what do you figure the tide is right now?"

"Don't know, don't care."

"Well, you *are* going to take the northern route into the bay, aren't you?"

Tulley laughed, and as he did, it brought Darby right back to the intensely painful memory of Tulley laughing as he sailed their sailboat out of Salt Water Pond and into Nantucket Sound when Darby was just six. This laugh was the same, just deeper, more adult. It echoed in Darby's head.

"It's high tide," Darby said, "or pretty darn near high tide. Don't you think you should do as Dad instructed and take the northern route? With this much water above them, the shoals south of Egmont Key will be tough to see from a safe distance, but they'll still be dangerous."

Tulley stared at his younger brother with no emotion, an inscrutable blankness with which Darby was all too familiar.

After a moment, Tulley said "Who is the captain of this vessel? Am I the captain or are you the captain? Unless I am mistaken, I'm the captain, which means I chart the course and you follow my orders." It was enough to make Darby sit still and say nothing more.

The strong, steady wind out of the north propelled the *Wateska* to the northeast at a good clip, leaving a healthy wake in the dark blue water behind the stern. Soon the schooner was within a quarter mile of Egmont Key, as close as she should get before coming about and tacking to the north-northwest in order to put Egmont Key to the south before turning again to the east and entering the northern passage into Tampa Bay.

Darby was watching his brother, considering whether or not to bring up, again, the subject of which route to take. If Darby said anything more about it, Tulley would probably dig in his heels and be more resolute in his decision to disregard their father's instructions. Tulley was the most stubborn person Darby had ever known. He wondered which would bring Tulley more pleasure: disregarding their father's orders or ignoring Darby's reminder.

Finally, Darby decided he had no choice but to try again. "Tulley, I know that you're in charge of the *Wateska*. I'm not questioning your authority, but if you continue on the present course you are going to lay us up on the shoals south of Egmont."

"Hogwash! In addition to being the captain of this schooner, I'm a superior sailor. A much better sailor than you will ever be. I know about the shoals, and I know how to get around them. Now stop provoking me!"

After a few more minutes, the *Wateska* slipped past the southern point of Egmont Key, bound directly for the perils ahead, though the shoals weren't visible. Darby went back to where Manuel sat at the bow.

"Tulley is taking us in south of Egmont. This is exactly what Dad told him not to do."

"You've got to stop him!"

"I can't. Nobody can stop him. He says he knows the shoals and how to get around them."

"Does he?"

"No."

"Then you've got to at least warn the others. If we run into the shoals hard enough and they're not expecting it, they could get hurt."

"Good thinking. I'll go tell them to come up on deck."

Darby went below decks to where the other sailors were resting.

"I think you should both come up on deck right now," Darby said to the men after rousing them from their sleep. "Tulley is taking us south of Egmont Key and directly into Tampa Bay. I think he's going to ground us, and I don't want anybody to be hurt in a sudden impact."

"Have you told Tulley this is a mistake?" asked the sailor from Truro.

"Yes."

"He wouldn't listen to you, would he?" asked the sailor from Chatham.

"No."

The men heeded Darby's warning, and soon all the crew members were on deck exchanging nervous glances and scanning the horizon for any signs of shoals.

The *Wateska* was headed into a trap created by a strangely shaped shoal, an underwater rise formed by the strong currents at the southern end of Tampa Bay. The shoal was shaped almost like an "L" turned on its side, the long arm extending to the west and the short arm extending to the north. Had it been low tide, the crew of the *Wateska* would have spotted the shoal from a safe distance, since it would have been just below the surface of the water. However, it was not anywhere near low tide. To make matters worse, the floor of the bay was at its deepest levels directly adjacent to the shoal—meaning there was no gradual drop in water level to provide early warning.

Darby tried again. "Tulley, we're headed right for the worst shoals. If you don't turn back now, we're in for big trouble."

"Shut up, Darby. I'm the captain. Leave me alone."

And rules are for babies, Darby thought to himself.

At just about the same moment, the shoal, perhaps three feet below the water, suddenly popped into view not far ahead, the strength of the northerly wind dropped precipitously, and the *Wateska*, burdened with fish, began to lose speed.

Darby realized that the only way to turn the *Wateska* around was to jibe, an awkward and sometimes dangerous process of turning away from the wind, instead of into it, then letting the sails snap suddenly from one side of the vessel to the other. Darby knew that by doing this, as opposed to coming about into the wind, the boat would lose almost no forward momentum, and the reversal of direction would succeed. The risk of capsizing the boat would be negligible because there were 8000 pounds of fish stabilizing the hull, and even that limited risk could be reduced by pulling in the sails as tight as possible before the wind was directly behind the stern. Darby knew that if Tulley tried to turn in the usual way, the boat would probably end up "in irons"—the mariner's term for "stalled."

"Tulley, you've got to jibe!" screamed Darby.

Darby looked at his brother, pleading. There was still no emotion in Tulley's face.

"Jibe!" Darby screamed again.

But Tulley did not jibe. Instead, he stubbornly turned the boat into the wind, beginning the common process of coming about. The bow of the *Wateska* began the turn to the north.

Loaded down with a hold full of fish and having slowed dramatically before any change in course was attempted, the *Wateska's* bow turned to the north grudgingly. As it did so, the sails began to lose the wind that had filled them, and the heavily burdened *Wateska* slowed even further. For a moment that seemed like an eternity, the crew watched as the bow ticked across the compass points from east to east-northeast, from east-northeast to northeast, from northeast to north-northeast, and then from north-northeast to north, all the while slowing, slowing, and slowing even more.

As the *Wateska* left its easterly heading, its sails flapped, first just a little bit, then more, and then more still until they were noisy and out of control. When the *Wateska* was finally heading due north, directly into the wind, she was no longer moving forward. It was a dead stop. Under the command of

Tulley Walker, and for the first time ever in its history, the *Wateska* had missed stays. The *Wateska* was in irons.

Everyone aboard, including Tulley, knew they were in trouble. They might have tried turning the rudder back toward the starboard, letting the wind push the boat *backward* instead of forward, and then completing the turn to the west by reversing the direction of the rudder at the moment the wind caught the sails again. But there wasn't enough wind nor enough water between them and the shoal to carry out this last-ditch effort.

The *Wateska* sat motionless for an instant, then began slipping backwards as the diminished wind lazily pushed her south. All eyes looked beyond the *Wateska's* taff rail to gauge how far they were from the westward pointing finger of the shoal behind them. It was not far. They were helpless.

Very suddenly the depth of the water decreased from fifteen feet to ten feet to five feet. The water continued to appear a lighter and lighter blue as the depth kept lessening. The *Wateska* was pushed slowly backward toward the shoal, and then the sailors heard the dreaded and extremely unpleasant sound of their vessel's keel digging into sand.

A light wind continued to push the helpless *Wateska*, and the bow slid around to the southerly position of the stern, so the entire length of the keel was in contact with the sand. As she was pushed against the shoal, she was pointed, as if it even mattered, in an easterly direction toward the inside of the curved shoal rather than westward toward open water. The sails were once again filling up with wind, but the keel was firmly planted in the sand. The only effect of the wind, had it been strong enough, would have been to blow the *Wateska* over.

The crew released all the sheets so the sails would luff rather than strain the ship's rigging. The *Wateska* was grounded.

Darby approached his brother. "We're grounded, Tulley. What's your plan now?"

"If we're patient, the rising water will lift us off the shoal."

"Tulley, it's already high tide. If it were anything other than high tide, I would agree with you. But the water is dropping, not rising. As time passes, the *Wateska* will become only more firmly stuck in the sand, not less."

"Well then, Darby. You think you're so smart. You want to be in command of the *Wateska* now? Okay, you're in command! Now if the *Wateska* is lost it will be on your watch, not mine!"

Darby looked at his brother. If this sort of statement had been at all out of the ordinary for Tulley, Darby would have been angry. Instead, he started thinking.

The only possible way to save the *Wateska* would be to pull it off the shoal with a steamship, but Tampa Bay was not a busy place in 1883. At that moment, there were no other vessels in sight. Darby ordered the others to remove the *Wateska's* rowboat from its place on the deck.

The five sailors climbed into the rowboat and rowed the twenty-four miles up to Tampa, rotating the rowing duty among them as they went. The arduous trip took several hours. When they arrived in Tampa, they secured the assistance of a steamship owner, who agreed to use his steamship to try and pull the *Wateska* off the shoal.

The steamship reached the scene late in the day, right around the subsequent high tide. A cable was secured from the stern of the steamship to the bow of the *Wateska*, but the effort to pull the *Wateska* off the bar failed.

The sailors spent an hour removing the fish from the hold, but even then the schooner could not be pulled free. The wind and the waves had jammed the hull into the sand. Darby and his fellow sailors then transferred everything moveable from the *Wateska* to the steamship. The *Wateska* would be a total loss.

Captain Walker and Emily had decided to spend their time together exploring the Ocklawaha River and Silver Springs. They returned to Tampa late on the day after the *Wateska* was lost. The captain was told of the tragedy as soon as he and Emily arrived back at their hotel. If the news shook him to the core, he did not show it. He quickly confirmed that all aboard had returned to Tampa safely. He summoned his sons and the other crew members to his room. When they appeared a few minutes later, he calmly asked Tulley for a full report. Tulley gave the captain an account of what had happened, omitting key facts that would have made it clear that only Tulley had been at fault.

"Who was the captain of the *Wateska* when it ran aground?" the captain asked Tulley.

"Darby was at the helm when we were on the shoal."

Darby shook his head as Tulley said this but said nothing.

"No, Tulley. I'm warning you that I'm just about at the end of my towline. I asked you who the captain was when the *Wateska* ran aground."

Tulley hesitated before saying, in a quieter voice, "I suppose that I was the captain, technically."

"Tulley, there is no technicality involved. You were the captain of the ship. By my reckoning, the captain of the ship is always responsible for what happens to her. It doesn't even matter who was at the helm. All I can hope for at this point is that you have learned a lesson. It better be a valuable lesson, because it is an extremely costly one. I was not able to fully insure the *Wateska*. This will be a huge financial loss for me, and it will take a long time to recover from it. Do you understand, Tulley?"

"Yup," said Tulley, looking down at the floor.

"I am extremely disappointed in you, Tulley. You deliberately chose to disobey my orders. You broke your promise to me. As a result, you wrecked my schooner."

Manuel, along with Darby and the sailors from Chatham and Truro, were present for the entire exchange between the captain and Tulley. Later that evening, Darby and Manuel went off on their own for a walk through town.

"Your brother tried to blame *you* for the loss of your father's schooner!"

"Yes, he did, but Dad knew it was Tulley's fault."

"Aren't you mad as the devil at Tulley? What an unbelievably rotten thing to do!"

"Well, I can't take it seriously. That's just what he does."

"Has he done anything this awful to you before?"

"Yes, he has." Darby paused. "When we were little, he nearly drowned me."

"On purpose?"

"Hard to say if it was deliberate or just reckless. Anyway, he's done monstrous things to me all my life. There was the time he stole my paper and claimed it as his own. I'm sure you remember me telling you about that."

"Yes, I remember. Darby, if my brother treated me the way your brother treats you, I swear I'd kill him."

"You don't have a brother."

"That's true."

Darby ran his right hand through his hair. "You don't seriously think I should kill Tulley?"

"You might have to someday."

"But then I'd be caught, and I'd be put away forever, if not hanged."

"No, you wouldn't. It would be self-defense. Or if it weren't self-defense, you could make it look like it was." Manuel thought a moment. "Or, better yet, you could make it look like a suicide. Listen, if you don't stop Tulley, someday Tulley's going to kill someone, and that someone might be you. Darby, you're my best friend. I guess I'm the one who has to tell you this, but I mean no offense. You're far too kind, especially to people who don't care about you. If you're going to make it in this world, you're going to have to find the fighter inside."

Darby considered this a moment. "You're right," said Darby. "If only I knew where to look."

The Grippe

March 1883

The loss of the *Wateska* forced Captain Walker to change his plans. Captain Walker and his family and crew returned to the Cape, where the captain lined up work with local ship owners for himself, Tulley, and his crew. Life resumed a regular routine. But ill winds were blowing across New England. The grippe, as influenza was called, was prevalent across the region, and several people on the Cape had already died of it.

Emily Burgess Walker was not particularly worried about the grippe. Just as she knew that her youngest son would never die at sea, she knew she and her children were not destined to die from any common infectious disease. The men in her family who were not lost to the sea typically died of some age-related organ failure or another. The women who made it through childbirth tended to live to an advanced age.

In part because of Emily's certainty on this matter, though more because of the tremendous generosity of her soul, Emily had always been happy to help tend the sick in the community and, as needed, take over some of their household chores. "I have trained my husband and sons to be self-sufficient when necessary," Emily would say when anyone expressed reluctance to accept her kind assistance because that would mean taking her away from her own family.

Captain Walker, Tulley, and Darby were proud of Emily for the service she so willingly gave to others. And just as she expected, Emily never picked up any of the illnesses of those she cared for. Until now. Emily had been spending a lot of her time in recent weeks helping at the homes of two neighbors where influenza was wreaking havoc.

For one of the first times in her life, Emily didn't feel well. She was unusually tired, and her throat felt scratchy.

It was a Saturday morning. Darby had the coming week off from school and had agreed to take Tulley's place as a crew member with the captain on a run to transport textiles from Providence to Charleston, and then return to Providence with a load of lumber. They would be heading out that morning on a large schooner owned by local investors. Tulley had requested a break from work and the captain had granted it to him.

As Emily served breakfast to her family, she thought about her lack of energy and her scratchy throat and wondered if she was starting to feel a bit feverish. Then she remembered a strange incident that had occurred when the Walkers were in Florida. On the day the *Wateska* set out on her final voyage, shortly before Emily and the captain set out on their trip to Silver Springs and the Ocklawaha River, a herring gull flew through an open window into their Tampa hotel room. Without much difficulty, a member of the hotel staff had been able to persuade the gull to leave the room, but for Emily this had been a significant event. She thought back to her exchange with the captain that day:

"Ken, I'm worried. Do you know what it means when a bird flies into a home?"

"It doesn't mean anything at all, my dear. But I know you'll tell me what you think it means."

"It means someone in the family is going to die, and in the case of a *white* bird, such as the gull that came in this morning, it means a female is going to die."

"My dear, wonderful Emily, this is nonsense. If a person died every time a bird flew into someone's home—even putting aside the fact that this hotel room is *not* our home—you can be sure that nobody would ever leave a door or a window open, and birds would be eradicated from residential areas. There is nothing to this. It's a silly superstition passed down to you by your grandmother, that's all."

"Oh, Ken, I wish I could agree with you."

"My dear, do you think you're about to die?"

"No, I don't. But perhaps some other female in the family will."

"According to your theory, how far out into the family might we have to look to find the victim about whose death the gull has just warned us? If you look far enough, perhaps you will find a fourth or fifth cousin who will die in the next month.

Maybe a ninety-year-old spinster in Connecticut—will that prove you right?"

"You can't dismiss age-old wisdom so easily. Somebody is going to lose her life soon. I can feel it."

Emily had let the matter drop, but in the following days she was just waiting for news of a family member's death, and she told the captain as much. The night they returned to Tampa, as they lay in bed, the captain embracing his beloved wife from behind, the captain had brought it up:

"Emily, perhaps you were right about the gull that flew into our room."

"What do you mean?"

"The *Wateska* was like a daughter to me. Now she's gone. Perhaps the message from your gull *was* real, and I was wrong to doubt it."

"Oh, Ken. That's not how it works. The *Wateska* wasn't a person." Emily released herself from the captain's embrace. She turned around and looked into his eyes. Her mouth twisted into a grimace.

"You said that a female member of the family was going to die. My beautiful, beloved *Wateska* is no more. Why shouldn't she count as the doomed female member of the family?"

Emily almost never won an argument with the captain by convincing him of anything, but on her own account she could always win by falsely conceding that he was right. She didn't know whether the captain knew this was how the game worked for her, but that didn't seem to matter. She kissed her husband and smiled. "All right. I was being foolish. Nobody's going to die."

"You know, Emily, I'm the luckiest man in the world."

Emily looked into her husband's eyes, already knowing what he would say next.

"I'm the luckiest man in the world because I have you." They kissed, and the kiss turned into love-making.

But back in her kitchen in Harwich, as Emily and her family ate their breakfast, the incident of the herring gull was at the forefront of Emily's mind, and she wondered to herself: *Was the gull's warning about me?*

Emily and Darby were the only ones remaining in the kitchen after breakfast was finished. Darby was washing the dishes as Emily dried them and put them away. The captain had gone to pack for the trip he and Darby were about to take. Tulley had gone off to the post office.

"Darby, there is something I've been meaning to discuss with you for some time, and I might as well do it now."

Darby turned. "Sure, Mother, what's on your mind?"

"You know that you and Tulley won't always have your parents."

"Of course, I know that. Is everything all right? Should I be worried?"

"Everything's perfectly fine. No, I'm just saying that a day will come, I hope many years from now—but that's up to the Lord—when your Dad and I will no longer be around."

"I know." Darby continued washing the dishes and putting them in the rack, but Emily put down her drying cloth.

"I know you know, dear, but I need you to promise that you'll do something after Dad and I are gone."

"Anything, Mother. You know I'll do anything you ask."

"I know you will. This is about your brother. You know as well as anyone does that Tulley isn't like most other people. He doesn't understand people like most of us do."

"Right. I know that."

"Darby, I'm worried that after Dad and I are gone, Tulley might choose the wrong course, or he might associate with people who will take advantage of him. If Dad and I aren't around to guide him, or give him a helping hand here and there, Tulley could end up in real trouble."

Darby stopped washing dishes, looking at his mother.

Emily continued. "Darby, dear, I want you to promise that after Dad and I are gone from this earth, you'll keep an eye on Tulley. You know, do your best to steer him in the right direction. Help him out of trouble when he finds it. Will you do that?"

"Of course, I will."

"Promise?"

"Mother, you know I'll do it. I promise."

Emily embraced her youngest son. "I know, Darby. Thank you." She kissed Darby on the cheek. "I have the best sons a mother could ask for."

An hour later, the captain and Darby and four other Harwich men were aboard the *Village Belle* on a southwesterly course to Providence. By the end of the day, Emily's scratchy throat had become a sore throat, and she felt feverish and achy, sensations almost completely foreign to her. She stayed home all day to rest and went to bed early, but she awoke the next morning feeling far worse. She asked Tulley to summon Dr. Sturgis.

When Dr. Sturgis arrived at the Walker home, it did not take him long to determine that Emily had contracted influenza. He instructed Tulley to stay with his mother until he could arrange for someone else to come and look after her. Less than an hour later, at the doctor's request, Emily's sister arrived at the house and took charge of the patient.

Several days went by during which Dr. Sturgis called regularly. Emily's sister forced her chicken soup into Emily and did her best to keep her warm, clean, and comfortable. But Emily was getting worse. Her body was burning with fever. She became unresponsive. After another day, when Emily's sister asked the doctor if he felt that Emily would pull through, the doctor indicated that he was not hopeful. This was a bad influenza season and many people on the Cape had died in the preceding weeks. There was no way for anyone to reach the captain and Darby to tell them they should return home at once.

Tulley never left the house during this time, and did whatever his aunt asked to help care for his mother. He sat by his mother's bedside, holding her hand for the last hours of her life. Emily's sister mostly stayed out of the way so Emily could have her last moments with her firstborn.

Shortly after it was clear that Emily had drawn her last breath, Dr. Sturgis came to the house to make an official pronouncement of death. Emily's sister hugged Tulley, and then Tulley left, saying only that he'd be gone for a few days.

He didn't know where he was going, only that he had to get away. Tulley was completely devastated. His mother was the one person in the world who never doubted him, never crossed him, and had at all times demonstrated her unbounding love for him. From the moment of his birth, she had meant the world to him. Other than Darby, nobody fully recognized how deeply devoted Tulley had been to Emily. Other than Darby, nobody would have believed that Tulley had been so attentive to his dying mother. Nobody, not even Captain Walker, would be more profoundly impacted by Emily's death.

When the *Village Belle* arrived at the wharf the following day, Dr. Sturgis, who had arranged to be alerted upon the first sighting of the returning ship, boarded her even before her lines were secured. He gave the captain and Darby the tragic news. The captain collapsed to his knees and buried his face in his hands as he began sobbing.

Darby knelt and embraced his father as his own eyes welled with tears. He understood that this would be one of the major turning points in his life, that nothing would ever be the same for his father, for his brother, and for himself. And he understood that, as hard as it would be for him to bear this loss, it would be even harder for his father and brother.

Jacksonville

Saturday, January 26, 1884

Five miles off the coast of South Carolina, the *Valley City*, a 320-ton, wooden-hulled, screw-propeller steamer, 130 feet long, with a 22-foot beam, pushed south at a steady fifteen knots. The clock in Captain Walker's cabin had just chimed eight times. Captain Walker stood in command in the wheelhouse. Darby, eighteen years old, stood by his side. Tulley, twenty-one, was sound asleep in his cabin, having stayed up most of the night reading.

The morning sun shone down on a flat sea. The thermometer indicated a pleasant sixty-five degrees. Not a single cloud floated in the sky.

This was the first voyage of the *Valley City* under the new ownership of Captain Walker and Miller & Henderson, a Tampa-based steamship company. Together they had purchased the vessel in New York for service on Florida's West Coast.

The *Valley City* had been built twenty-five years earlier in Philadelphia. The Union Navy purchased her in 1861 and used her actively during the Civil War before selling her back into private service in 1865. Both during the war and after, the *Valley City* had suffered numerous damaging blows requiring extensive repairs. Though properly repaired as necessary and well maintained, this wooden ship was entering the final stretch of a useful life.

According to Captain Walker's careful calculations, the *Valley City* was now south of Savannah, off the southernmost part of South Carolina where the coast was beginning the turn east. The captain needed to adjust the *Valley City's* course from southwesterly to southerly in order to maintain the desired distance from the shore. After consulting a chart laid out on the table, the captain turned the ship's wheel a few degrees. He could feel the tension in the steering cable suddenly and completely dissipate. Something had broken. The rudder was no longer under his control.

The captain grabbed the handle on the engine order telegraph and quickly moved it to the stop position and back three times, leaving it on stop. As he did, a bell rang three times below decks in the engine room, alerting the engineer to the urgent order. The engineer moved the handle on his own E.O.T. dial to the stop position, signaling he had received the order, then quickly throttled the *Valley City's* giant steam engine to a stop. The *Valley City* slowed down, but the great inertia of the heavy vessel meant it continued moving straight ahead.

"Darby, run to the engine room and ask the engineer to report to me as soon as he knows what happened."

"Yes, sir," said Darby, and off he went.

In a couple of minutes Darby was back up in the wheelhouse, accompanied by the engineer.

The engineer addressed the captain: "Captain, the top portion of the bulkhead to which one of the turning blocks is attached has broken apart, leaving the steering cable hanging loose."

"As I suspected. What do you propose as a fix?"

"I can attach a beam across the split in the bulkhead and attach the turning block to the beam. It will take a half hour or so. This will restore the steering, but I'm afraid the whole length of the bulkhead may be compromised. I suggest we head to the nearest port where we can get the entire bulkhead replaced. I would advise against waiting until we get to Tampa."

"Right. Thank you. Please go ahead and complete the temporary fix. Then we'll make port at Jacksonville, where we can have the repair work done. We're only about ten miles north of the mouth of the St. Johns River. This is going to set us back two or three days. I'm just glad that we have no paying passengers onboard and no perishable cargo."

The engineer set off to work on the temporary repairs to the steering system.

"Well, Dad, I guess our good luck has run out," said Darby.

"Stuff and nonsense! By my reckoning, what just happened seems more like good luck."

Darby looked at his father without beginning to comprehend how their current disabled state could be good luck. Darby's eyebrows were raised, reflecting puzzlement. His father was known for his even temper — he was almost never noticeably upset by anything — but a broken steering system couldn't be good luck, thought Darby.

The captain continued. "The steering was going to fail at some point. It's good luck that it failed on one of the calmest seas I've ever seen and at a time when we are not facing a hard deadline for arrival anywhere. More important, Darby, life is an adventure, and sometimes the best events are the ones you don't plan and don't expect. I've been to Jacksonville several times. Once with your mother. Tulley was even there with me a couple of years ago. It's a fantastic town and I know you're going to love it."

Shortly thereafter, with the turning block mounted to a beam attached across the split bulkhead, the *Valley City* steamed south for another hour. Half a mile off the mouth of the St. Johns River, a pilot boat greeted them. A pilot came on board to guide them the twenty-five miles up the north-flowing St. Johns River to Jacksonville. By noon, the *Valley City* was secured to a wharf adjacent to a ship repair facility on the town's western edge.

The captain called his sons to his cabin. "My boys, we are going to see how rich people live. Instead of staying on the ship until the repairs are done, we're going to stay at Carleton House, one of the finest hotels in Jacksonville. I know the owners. In the summer they operate Ocean Bluff Hotel in Kennebunkport, where your mother and I always had our little getaways. William Davis, one of the proprietors, is a good friend."

Darby was thrilled by the idea. Tulley didn't seem thrilled, but Darby could never be sure what he was thinking. Nobody could.

Carleton House was a large, handsome, four-story brick structure, with accommodations for 250 guests. The captain reserved a room for himself and a second room, just down the hall, for his sons.

The hotel had been built in 1876, and it was equipped with many modern conveniences, including a passenger elevator, a firehose on each floor, and a new contraption called "Creighton's Oral Enunciator," enabling the immediate summoning of hotel staff. Darby was struck by the bright, fragrant flowers everywhere, outside and in. It had been cold and damp when they'd left Massachusetts, but here in Florida it felt like summer. The captain had previously been in hotels much like this one, but Darby never had. Darby was bowled over by its scale and opulence.

From their room on the second floor, Darby and Tulley had a magnificent view across Bay Street to the St. Johns River. Directly across from Carleton House was George DeCotte's Lumber Yard, not an especially attractive operation but it did not impede the view of the broad river beyond. Schooners, steamships, and various pleasure craft were floating serenely on the river. A couple of small sailboats tacked across the river at different points, and rowboats passed here and there. Most of these smaller boats were rented by the day or by the hour from St. Johns River Boat Yard at the foot of Market Street or from Donnelly & Green's Boat Yard at the foot of Laura Street.

Excursionists on steamboats were headed up the St. Johns toward Tocoi, where they could catch a train on the short St. Johns Railroad to St. Augustine. Steamboats of more modest size were destined for the Ocklawaha River which promised a long, unusual, and enchanting voyage through the wilderness up to Silver Springs. A gigantic sailing vessel, the largest one Darby had ever seen, was anchored in the middle of the river.

"Hey, Tulley, come look at this gigantic yacht!" Darby called to his brother.

"Yup. Already saw it," Tulley answered.

"I wonder what it is."

"It's the *Ambassadress*."

"What's that?"

"The *Ambassadress* is the largest sailing vessel in the world. Four hundred feet long."

"Who owns it?"

"William Astor, one of the grandsons of John Jacob Astor."

"How do you know all this, Tulley?"

"I overheard a desk clerk talking about it with one of the guests."

Shortly after Darby and Tulley had arrived in their room and familiarized themselves with its offerings, the captain knocked on their door.

"Boys, let's go get some lunch and explore the town," Captain Walker said.

"That sounds great, Dad! I'm ready," said Darby.

Tulley wasn't interested. "Dad, thanks, but I think I'll just stay here for now. I was up late last night and could use a nap. Remember, I saw Jacksonville when you and I were here two years ago, so I know what it's all about."

"That's fine, Tulley. If you get up and need something to eat, just go down to the dining room and they'll get you whatever you want. But be sure to leave room for dinner, which is at seven."

Darby and the captain set off on their afternoon exploration. Darby fell in love with the town almost instantly. With about 15,000 residents, plus several thousand tourists this time of year, the population of Jacksonville, packed almost entirely into its grid along the river, was more than six times the population of Harwich. Darby found the two- and three-story brick buildings lining Bay Street attractive and pleasant. Unlike the commercial buildings in the villages back at the Cape, which were mostly just like the residential structures among which they sat, the brick buildings on Bay Street had been specifically built to house shops and other business enterprises. They had large, plate glass windows on the street level through which people strolling by could admire wares being offered for sale or see the goings on inside.

Darby had been to Boston several times, and Boston was, of course, a much larger city than Jacksonville. But Jacksonville had a softness and warmth to it that Darby hadn't felt in Boston. The streets were wider and unpaved, and the pace slower. The sidewalks were fashioned out of planks of wood, not stone. The people were friendlier. Of course they were friendlier, Darby mused. Many were on vacation, and none of them were struggling against ice, snow, and the darkness of winter. This afternoon was unusually warm, nearly eighty degrees. Darby had no complaints.

Captain Walker took Darby to lunch at California Chop and Coffee House at 22 West Bay Street. They ordered thick roast beef sandwiches and apple pie for dessert. Captain Walker recounted prior visits to the city, including the visit when Emily had accompanied him.

"Your mother loved our brief time here in Jacksonville," Captain Walker said after taking a bite of apple pie. "I remember how happy she was when she first arrived in the warmth and sunshine. You know, your mother was the sweetest, most beautiful woman I ever laid eyes upon."

Captain Walker became silent, evidently thinking about his beloved Emily. Darby didn't interrupt. After a moment, Captain Walker returned to the present. "We even talked about spending the winters in Florida someday."

"Do you think Mother really would have done that?"

"I don't know, Darby. She said she liked the idea, but not while her mother was living. She couldn't be so far away from her for too long."

After lunch, father and son went into Alvord & Kellogg Booksellers & Stationers on West Bay Street, spending nearly an hour looking over an impressive selection of the day's most popular books and magazines. Darby and the captain each selected a book. Not being entirely sure what sort of book Tulley might appreciate, the captain picked out a magazine for him, something of general interest, with shorter articles on diverse subjects. Next, they crossed the street and stopped in front of the window of Irving Webster's Shop, where several birdcages contained canaries. Darby was entranced, never having seen such creatures. After, they went into J. Gumbinger's Jewelry Shop, where they admired the fanciest gold watches Darby had ever seen. "Baubles for the rich," the captain said to Darby.

Once in a while the captain enjoyed a good cigar, so at G.H. Gato & Company he purchased a box of the shop's best Havana cigars. Then they went into L. Warrock's Confectionary, marveling at the vast array of chocolates, candies of all kinds, and cakes. They tried a sample of Warrock's orange marmalade. It was so delectable they felt compelled to purchase two jars of it.

After that, they went next door into J.D. Bucky's Clothing House, where they found a large inventory of fancy suits, hats, and shoes. The captain spent several minutes looking through the selection of hats. He nearly purchased a wool cap he liked, but in the end told Darby that he really didn't need it. He asked Darby if Darby wanted anything, but Darby said he didn't. He was just happy spending the time with his father and taking everything in.

It seemed to Darby that anything one wanted or needed could be purchased in the shops on Bay Street. Entertainment and all kinds of services were also available. Darby and the captain passed several saloons, a theater, a couple of billiard halls, and a new bowling alley. The upper floors of the buildings on Bay Street housed offices of doctors, lawyers, engineers, architects, real estate and insurance agents, and various other businesses.

The last shop they went into before returning to Carleton House was Buker & Harris, purveyors of fruits, produce, groceries and provisions. Captain Walker showed Darby a selection of fresh fruits and vegetables that was beyond Darby's wildest imagination. There were fruits for sale which Darby had never even seen, including yellow-green apple guavas. Some of these guavas were cut open and set on a table for the customers to sample, their pink, ripe flesh nearly impossible to resist. They tasted the guavas, then purchased several of them, along with a sack of oranges to take back to their hotel.

Captain Walker and Darby got back to Carleton House at around six o'clock.

"Dad, this was a really great afternoon. Thanks for spending it with me."

"Yes, it was, Darby. I'm glad we could do this." The captain hugged his son. "I'll come by your room a little before seven, and we'll all go down to dinner together."

Tulley had gone out on his own, but was back at the hotel at 6:15.

At about 6:30, a porter knocked on the door of Darby and Tulley's room. The porter had brought up a suit for each of the young men, "per the instructions of Mr. Davis," he said. Dinner at Carleton House was a formal event, and Mr. Davis, the captain's friend, had confirmed that his sons did not have formal attire with them. The captain appeared shortly after the Walker boys finished putting on the fine suits and ties. Even

Tulley's suit was a good fit, which was surprising because he was so unusually tall and lean.

"Fine feathers make fine birds!" said the captain to his sons. The three Walkers made their way down to the dining room.

A huge dining room was filled with a large number of round tables, each elegantly set for twelve. Darby and Tulley were placed at a table of people about their ages, the younger members of vacationing families.

The captain was seated at another table at the far end of the room. His table included the president of a Burlington, Vermont bank, the owner of a Maryland distillery, the owner of a Rhode Island textile mill, a wholesale grocer from New York, and a lawyer from Boston.

The captain did not feel the least bit uncomfortable at his table, though he knew that all his dining companions were far wealthier than he would ever be. The captain's attire was faultlessly respectable. Though lacking formal education beyond high school, he was articulate and well-informed. Always curious, he was an avid reader, had traveled the world, and always kept up with the news of the day. He was also in command of social skills more than sufficient to enable him to thrive in any social environment. All this helped make Kenelm Walker the popular captain he was.

Two individuals would stand out in the captain's memory of the evening. The first was the lawyer from Boston, a black man of about fifty who had built a successful law practice in Boston. The lawyer was seated to the captain's left, and for several minutes toward the end of the dinner they were engaged in a private conversation initiated by the lawyer. The captain learned that the lawyer handled the legal matters of the owners of Carleton House. He was favorably impressed to find that Davis and his partners were as progressive as he was, and as his father had been, in matters of race. A black man dining in a fine hotel in the South was a rarity indeed, although in this case all of the diners were educated northerners, most of whom would be supportive of his presence.

The second standout was Mrs. Humphrey Loomis, the elegant and alluring young wife of the Vermont bank president. She was seated to the captain's right. Mrs. Loomis — Henrietta — was, at age thirty-nine, nearly thirty years younger than her husband. She had unusually pale blue eyes, a perfect figure, and an aura of great kindness and confidence. She was the most strikingly beautiful woman the captain had ever encountered, setting aside, of course, his late wife, Emily. It was only through consistent and focused effort that the captain was able to keep himself from inappropriately gazing at Mrs. Loomis throughout the meal. He had the feeling Mrs. Loomis was afflicted with the same magnetic attraction, problematic given that Mrs. Loomis was, unlike the captain, married.

Tulley and Darby did not fit in with their fellow diners, all of whom came from wealthy backgrounds and were on extended vacations, but nobody emphasized that fact and everyone was polite. Their dinner ended early when Mr. Davis came by their table, chatted with the group briefly, and then suggested that the group go over to the Friday night dance at the Florida Yacht Club. He was inviting them on behalf of the club, of which he was an officer. The dance was already starting, he said.

A few at the table, including Darby, embraced the idea of going to the dance. Others indicated that they'd already made plans. Tulley was not interested in a dance or any other organized event, and excused himself to wander off on his own on a self-guided tour of Jacksonville saloons.

The few other diners at Darby's table who had decided to go to the dance each returned to their respective rooms to prepare for an evening out. Darby went to tell his father about his plans. The captain introduced Darby to his dining companions, and then Darby set off to the Florida Yacht Club.

It was already dark out, but gas lights blazed all the way up Bay Street, illuminating the brick buildings and their large front windows. Plenty of people strolled up and down the wide, sandy street.

At the Florida Yacht Club, the dance was just beginning. Well-dressed partygoers were arriving in small groups. The yacht club was on the waterfront diagonally across Bay Street from Carleton House, just east of the lumber yard. Its proximity was reassuring to Darby: he could leave the dance at any point and easily return to his room.

Three greeters with white carnations in their lapels were checking invitations and making introductions just inside the front door. Darby approached one of the greeters, indicating he was a guest at Carleton House and that Mr. Davis had extended an invitation. This was enough to result in a hearty handshake and a warm exhortation to follow the other guests up the front stairs to the second floor.

The Florida Yacht Club building, though not unattractive, was unremarkable, Darby thought. It was a large, wooden structure built on pilings out into the river, plain except for some raised paneling and gingerbread accents on the exterior. The dance space on the second floor was one large, well-lit activity hall with many windows and doors, all thrown open to the warm Florida evening and to the exterior porch circling the building.

At the end of the room nearest the shore, tables of refreshments, including finger sandwiches, fancy cakes, and large punch bowls, had been set up for the attendees. An ensemble of musicians was at the far end of the room, already engaged in filling the air with a perfect rendition of Strauss's *Blue Danube* waltz. Several beautiful young couples were already in the middle of the room, brilliantly turning to the music.

"What am I doing here?" Darby asked himself. He had no money and was a nobody from a nothing town on Cape Cod. Based on the people he had gotten to know a bit at dinner, he was sure everyone else at the dance came from wealthy families, many from New York City. These people intimidated him without even trying.

On the other hand, Darby enjoyed meeting people. He had been given a good education through high school and had been taught manners. He also knew that people liked him.

One other thing worked in Darby's favor that evening. In the fall of his second year at Harwich High School, a private dance instructor had offered dance classes that extended through the entire year, and Darby's mother had encouraged him to attend, saying that knowing how to dance would open up a world of possibilities. Darby had enjoyed the classes and had become a good dancer, especially for a man of only eighteen.

Darby was happy to be wearing the suit from Carleton House; it did a reasonably good job of concealing his true social status. However, despite the suit, the dance lessons, the good manners, and his natural confidence, Darby felt like an intruder, a pretender, a fake, a fraudster. His presence at the Florida Yacht Club was a charade. His family were everyday people. He was the son of a fisherman from Cape Cod masquerading as the son of an industrialist. Surely the truth would be quickly exposed and then Darby would be ejected from the Florida Yacht Club Friday Night Dance, into the dark, dusty street.

Darby felt more comfortable working for people like this than pretending to be one of them. He had worked one summer at Sea View House, the hotel in Harwich Port. He had been hired to do whatever was needed, which included meeting guests at the railroad station, helping guests with their trunks, bussing tables in the dining room, cleaning and readying rowboats for guests to row around Salt Water Pond, if they could figure out how to do that, delivering messages, and running errands.

These partygoers here at the Yacht Club were just like the guests at the Sea View; they came from the best addresses in Boston and New York City, and Darby felt like an imposter while his own people scurried around unnoticed, keeping the refreshments coming, cleaning up spills. Not only was Darby a fraud, he was a traitor to these hardworking people.

He picked up a glass of punch from a hostess at the refreshments table, one of *his people*, then made a quick tour of the dance hall, eventually settling on an unoccupied patch of wall against which he could stand and unobtrusively watch the action.

As Darby stood against the wall, people continued to flow into the hall. The dance floor filled, and the volume of the noise created by the people dancing, laughing, and trying to make themselves heard above the music increased.

Only a few moments passed before the gloved hand of an especially radiant, finely dressed young lady reached out from a swirling constellation of dancers at the edge of the dance floor and yanked Darby into her group.

"What is this?" Darby wondered to himself, but he went along willingly, quickly finding himself the eighth member of a group of four couples dancing the quadrille. Happily, he knew the quadrille, and was able to acquit himself extremely well in that first dance. His dance partner and her friends smiled at him, laughing with pleasure as they swirled around the room among a sea of dancers, all apparently without cares.

The band paused only for a moment when the quadrille ended, and the next dance, the Lancers, commenced. Darby was handed off by the first young lady to a second, who gladly partnered with him as part of the group of eight.

Again, Darby more than held his own, and the only attention he drew was of the most favorable kind. When that dance came to an end, Darby was whisked off to a third young lady in the group just as the band began playing a waltz. Darby was able to delay his unmasking. He was actually having fun.

When the waltz ended, two of the eight-party dance group drifted off in another direction, but just as Darby concluded that his temporary admission into the Yacht Club crowd had expired, the first young lady, the one who had first pulled Darby away from the wall, again grabbed his hand. "Come with us, mystery boy."

Darby followed his beautiful captor and her four remaining satellites out an open door and onto the porch. They commandeered folding chairs in a quiet, more remote corner.

Now seated and starting to cool off from the fast-paced dancing inside the hall, Darby's captor and her friends introduced themselves. "I'm Charlotte," said his beautiful captor, gazing at her prey. "Michael," said the tall, handsome young man who, Darby imagined, was her suitor. The other three members of the group gave their names too.

"I'm Darby Walker. From Boston." Based upon his experiences with the summer tourists back in his Sea View House days, Darby was pretty sure that his captor and her friends were from New York City. New Yorkers had identifiable ways of comporting themselves that were unique to their place of origin. If he was right, it would be unlikely that they would catch him in his lie about being from Boston. He was certainly *not* going to admit that he was a Cape Codder. Aristocracy did not hail from Cape Cod.

It was clear to Darby that these five individuals were close friends, all a couple of years older than Darby. It was also clear that they were wealthy — everything about them indicated as much. They had a confidence about them that Darby had seen in many guests at Sea View House. It probably arose from never having to worry about money and from always getting what they wanted. In addition, they were full of themselves, though not in the worst possible way, and, it turned out, they were full of something else. After making sure the coast was clear, Michael withdrew from his coat pocket a large silver flask, already half empty. He passed it first to Darby.

"Darby Walker of Boston, meet Johnnie Walker of Scotland," said Michael.

Darby was expected to drink from the flask, and he did. The flask got passed around, at a couple of points being refilled from a bottle secreted just outside the premises. For the next hour, Darby and his acquaintances were talking and laughing. Darby's experience with alcohol up until that time had been limited to small amounts of beer and wine. This would be his first experience with inebriation.

In the course of the conversation, while doing his best not to seem like the spy he felt he was, Darby managed to find out quite a bit about these people adopting him as their new friend. They were indeed all from New York City.

The fathers of three of them were captains of industry. Charlotte said that her father did "what he pleased," and left it at that. Michael said his father "did a little of this and little of that."

"Well, Darby," said Charlotte at one point in the conversation. "Our little mystery boy from Boston, tell us about yourself. First of all, how did you get the name Darby? Are you a Bostonian of Hibernian extraction?"

"Hmmm," said Darby. "Darby *is* an Irish name, but most of my ancestors weren't from Ireland. Darby Field, one of our immigrant ancestors, was one of the first settlors of New Hampshire in the 1630s. He was born in England but was from an Irish family. He also happens to have been the first European to climb Mt. Washington. He did that in 1642."

"I'm impressed, Darby. That's quite a pedigree!" Charlotte said. "It sure beats mine! Compared to that, my family is practically just off the boat. Tell us more!"

Darby hesitated. The jig was up. Before considering the consequences, and before he even knew what was happening, he opened his mouth and out sprang the following false narrative: "Hmm. All right. I finished high school last spring. I haven't yet decided what I want to do next, so I'm taking time off. My father owns a steamship company. The company just purchased another steamship in New York which is going be placed into service at Tampa after it's refurbished. My father wanted to take the first sail on her, and he asked me to come along for the fun of it. We decided to stop at Jacksonville for a brief exploration of the area. We just arrived earlier today."

"That's marvelous!" Charlotte exclaimed. "You simply must take us on a tour of the new steamship. Let's go right now!"

Charlotte was clearly the driving force behind her little group, and at once everyone stood, eager to go on an extemporaneous nocturnal adventure. Darby melted into his chair.

The Dancer

Darby's friends did not seem to notice how disturbed he was by the prospect of taking them on a tour of the *Valley City*. They indicated to him that they attributed his slump into his chair to a brief moment of alcohol-induced fatigue from which he would quickly rally.

Darby did rally. After a second, he ran his right hand through his hair and seemed to regain his composure. "Umm, well, you see, the ship is in a shambles. We have contracted to have it done over at a shipyard at Tampa. I don't think it would be much fun for you to see it right now." Darby figured that his new friends had sailed on much larger and finer ships than the *Valley City*.

"Nonsense, Darby of Boston," said Charlotte. "We'll have a ball!"

Darby could tell that there was no talking Charlotte out of her idea of touring the steamship owned by Darby's father's steamship company, so off the group went, with Darby as their extremely reluctant guide. They had to walk west the entire length of Bay Street to reach the *Valley City* where she was berthed until her repairs could be completed. As they walked along Bay Street, the party continued gaily on, with a little help from Johnnie Walker of Scotland.

When they reached the *Valley City*, Darby asked the group to wait on the wharf while he went onboard to fetch lanterns. He was delighted and relieved to find the engineer in the main cabin playing cards with another crew member.

After Darby explained the situation, the engineer assured Darby that he would play along with Darby's story. He even volunteered to give the group a guided tour of the ship himself, and Darby quickly accepted the offer, figuring that he was not up to the task in his present state. He also figured that without a sober, responsible adult keeping things under control, a group of intoxicated rich kids from New York City stumbling around the *Valley City* carrying burning lanterns could do more than a little damage.

Charlotte, Michael, Darby, and the other three group members took a tour of the *Valley City*, a tour carefully defined and limited by the engineer so that they would leave with the most favorable opinion of the aging vessel one could possibly acquire. He repeated to the New Yorkers the story "young Mr. Walker" had told them of the ship being scheduled for a total overhaul at Tampa.

The engineer began the tour at the lowest of the three below-decks levels of the ship and worked his way up so that the most respectable parts of the ship would be the last thing the kids would see and remember. They were shown the massive steam engine, planted in the very center of the bottom of the ship with its long shaft disappearing off to the screw propeller behind the stern. Huge boilers sat on either side of the steam engine. A gigantic fire box with multiple feeding ports sat just in front of the engine, and seemingly endless coal bins filled up most of the lowest level. The smell of coal permeated the space.

The next level up consisted mostly of the ship's four cavernous storage bays, which were empty. Charlotte commented about the somewhat sour, somewhat fruity smell that hung in the air there, and the engineer explained that the *Valley City* had most recently been transporting citrus from Cuba to New York. Up one more level and the party was now inside the main cabin, a narrow room of about fifty feet in length in the middle of the ship, with colorful but somewhat worn oriental carpets covering the floor and a row of windows facing out the stern. A wood stove sat at the center of the space, its pipe extending upwards through the ceiling. The engineer explained that this luxuriously appointed space served as dining room, drawing room, study, parlor, and meeting room all rolled into one. Several tables and fancy chairs and couches confirmed that explanation.

On each side of the main cabin were six passenger staterooms. They were fitted up with rich wood paneling that smelled as if it had just been polished. Next they were shown the galley, which was just in front of the main cabin, then the quarters of the ship's crew, and then the captain's cabin, which was the most beautifully furnished space of all, with plush carpeting, fancy lanterns, and an intricate built-in desk and bookshelves. Then the party went back up on the deck. The last space the party saw was the wheelhouse, the glass-enclosed structure forward of the stack coming up from the boilers down below. Everything in that space was orderly and beautifully maintained.

Darby was relieved and amazed that nothing went wrong on the tour and that his dancing partners were completely uncritical of the *Valley City*. It was clear that his new friends had thoroughly enjoyed the experience. The engineer, with his colorful descriptions of the ship and his salty sailors' jokes, perfect in that moment for Darby's fellow party-goers, had snatched victory from the jaws of defeat.

When the tour ended, it was after 2:00 in the morning. It was time to call it a night. Charlotte and Michael and their New York friends were all staying at the St. James Hotel, a few blocks back from the river on West Duval Street. As they said their goodbyes, Michael volunteered to walk Darby back to Carleton House, a few blocks east.

"No, Michael, you don't need to walk me back to Carleton House," Darby protested. "I'm sure I can manage."

"Darby, I won't hear of leaving you on your own to find your way back to your hotel. You don't know this city, it's late, and you could encounter rough characters looking for trouble. You can't change my mind." Michael grabbed Darby's arm, and off they went as Darby looked over his shoulder and waved a final goodbye to his new friends.

By this point, the effects of the Scotch which Darby had consumed earlier in the evening had substantially abated. He was feeling deeply ashamed by the lies he'd told. He was disappointed in himself for telling the lies, and didn't really understand why he'd felt the need to do it. As they headed east, Darby was aware of the fact that Michael had not removed his arm from Darby's, but nothing about that seemed unusual at that moment.

"Michael," said Darby, "I am so ashamed of my behavior tonight."

"Balderdash! You were a perfect gentleman, Darby, and a wonderful dancer. Charlotte thinks you're the catch of the season."

"Wait a moment. Aren't you courting Charlotte?"

"Whatever would make you think that? I like Charlotte, but not in that way. I doubt that her parents would approve of such a financial mismatch anyway. I trust you know that the gigantic yacht out in the middle of the river belongs to Charlotte's father."

"You mean Charlotte is Charlotte Astor?"

"One and the same."

Darby was stunned. He had spent the evening dancing and drinking with one of the wealthiest people in the world, and then he had taken her on a tour of a decaying old steamship and lied about its ownership.

"Oh, boy. I've really dug my own grave."

"Darby. Charlotte's a sweetheart. You have nothing to worry about. As I said, you were a perfect gentleman. And

I always say that if you must have friends, you might as well have rich ones." He looked at Darby and winked.

"Appearances are often deceiving, Michael. I'm not like you," said Darby. "Everything I've told you this evening is a lie. My father doesn't own any steamship company. He's a hard-working captain who comes from nothing. He was offered a modest ownership stake in the ship so that the real owners could be sure he would have the incentive to maximize the ship's profits."

Michael and Darby kept walking for a moment in silence. Darby was sure that this would be the end of this friendship, and that Michael would stop, turn around, and go back to the St. James and tell the others that Darby had deceived them.

"Darby, my dear sweet boy, you are so young. There is so much you don't yet know. Just because my family has money doesn't make me any different from you. And being rich isn't what it may appear to be to you. Money doesn't buy happiness, and in my experience, too much of it can buy unhappiness. I've met some of the wealthiest people on the planet, so I believe I am qualified to comment. Some of these people suffer from crippling angst, and endless parties and receptions only worsen the affliction. Some conclude that they are worthless creatures because they have never had to prove otherwise. Some question whether their friends are genuine or are just after their fortunes. Some become addicted to the game of increasing their wealth, forgetting everything they ever knew about decency, or kindness, or having fun, or enjoying their

family and friends. Sometimes too much money leads people
to dance on the edge of insanity."

Michael thought a moment. "Take Charlotte's father, for
example. He's a perfectly good fellow, but I've spent some time
with him, and I promise you that he's no happier than you are.
You can sail a long way on the world's largest yacht, but it won't
necessarily take you any closer to happiness than you can get
on the world's smallest dinghy in a small pond."

"What about you, Michael. Do *you* suffer from angst or
feelings of worthlessness?"

"No. If you really think about it, those problems are nothing more than a stupid waste of time. Anybody who has more
than they need and too much time on their hands should be
helping people who have less than they need. If you're busy
helping others, you won't wonder what you ought to be doing
and you won't feel worthless. In the final analysis, I think we're
all here to help one another. I'll be going to law school next
year. When I have my law degree, I shall work for housing
reform in New York City. The way poor people in New York
are forced to live is inexcusable."

"Good for you, Michael."

"Well, I happen to know what it means not to have anything. Unlike some of my friends, I wasn't born into money.
When I was a kid, my family had nothing. We lived in a run-
down apartment building at an address that was anything but
aristocratic. Then, eight years ago, one of my mother's cousins
died. I'd never even met him. He was a brilliant inventor who
conjured up an arcane but incredibly useful machine compo-

nent. He died with a huge pile of cash, no wife, no kids, and no will. Suddenly my family went from being poor to being very wealthy. It's been a roller coaster ride since, but my family is no happier now than it was then. We just live in a bigger house at a better address, have better clothes, and take more exotic and longer vacations. But we're not happier. Actually, my father is depressed most of the time. He no longer seems to know what he's doing. That's the honest truth."

They continued walking as Darby pondered this. "You don't think I'm a fool for making up my story about the steamship company?"

"No, Darby. You're no fool. You were caught up in the moment and you had never been in the presence of a force like Charlotte. I'm sure I would have done the same thing in your shoes. I knew you weren't from a wealthy family anyway. You didn't fool me."

"How could you have known?"

"I saw you earlier today in Bucky's. I think you were with your father, who was looking at hats. Your father might have passed as the owner of a steamship company, but, Darby, I'm afraid that this afternoon you simply weren't dressed to play the part of a privileged young man."

"Then you mean you just let me go on with my story this evening, knowing all the while it was false?"

"What should I have done, Darby? Announce in front of everyone that I doubted what you were telling us? Take you aside and tell you that you weren't fooling me? Wouldn't that have spoiled the fun? You're a good storyteller and I'm sure

I'm the only one who knew your story wasn't true. In addition to being a lot of fun, the tour of the steamship was especially convincing."

Darby smiled at Michael. He was grateful and relieved to hear Michael's reassuring words. Now as they approached Carleton House, Darby said, "I doubt you would have done the same as I have done, Michael, but thank you for saying so. It makes me feel somewhat less foolish."

The gas street lamps were still burning, but all of the shop windows were dark and Bay Street was quiet at that hour, except for a random shout or laugh as the last nighttime revelers retreated to their hotels. Darby and Michael were standing not far from the southwest corner of Carleton House. A dozen yards behind them, and on the far side of Bay Street, another man had been following them since they separated from Charlotte's group at Hogan Street. He had started following them as soon as he stepped out of a saloon at the corner of Hogan Street and Bay Street and observed them. He had kept a safe distance and had been unnoticed in his pursuit.

"There's something else, Darby. A while back you said that you weren't like me." Michael paused and looked into Darby's eyes. "I think you *are* like me."

As he said this, Michael put his hands on Darby's narrow waist and firmly maneuvered him into the darkened alley adjacent to Carleton House. He pulled Darby's body against his own, pressed his mouth tightly against Darby's open mouth, and kissed Darby deeply. The kiss went on forever and for no time at all.

Darby was too shocked to resist Michael. As Michael's tongue made the acquaintance with his own, and as Michael's strong arms held Darby's body against Michael's, things happened elsewhere in Darby's body that had never happened before. Darby was feeling a kind of electricity that was completely new. He wondered if all this was the result of whisky.

Michael eventually pulled back from Darby, but continued gazing into his eyes.

"You are a beautiful, kind, and intelligent creature, Darby. I hope to see you again soon."

Michael handed Darby his calling card. Then he turned, retreated out to Bay Street, and started walking back to the street that would take him up to the St. James.

Darby was dazed and bewildered. He glanced briefly at the calling card. Michael Chamberlain, it said, also indicating an address on Park Avenue, New York. Then he tucked the card in his pocket, exited the alley, and slowly made his way back to his room inside Carleton House to prepare for bed.

The man pursuing Darby and Michael had been watching them as they dipped into the alley, by which point he was almost directly across the street, standing at the edge of the lumber yard in the lee of the brick building housing Lorenz Stein's Bakery and Confectionery at 37 East Bay Street. Though the alley into which Michael pulled Darby was darker than the surrounding area, there was no mistaking the fact, even from the vantage point of the man across the street, that Darby and Michael were engaged in an intimate act. The man smiled when he realized what was happening, but the smile was of a dark, malevolent variety.

The captain would finally know that he, Tulley, was the good son, and that Darby was an abomination. Tulley would be restored to his proper position in his father's heart.

As Tulley watched his brother in the alley, upstairs inside Carleton House the captain heard a soft knock on his door. He opened the door to find Mrs. Loomis.

Since his wife's death several months earlier, the captain had not considered it possible that he would ever again be with a woman. The captain started to say something, but Mrs. Loomis placed her finger on his lips, pushed him back from the door and closed the door behind her.

The captain and Mrs. Loomis were suddenly in each other's arms. The thirst that the captain felt for Mrs. Loomis's touch matched the exhilaration caused by her kiss and warm embrace. Because Mrs. Loomis was a married woman, what they were doing was highly improper, even criminal, but soon the captain's best suit and Mrs. Loomis's fine dress were on the floor. Their naked bodies were fully engaged. Soft moans of ecstasy could be heard from just outside their door.

The Informant

Tuesday, January 29, 1884

The shipyard completed the repair work on the *Valley City* by mid-morning Tuesday, and at three o'clock the *Valley City* was steaming south along the coast under the command of the first mate. All was well, and the captain sat at his desk in his cabin, taking care of paperwork associated with the unplanned stop in Jacksonville.

There was a knock on the cabin door.

"Come in," called the captain. Turning his gaze from his desk, he looked up to see Tulley enter the cabin and close the door behind him.

"Hello, son. I was just catching up on a report for Mr. Henderson. What can I do for you?"

"Dad, I need to talk with you about something disturbing. Something I recently observed."

"Take a seat, Tulley," said the captain. Tulley sat on the bench near the desk.

"What sort of disturbing observation would this be, son?"

The captain, having just had an illicit sexual encounter with a married woman less than three days earlier, considered the possibility that someone in Carleton House, possibly even Tulley himself, had learned of his late-night encounter with Mrs. Loomis.

"I observed my brother committing a vile sin. I have been wrestling with the question of whether or not to tell you, but I feel it's my obligation."

"Is that so, Tulley? Are you your brother's keeper?" asked the captain, maintaining his placid demeanor.

"No, sir, I'm not. However, in addition to blackening his own soul, Darby is bringing shame and dishonor to this family."

"Did Darby take advantage of anyone?"

"No, Father."

"Did Darby steal from anyone?"

"No, Father."

"Did Darby kill anyone?"

"No, Father."

"Did Darby harm anyone?"

"No, Father. On Saturday night, when I was returning to Carleton House, I saw Darby involved in an intimate act with ..."

"Stop!" the captain interrupted. "I am not going to listen to whatever you came to tell me. I am not going to allow you to pass judgment on Darby. He has not harmed anyone, and by my reckoning he never will."

"But ..." Tulley started saying.

"No!" the captain responded, raising his voice to a level few people ever heard it raised.

Tulley was dumbfounded. The captain stood up and walked to a bookcase on an interior wall of his cabin, scanned the spines of the volumes on one of the shelves, then withdrew a small, brown book.

"I'm sure you remember what your grandfather, my father, did here in Florida many years ago."

"Yes, father, of course I know all about that, but what has that got to do ..."

The captain cut him off again: "I'm going to read you a passage from the book your grandfather wrote just after he was released from his year of imprisonment for helping slaves escape to their freedom." The captain opened the book, found the page he wanted, and began reading:

> If we are to be true to ourselves and to the stan-
> dards clearly set forth by the founders of this
> nation, then we cannot tolerate, let alone sup-
> port, a system that enslaves any of our brothers
> and sisters. We cannot tolerate or support any
> system that condemns or relegates to an inferior
> status any individual on the basis of that indi-
> vidual's identity, including his race, skin color, or
> country of origin, or on the basis of that individ-
> uals beliefs, including religious beliefs, or on the
> basis of the associations that individual makes
> with others. Our shared realization that "all men
> are created equal" necessarily requires that no

individual ever be treated, based upon his own
identity, as anything less than equal, and it re-
quires that no individual ever be given any cause
to believe that he is anything less than equal.

Upon completing the reading, the captain regarded
Tulley with an expression suggesting that the matter was
fully addressed.

"Dad," said Tulley, "Grandpa was writing about slavery.
This has nothing to do with the sin committed by Darby on
Saturday night, a sin which you haven't even allowed me
to describe."

"Tulley, your grandfather's words I just read, and with
which I agree absolutely, have *everything* to do with what you
came to tell me about. You saw Darby with someone you did
not expect to see him with. Darby is eighteen years old. He is
finding himself. He may or may not have been with the sort of
person who might ever mean something to him. I don't care
what kind of a person he was with. Your grandfather understood, as do I, that we are free to pursue happiness, and free
to love, however we wish and with whomever we wish, just as
long as we do not trample on the rights of anyone else. It is not
your job, nor my job, nor the government's job to police the
private affairs of others, provided that no harm is done and no
rights infringed."

Tulley was astounded. He could hardly believe his ears.
He had been expecting that his father would be beyond irate
and would storm out of his cabin, find Darby, and dump Darby off at the nearest port, ejecting him from the family. Any

normal father would have done exactly that. But this was not what was happening. Tulley struggled to make sense of what the captain was saying. He hadn't even told his father the worst part, because his father wasn't letting him tell it.

"But, Father," said Tulley, "Darby was kissing a man! What Darby was doing was criminal!"

The captain fired back immediately. "Tulley, are you not paying attention? Your grandfather was imprisoned for *a whole year* in a Pensacola jail, and they used a *branding iron* to burn the letters SS into his hand. You know all this. Your grandfather's loving hand, his branded hand, caressed you when you were a child, and he took your hand in his hand on countless occasions. In rescuing slaves forty-five years ago, your grandfather committed a criminal act! Was your grandfather wrong, or was the law wrong?"

Tulley looked down at the floor. His plans were being thrown into the discard bin. He was not going to displace Darby as the favored son.

"Tulley! Answer me!"

"Yes, Father. The law was wrong about slavery. I know that. But Grandpa was an abolitionist, not a defender of sodomites!"

"Tulley, I'm sorry that I haven't had this discussion with you before now. What your grandfather wrote, though he wrote it in response to his experience helping slaves get their freedom, is just as applicable to the unequal treatment of men who happen to love men, or women who happen to love women. My grandfather's brother, Zephaniah, was a man who happened to love men. I was told he was very kind and worked hard. He ran a shoe shop in the village. One day, Zephaniah, who was at the time about thirty, was found hanging from a beam in the barn. He had left a note in his room saying that he didn't fit into this world and couldn't go on. Your grandfather, just a boy at the time, loved his uncle Zephaniah deeply. He was devastated. From that day forward, your grandfather was a defender of a person's right to love anyone, of whatever gender or race or social position. He was as committed to this idea as he was to the abolition of slavery."

Tulley didn't know what to say. His shock was transforming into anger.

The captain continued. "Tulley, I love you and I love Darby. I love both of my sons forever and there is nothing either of you could ever do to make me stop loving you. However, I am profoundly disappointed that you have come to believe that your brother could be anything other than the wonderful Darby we have always known. Darby's personal affairs are none of your business unless he wants to discuss them with you, and if I ever find out that you have revealed to others anything Darby would not want revealed, there will be serious consequences for you. In any case, what Darby does in his life does not require your approval, or mine, or anyone else's. If you can't accept this truth, and if you don't understand why I am so extremely disappointed in you at this moment, then perhaps you need to take some time away on your own to work it through."

Now Tulley was fuming. "I think I'll do just that. When we get to Key West, I'll get off and catch a steamer back to

Massachusetts." Tulley stood up abruptly and stormed from the captain's cabin.

The captain was deeply troubled by what had just transpired. He wondered what Tulley's actual motivation was for reporting what he had witnessed in Jacksonville. Did he think the captain was going to disown Darby? "I guess it's time for a talk with Darby," the captain said to himself.

The Summons

Thursday, January 31, 1884

The *Valley City* arrived at Key West early in the morning. Tulley had packed his things the prior evening and was ready to leave the ship as soon as it landed. After leaving his cabin, he stopped briefly in the doorway of the captain's cabin.

At his desk, the captain turned and looked at his elder son. He stood, walked to the door of the cabin, and handed Tulley an envelope. "Tulley, take this money. You will need it to tide you over until you have your next job. Whenever you're ready to come back, there is always a position for you on my ship."

Tulley looked down at the floor and said nothing.

"You know I love you, son. All I want is for you to be happy. That's all your mother ever wanted too. I'm disappointed in you at the moment, but love you no less than ever. We all make mistakes, but every mistake is a learning opportunity. It is through our mistakes that we become stronger and more caring people."

Tulley had no response.

The captain put his arms around his son, who half-heartedly returned the embrace. After a moment, Tulley pulled back from his father, slid the envelope into his pocket, turned and made his way off the ship. He quickly disappeared into the activity of Key West's waterfront.

The captain was sad to see Tulley go, but he also knew his elder son better than anybody else did, and knew that he could never change his elder son's mind. Only Tulley could change Tulley's mind.

After Tulley was off the ship, the captain stood and opened the door to his cabin. The engineer was in the passage just outside the door, and the captain asked the engineer to go find Darby and ask Darby to come to the cabin.

Moments later, Darby entered the captain's cabin.

"Good morning, Dad. You wanted to see me?"

"Yes. Have a seat, Darby," said the captain, motioning to a bench. "There is something I need to discuss with you."

Darby took a seat on the bench adjacent to the captain's desk.

"Darby, your brother has been envious of you since the day you were born. We both know that. His life is a difficult one, and you already know that too. He can't change his fundamental nature any more than you can change yours or I can change mine. Once we develop an understanding of who we are, however, we can learn to minimize and manage our weaknesses and build upon and take advantage of our strengths.

Tulley has a long way to go in this process. He needs time to work things out."

Darby nodded. He had no idea where this conversation was headed.

The captain said, "Your brother told me that he saw you with another young man one evening in Jacksonville."

Darby's jaw dropped, and his face began to flush. "But ..."

"It's all right, Darby. You don't need to say anything about what did or did not happen. I've been all over the world. I've seen a lot of things and met a lot of people—perhaps more things and more people than are encountered in an average American's lifespan—and I can't even see the end of my days with a spyglass. I've known sailors who had relations with other sailors in their youth and later married women and raised families. I've known men who fell in love with men and spent their lives together. I've known women who have lived together as married couples. You're only eighteen years old, and you're just starting out. I wouldn't expect you to know all there is to know about yourself at this point."

Darby wasn't sure what to say in response to the captain, so he said nothing.

"I told your brother I was extremely disappointed in him for sharing with me what he observed, and that it was none of his business, or mine. I also told him there would be serious consequences for him if he ever did such a thing again. I am afraid, however, that he didn't expect me to react the way I did, and it troubles me to consider what he *did* expect. I suggested to your brother that he should take time away until he could understand why I was so disappointed in him. He decided to get off here at Key West. He's on his way back to Cape Cod."

Now Darby understood why Tulley had not said more than two words to him since the morning after the passionate encounter with Michael.

"Darby, just now, before your brother left, I told him that all I want is for him to be happy. The same is true for you. I love you forever and without condition. It doesn't matter to me whom you fall in love with. I want you to find the love that your mother and I had for each other."

The captain paused, his expression clearly indicating careful consideration of his next statement. "There is one other thing you need to know, Darby. My father was known for being an abolitionist, but he also believed strongly in the equality of people who are attracted to members of their own sex. He knew, as I know, that we can't choose to be attracted to one gender or the other any more than we can choose our skin color. His uncle Zephaniah took his own life when a young man, long before I came along."

"Wait, Dad. Are you saying that Zephaniah, the man whose portrait hangs above my bed back at home, took his own life because he was attracted to men?"

"Yes, that's right. That's what my father told me."

"Oh my gosh! Freeman told me that Zephaniah had committed suicide because Eleazer threatened to expose Zephaniah's secret, but Freeman wouldn't tell me what the secret was. Now I finally know!"

"Yes, Darby, now you know."

Darby also realized, in that same moment, that Freeman had been talking about Zephaniah when he told Darby about having been in love with someone, a relationship that "had not been countenanced," as Freeman had put it. Freeman had given Darby his most prized possession, his portrait of his lover whom he had lost to suicide.

"Um, Dad, did your father ever say anything to you about Zephaniah and Freeman?"

"Yes, Darby. He did. They had been in love with each other."

Darby was shaken to his core. The sadness of it all was almost too intense for him to contemplate. So was the love. He looked down at the floor of the cabin and ran a hand through his hair as he considered the meaning of everything he had just learned. His eyes filled with water.

The two men sat in silence. Darby reflected on the hardship endured by Zephaniah and Freeman and on the fact that Tulley, by exposing Darby's encounter in the dark alley, had just done to Darby what Eleazer had threatened to do to Zephaniah. But Tulley failed in his effort to hurt Darby, and failed for one reason alone: Captain Walker's unconditional love. Darby could think of no other father he had ever known who would be as accepting as his own father.

"Darby, things are changing, and as time passes it will be easier for people like Zephaniah and Freeman, and like you, if you discover this is who you are. Don't forget that only thirty years ago it was both legal and ordinary in much of this country for white people to own colored people as their possessions, and to abuse them. Think of that! As time goes on, our civilization is becoming more enlightened."

Darby was overcome with emotion. He thought of his dear friend Freeman losing the person he loved and then spending the rest of his life alone. He thought of Tulley trying to destroy Darby's relationship with his father. How fortunate he was to have a father who loved him so much. Another thought suddenly entered Darby's mind. Freeman must have known what Darby had not known himself until recently: that Darby was, like Freeman, a man who would love other men. And yet Freeman had said nothing about it to Darby because he had understood that Darby was then too young for that sort of discussion.

Tears rolled down Darby's cheeks. The captain got up from his desk and sat on the bench beside his son. He put his arms around him. Darby, now a young man and taller than his father, buried his head in his father's chest. As his father embraced him, Darby's body quivered, and his tears became a river.

Spoliation

September 1886

For over two years after Tulley left the captain and Darby at Key West, Tulley stayed away. He signed on for various trips up and down the coast and across the Atlantic. Meanwhile, Darby worked alongside his father on the *Valley City*, transporting cattle, produce, and passengers to and from all the ports between New Orleans and Key West, and to and from Havana.

The captain rented for himself and his son a modest house in Tampa. This became their home base. At the same time, the captain continued to maintain the family home back in Harwich Port, which served as Tulley's residence when Tulley was not on the sea.

The captain sent regular correspondence to Tulley, recounting what he and Darby had been up to and inquiring about Tulley's life. In reply, he would only occasionally receive a short note saying only, "Everything is okay in Harwich. Tulley."

But then the captain received a longer letter from Tulley. As he read it, the captain felt that it just didn't sound like the Tulley he knew, but, he reasoned, perhaps Tulley was at long last maturing. Also, the captain realized that he had never read anything written by Tulley of this length or importance. This made the captain think back to Tulley's final high school paper, the one that had earned high praise from Tulley's teacher. He remembered that Tulley, oddly enough, had never brought it home for the captain and Emily to read.

Harwich Port

September 6, 1886

Dear Dad:

Hello to you from Harwich Port. I hope that you and Darby are in good health and good spirits.

I have much to tell you.

First of all, I am engaged to be married. I met my future wife in Maine at the beginning of the summer. Her name is Martha Gould.

I first met Martha when I was playing chess with a sailor I met at the waterfront in Portland. She came up to us and asked if we would mind if she watched us play chess, which we didn't. Then she asked if she could play whichever one of us won the game, and that was of course me. I doubted she even knew how to play chess, but it turned out she did, and she is an excellent player. She is the best chess player I have ever met, besides myself. I asked her who taught her to play the game and she told me she taught herself.

After the chess game ended, she tarried, finally telling me she would be pleased to accompany me if I would care to invite her to dinner, which I hadn't even thought of. Anyway, I ended up spending all my free time on that trip with Martha, and when I returned to Portland the next time, the same thing happened. On the most recent trip up there, from which I am just recently returned, I asked Martha to marry me, and she said yes!

Martha is very pretty and very intelligent.

We would like to get married as soon as possible. I told Martha I would not marry her until my father could be present, so I am hoping you will write me back at your earliest convenience and let me know when you are able to get back home. Martha's parents can be available any time you are.

The other thing I need to tell you is that you may be about to become a very wealthy man.

I suppose you remember all about your grandfather's schooner, the "Caroline", which was destroyed by a French privateer in 1798 on Nantucket Shoals. This was when America was in an undeclared war with France and this sort of thing happened on many occasions.

There was an article in the Boston Globe a while back all about the French taking of ships around the time the Caroline was taken. The article explained that Congress recently passed a law that allows people to submit claims to a court in Washington, DC, for the value of the vessels and cargo taken by French vessels during the relevant period, and that the U.S. government will pay those claims, plus interest from the date of the taking, to the heirs of the owners whose ships were taken. These are called "French Spoliation" claims.

I felt certain that you would be happy if I pursued this for you, so I have done the research and I have discussed everything with Eldon Doane, who says he would be happy to represent us in the claim.

Only two of your grandfather's five children had children, namely your father and your Uncle Warren. Each of these two children would now be entitled to one-half of your grandfather's interest in any claim, if they were still alive, but they're not. Your father's half of your grandfather's claim would now pass in equal thirds to you and to your brother and sister. That means that each of the three of you would be entitled to one-sixth of any award made on the claim. By my calculations, which Eldon has double-checked, the value of what your grandfather lost in 1798 was $18,780. That includes the value of the Caroline plus a full cargo of fish plus all the gear and equipment on board.

Here's the really good news. At a rate of 4% for the 88 years since the loss occurred, the full value of the claim is now about $600,000. Your share in that is about $100,000. You read that right! $100,000!

Now we need to re-open the probate of your grandfather's estate and get one of us appointed as the administrator of the estate, and then we file the claim in Washington. Eldon says it may take a couple of years beyond that for the claim to be processed by the government.

I thought that since I'm here in town to take care of details, it would be best if I ask the court to make me the administrator of the estate. I have already spoken with your brother and sister and your cousins, and they're all in agreement. All you need to do is sign the assent form Eldon has prepared. I have enclosed it with this letter. Please sign and mail it back to me. I'll take care of the rest. When you are a very wealthy man, perhaps you will give me a commission!

I will wait for your reply about when you can come up for the wedding and for your signed assent form. One last thing: we only have until the end of January to file the French Spoliation claim, and before that the administrator of your grandfather's estate has to be appointed, so please return the signed assent form to me as quickly as possible.

Thank you.

Your loving son,

Tulley

Tulley didn't tell his father that Martha was already essentially living with him in the house in Harwich Port. He knew that his father would not have approved of that arrangement. In an attempt to maintain an appearance of propriety, Martha was also renting a room in the least expensive boarding house in the village.

Tulley also didn't tell his father that it had been Martha who had come up with the idea of filing the French Spoliation claim and that Martha had done the background research. Martha had even written the September letter to the captain and had dictated it to Tulley so that it would be in his handwriting. But Tulley was going to claim full credit for this project himself.

Surely the French Spoliation claim, along with his marriage, which was something his brother could never compete with, would make him "son number one" in his father's eyes. Furthermore, once he and Martha started producing grandchildren, there would be no question who was the favorite son, and it wouldn't hurt at all that Martha was as pretty as she was. She had sparkling blue eyes and perfect, soft, symmetrical facial features. She had abundant natural charm and carried herself with unusual grace. In fact she was so attractive in every way that Tulley sometimes wondered why she was interested in him.

The captain was thrilled to get this letter from Tulley. It indicated to the captain that his eldest son had undergone a positive transformation. He had never known Tulley to seem so happy.

The captain was also greatly pleased that his son was about to be married. He would find a substitute to take his place on the *Valley City* as soon as possible, then he and Darby would travel up to the Cape to attend the wedding.

As for the French Spoliation claim, the captain was dazzled by the thought that he might come into the grand sum of $100,000. It seemed impossible!

At the same time, something about Tulley's proposal bothered him. Eleazer Walker, the captain's grandfather and owner of the *Caroline*, had died before the captain was born. The captain had never met him, but remembered very well his father mentioning the *Caroline*, and he remembered hearing that it had been destroyed on Nantucket Shoals in 1798. The captain understood as well as anyone that Nantucket Shoals was a large area of shifting sands south and east of Nantucket where the water is as shallow as three feet in places, a hazardous area which mariners avoided.

However, the captain could not remember anyone ever suggesting that the *Caroline* had been destroyed by a French vessel. He had always believed that the *Caroline* was just one of a number of shipwrecks on Nantucket Shoals over the centuries.

The captain reflected on the situation, finally concluding that if Tulley had researched it, and if Eldon Doane was willing to handle the claim for the family, Tulley must be right about the facts. Perhaps the fact that the *Caroline* was destroyed by a French vessel wasn't mentioned because it wasn't considered important or was considered some kind of an embarrassment. Perhaps the captain just didn't remember this detail of the ship's destruction, which until now wouldn't have been of much significance to anyone.

There seemed nothing to lose if Tulley filed the French Spoliation claim. If the claim succeeded, the Walkers would be wealthy. If the claim failed, Tulley would have gained experience in the workings of the federal government. It would be a beneficial experience either way.

The captain signed the probate assent form and promptly mailed it back to Tulley, indicating that he would respond as soon as possible with the earliest date he and Darby could return to Cape Cod for Tulley's wedding. In the return correspondence, the captain also told Tulley how happy he was to get Tulley's news and how proud he was of his eldest son.

The marriage of Tulley and Martha took place on the day before Thanksgiving, 1886. The captain and Darby were there for the event, as were Martha's parents and various relatives from both families.

The captain somehow didn't get a warm feeling about his new daughter-in-law, despite her outward beauty and poise, but the important thing was that she made Tulley happy. Martha was welcomed into the Walker family with open arms. The captain was overjoyed to see his eldest son doing so well.

Martha and Tulley had a number of meetings with Eldon Doane about the French Spoliation claim. It turned out that many of the pre-1800 records of vessel registrations were missing from the Customs House in Barnstable, including records of the *Caroline*. Eldon advised Tulley that the lack of official records was not fatal to the claim, provided that Tulley could come up with other substantiating documentary and circumstantial evidence. In particular, he suggested getting affidavits from every neighbor and relative who could report hearing about the 1798 taking of the *Caroline* by the French privateer eighty-eight years earlier. Tulley wasn't comfortable going out and talking with lots of different people, but Martha told Tulley she was happy to take care of it. She said it would be a good way for her to meet people throughout Harwich.

When Martha completed her work, she had collected over two dozen affidavits of people stating that they remembered the story of the taking of the *Caroline* in 1798. One of those people was a ninety-six-year old woman who said that her father had been one of the crew members the day the *Caroline* was taken. He had told her all about it at that time, when she was eight years old. Her affidavit contained details consistent with those that would go on the actual claim form. The other affiants were only able to state that they had heard the story of the *Caroline* from elderly friends and relatives, now deceased, who had been connected to the event or had learned about it at the time the *Caroline* was destroyed.

Tulley, acting as administrator of his great-grandfather's estate, signed the French Spoliation claim and filed it by the due date in January 1887.

Nothing much happened with it for more than two years. Then, in the summer of 1889, Eldon contacted Tulley to advise him that the claim was going to be denied unless Tulley could produce additional documentary evidence of the loss. The Court of Claims notified Eldon that the affidavits that were submitted did not, by themselves, have sufficient evidentiary value to support the claim. All but one of those affidavits was only second or third-hand testimony, and the one firsthand statement by the ninety-six-year old woman, who had since died, was not thought to be entirely reliable.

Within a couple of weeks, Tulley delivered to Eldon an old letter which he said he had found in a collection of old papers that had belonged to his grandfather, Nathaniel Walker. The letter, dated February 25, 1838, was from Shubael Eldridge, Nathaniel's uncle by marriage. The letter read, in part:

I know how upset you still are about your father's death. I think you made a good dicision to git away for a while. You asked me in your last letter to tell you about your father's first schooner, the Caroline. As you know, your father and I were born the same year and we were good friends since we were young. I helped him build the Caroline in 1796. We built the Caroline down by the shore in front of your father's house. Several of us were involved in her construction, which your father's father oversaw and he also contributed the lumber, which came from his land. It took us a full year. The Caroline was 95 tons burthen, which gave her a value then of about $9,500. She was launched in the summer of 1797. I went on several fishing trips on the Caroline. Your *father was the captain and there were usually three to five others onboard. I was on the last voyage of the Caroline. We left Harwich in the middle of July 1798 for the fishing banks. At the end of August, the hold was full with 1,000 quintals of salted codfish and we were returning to Harwich. This was during the time we were in hostilities with France. On the last day of August, we were seized and boarded near the edge of Nantucket Sholes by the French Privateer, L'Union. The Caroline was rummaged, scuttled, and sunk, the vessel and its cargo a total loss. We pleaded with the captain of the French privateer to let us go, and he allowed us to git the rowboat off the Caroline before she was scuttled, which we did, and we got to Nantucket late that night. It was a devastating financial loss to your father.*

Eldon advised Tulley that he was optimistic that when the letter was added to the previously submitted material, there would be enough evidence to support the claim.

Tulley did not tell Eldon that this 1838 letter to Nathaniel Walker from Shubael Eldridge was handwritten in August 1889 by Martha's brother back in Maine, on old sheets of paper from the brother's attic. The forgery was based upon a real 1838 letter sent to Nathaniel that had included no information about the *Caroline*. Tulley did not tell Eldon this because Tulley didn't know it. Martha had not told him.

On top of that, Tulley did not know that Martha had been unable to find anybody in the entire town of Harwich, other than Tulley's few relatives who stood to gain from the claim, who remembered anything about the *Caroline*. The mind of the ninety-six-year-old woman had not been especially clear on the day Martha met with her. In a couple of cases, those signing the affidavits had been led to believe that there would be a gift coming from the Walkers if the claim were successful.

Several weeks after the 1838 forged letter was presented to Attorney Doane, Tulley and Martha were sitting down for supper in the Walker house in Harwich Port when a horse and buggy pulled up in front of the house. Tulley could see from his seat at the dinner table that it was Eldon Doane.

Tulley knew something was up. Eldon had not stopped by the Walker house since the death of Freeman Scott several years earlier. He and Martha had always met with Eldon at his office.

"This may be our lucky day, Martha," said Tulley. "Here comes Eldon. I can't imagine why he would be here unless it is to tell us that Washington has approved our claim." Tulley pushed back his chair, almost knocking it over, and rushed to the front door of the little house.

Tulley pulled the door open before Eldon had had a chance to knock.

"Eldon, my friend! Come in! Come in and tell us the good news!"

Tulley didn't notice the look of gloom on Eldon's face. As Eldon stepped into the house, he removed his hat and tipped his head toward Martha. "Good evening, Martha, Tulley," Eldon said in a subdued voice.

"Hello, Eldon," Martha said, no emotion registering on her face.

"Come, sit with us at the table, Eldon," said Tulley. "Martha, fetch this man a bowl of your fish chowder, and some coffee."

Eldon sat at the table. "Martha, really, I'm not hungry, but thanks just the same."

Martha did not rise from the table.

"Tulley, Martha," said Eldon, "I'm afraid that I have some bad news."

"What?" Tulley exclaimed. "You can't possibly be here to tell us the claim hasn't been approved!"

"Sadly, that *is* part of my news."

"What, then? Are we going to have to wait another year before these damned bureaucrats down in Washington can figure out how to add up the figures?"

"No, Tulley, it's not a question of waiting another year."

"You're not saying they *denied* the claim, are you?" Tulley asked.

"Well, Tulley, they *did* deny it. And it's rather worse than that. Let me explain. It seems that the Court of Claims has received a number of fraudulent spoliation claims since Congress established …"

"There's no fraud in our claim!" Tulley interjected impatiently.

The color drained from Martha's face.

"Let me finish. Because of the number of fraudulent claims received, and because of the large sums of money involved, the Court is looking at all claims carefully and critically. They have a team of professional examiners studying each claim to make sure everything is in proper order and fully supported by the evidence submitted."

"We submitted sufficient evidence! Our claim is in proper order," Tulley interjected again.

"Hold your horses, Tulley. I learned today that the Court has one of its examiners based here on the Cape looking into claims relating to vessels from ports on the Cape and Martha's Vineyard and Nantucket. The Court wanted to be sure the 1838 letter to your grandfather was authentic."

At this moment, Martha's face went from slightly off-color to white, even whiter than the underside of a flat fish.

Eldon continued. "One of the examiners in Washington sent up to the examiner here on the Cape a photograph of the 1838 letter you provided, and he asked the examiner here to find another sample of Shubael Eldridge's handwriting and see if it matched the writing in the 1838 letter."

"Well, Eldon, I'm sure that's a wild goose chase. Martha found just the one letter from Shubael up in the attic. Just the one. Shubael has been dead for over forty years. They could never possibly find another thing that he wrote himself. And if they did find another sample, it would just show that the 1838 letter is the real deal."

Martha looked as though she was about to melt into a puddle and drain through a crack in the floor.

"Tulley, my friend. I would have thought you were right about not finding a writing sample and about what would happen if they did find one. It turns out, however, that you are wrong. The examiner here did find a sample of Shubael Eldridge's handwriting. Apparently, the examiner went to the probate court in Barnstable and pulled Shubael's probate file."

"But there wouldn't be any letters written by Shubael in that old file," Tulley exclaimed, defiantly.

"No Tulley, there were no letters but there was Shubael's will. It was a holographic will."

"What's a holographic will?" Tulley asked.

"A holographic will is a will that is handwritten by the testator—that is to say, handwritten by the person whose will it is. Such wills were common in earlier days. In the case of Shubael's will, the witnesses even attest that they saw Shubael write the entire will in his own hand."

"Go on," said Tulley, more subdued.

"The handwriting in Shubael's will, which, coincidentally, was written in 1838, does not match the handwriting in the 1838 letter you submitted with the French Spoliation claim."

"And therefore what?" asked Tulley.

"And therefore, according to the Court of Claims, the letter you produced in support of your claim is a forgery, and you are about to be indicted by a federal grand jury on a charge of perjury for having submitted an affidavit swearing that the 1838 letter was authentic."

"Oh, dear God!" said Tulley. "How can this be? Martha found the letter along with a bunch of my grandfather's papers in a trunk in the attic! It can't be a forgery. How could it be a forgery?"

As he said this, Tulley looked at Martha, who by this time looked gravely ill and was staring down at the floor.

"Martha," said Eldon, "is there something you haven't told Tulley about the 1838 letter?"

Martha sat in her chair without responding. She continued staring at the floor.

"Martha!" shouted Tulley. "What did you do? Did you create a fake letter?"

More silence from Martha.

Tulley stood up and walked over to just behind Martha's chair. "Answer me, woman!"

Martha began sobbing. Finally, she started to speak, slowly and haltingly. "I did find an 1838 letter from Shubael Eldridge to Nathaniel Walker in that old trunk. It said everything that's in the letter given to the Court, except for the part about the schooner. There was nothing in the letter about the schooner. I made up that part. I sent what I wrote to my brother. He found old writing paper somewhere and wrote out what I had come up with on the old paper and sent it back to me."

After this revelation, there was a deafening silence while the gravity of the situation sunk in for Tulley.

"What does this mean?" Tulley finally asked Eldon.

"It means I can't help you any further. You're going to need the best criminal lawyer you can find, and it's going to cost money. You may want to contact your father and see if he knows anybody who can help."

The Family Reunion

– THE INDEPENDENT –
Harwich, Massachusetts
Tulley Walker of Harwich Indicted for Perjury

OCTOBER 10, 1889. The United States Circuit Court grand jury was convened in special session Tuesday for the purpose of having brought before the jurors the case of Tulley Walker of Harwich, whom they subsequently indicted on a charge of perjury. The case is an interesting one. Walker, as the administrator of the estate of his great-grandfather, the late Eleazer Walker of Harwich, filed a claim in the U.S. Court of Claims under the Act of Congress relating to French spoliations. It is alleged that Walker went before Norris Bennett, a notary public, and swore that a letter which he put in before the notary had been received by his grandfather in 1838, the letter containing a statement that his great-grandfather's schooner, *Caroline*, had been captured by a French privateer and destroyed. The letter materially strengthened the claimant's case. It is charged that the letter was a complete forgery, created by Walker based upon an actual 1838 letter that did not contain any reference to the schooner. Walker was brought to Boston on Wednesday where he was before U.S. Commissioner Gordon Rogers on the perjury charge. He is being held in lieu of $2,000 bail for trial in the Circuit Court. The affair causes great surprise through the Cape. Many are of the opinion that there is a mistake somewhere.

Darby answered the door of the Tampa home he was sharing with his father and found a boy standing outside with a telegram. Thanking the boy, Darby took the telegram and closed the door.

"Dad, there's a telegram for you," he called to the captain, who was back in his room taking care of paperwork.

When the captain walked out to the front room, Darby handed him the envelope from the Western Union Telegraph Company. There was a message inside which had been sent by his daughter-in-law, Martha:

October 10, 1889 Father Walker – I am sorry to report that Tulley is being held in Boston under a charge of perjury relating to the Caroline claim. The bail is $2,000. I don't know what to do.

Lovingly, Martha.

"Oh, hell's blazes!" exclaimed the captain.

"What is it?" asked Darby.

"The French Spoliation claim sounded too good to be true when your brother first wrote me about it, and it appears it *was* too good to be true. Your brother is in jail. This is a fine kettle of fish!"

"Oh, Dad, I'm sorry to hear this." As Darby contemplated this news, he placed a thumb and forefinger on his beard, a recent addition to his face that gave Darby a measure of badly needed confidence. Nothing about this development came as a surprise to Darby, but he sensed that the less he said about it at that moment, the better. He felt awful for his father, and the fact that his brother was in trouble didn't bring him any pleasure either.

"Son, listen, I need you to run over to the Telegraph office and send two telegrams. The first will be to Martha. Tell her I'm on my way to Boston on the next train. The second one will be to Attorney Andrew Beaumont … I have his card right here for you … Attorney Andrew Beaumont, 99 Newbury Street, Boston. Tell Andrew that Tulley is being held in Boston on a perjury charge. Also say that I need him to bail Tulley out and then keep Tulley at his house until I get to Boston."

"Sure, Dad. I can do that."

"Also, Darby, on your way back please run into the train station and find out when the next train will be leaving. I'm going to start packing."

Darby was out the door.

Four days later, Captain Walker, Tulley Walker, Martha Walker, and Andrew Beaumont were seated around the desk in Andrew's sumptuous, wood-paneled office.

"This is where things stand," said Andrew. "With the cooperation of Tulley and Martha I've assembled the relevant facts of the case. I've also been communicating with the federal prosecutor on this case since Thursday. It turns out that the federal prosecutor, Stockton Kenyon, is a friend from law school at Harvard, and that has helped."

The captain, Tulley, and Martha stared intently at Andrew, waiting.

"This is an extremely serious matter. The prosecutor has indicated that he is under pressure to bring the greatest possible weight to bear in these cases. The government needs to set examples wherever they can. I suggested to the prosecutor that his case against Tulley is far from ironclad, primarily because Tulley indicates he had no knowledge that the letter he was certifying as genuine was a forgery. Martha had not disclosed to Tulley that she herself arranged to have the false letter created."

Andrew paused a moment to survey the looks on the faces of the Walkers and to underscore the situation's seriousness.

He resumed, "There is supporting evidence that Tulley was not himself involved in the forgery. Eldon Doane, for one, is prepared to testify that he was present when Martha disclosed the forgery, and that it is his opinion, having known Tulley since Tulley was a boy, that Tulley's shock upon learning the news was genuine. Also, I have obtained samples of the handwriting of Martha's brother to show that the forged letter was not created by Tulley. All are in agreement that Tulley had no contact with the people in Harwich who were cajoled into signing affidavits in support of the claim. I also mentioned to the prosecutor other arguments into which I need not delve here, most of which would at least throw sand in the gears of the prosecutor's case."

Andrew took the temperature of the emotions in the room and made sure that the Walkers were following him. "The prosecutor indicates he is willing to have the charges against Tulley dropped if Tulley pays a fine to the Court of Claims. This fine will serve as a penalty and will cover the government's costs of processing and investigating the claim. I don't yet know what amount the prosecutor has in mind, but I'm sure it will be in the thousands."

If the captain was disturbed by this news, Darby could see no sign of it in his face. Martha looked like a shipwreck. Tulley appeared to be in a state of panic.

"There is another set of people who are unhappy with the current state of affairs," Andrew continued. "All of the individuals back in Harwich who signed affidavits were contacted by the prosecutor's office. I have communicated with most of them, and have passed along to them assurances from the prosecutor's office that if Tulley continues to cooperate, as I'm sure he will, the affiants are in no danger of being charged with any crime."

Again, Andrew took a break from talking to be sure that his points were being taken in.

"I have rarely seen," Andrew continued, "a group of citizens here in the commonwealth who are so angry and who feel so strongly that their honor and reputations have been unjustly impugned. My advice to all of you is that you not return to Harwich Port. If Tulley returns, he may be greeted by an angry mob. In any event, nobody on the Cape is ever again going to offer Tulley employment of any sort. The same holds for Martha. I believe there may be *some* sympathy for you, Tulley, but the best course will be to relocate and start over elsewhere. Over time, the people who feel wronged may forgive and forget."

The meeting ended when it was agreed that whatever fine the prosecutor ultimately insisted upon would be paid, and that the Walkers would not be returning to Harwich Port. The captain told his eldest son that he would cover the fines and costs, provided that his son and daughter-in-law agreed to relocate to Tampa Bay, where he could keep an eye on them. He also said that the fines and costs would be deducted from any inheritance Tulley might receive upon the captain's death.

Within a couple of weeks, the captain and his sons and daughter-in-law were living together in the rented house in Tampa. It wasn't much later when the captain, having directed inquiries to his fellow captains and associates in the area, learned the U.S. Lighthouse Board was looking for a place to build a lighthouse on the eastern shore of Tampa Bay, and that they were also looking for someone to serve as its keeper. Having sailed up and down the bay for the last fifteen years, the captain knew just the place.

Strings were pulled, and at the beginning of January 1890, Tulley paid the Internal Improvement Fund of the State of Florida the sum of ten dollars in exchange for a deed to "The Island Numbered One of Section Twenty in Township Thirty-Two, South of Range Eighteen, East, unsurveyed, containing an estimated area of one acre, and lying and being in the county of Hillsborough, State of Florida." The tiny island known locally as Indian Hill would now be called "Walker's Key."

A short time after that, Tulley signed a contract with the U.S. Lighthouse Board providing for its purchase of a 25-by-25-foot square piece of land at the highest point of his island, providing for a permanent easement to reach that tiny plot from the waterfront, and providing for Tulley's employment as keeper of the soon-to-be constructed Walker's Key light.

In the course of these inquiries, the captain also learned that the Tampa Bay ship pilots were looking for an additional pilot to join them at their station at Egmont Key. The captain had grown weary of the stress of managing a steamship. He applied for the position and accepted the pilots' offer to join them at the beginning of February 1890.

Darby had been serving by the captain's side aboard the *Valley City* for the prior five years. He had been considering his options for some time. He wanted to have his own boat to transport paying passengers and handle special deliveries around the bay. He evaluated the available transportation resources around Tampa Bay, and concluded there would be a great demand for a small, accommodating ferry service based at St. Petersburg.

Soon thereafter, Andrew Beaumont put out some feelers and located the *Shooting Star* in southern Maine. The owner had not yet listed it for sale, but one of Andrew's contacts knew the owner's story, and convinced the owner that Darby would be the right person to take her over. Darby knew she was the perfect vessel as soon as he laid eyes on her. Using his inheritance from Freeman Scott, he made the purchase. It took Darby a couple of months to get in place the necessary permits and licenses and hire an engineer to work on the boat with him. Walker's Ferry Service commenced business at the Electric Pier in St. Petersburg in the middle of April 1890.

The captain was glad to have both of his sons in close proximity. He was sure the Walkers would be happy at Tampa Bay.

And for the next ten years they would be happy, for the most part.

The Indian's Curse

Wednesday, February 5, 1890

"My goodness! Look at this view!" said Darby, sweeping his hand in an arc in front of him. "It feels like we're at the top of the world! You can actually see St. Petersburg all the way across the bay!"

"Indeed," said Captain Walker. "The prospect from this hill repays the ascent a thousand-fold. And the view from the lighthouse will be far more spectacular."

"This is thought to be the highest point in the whole county. Here, Tulley, take a look through my spyglass," said Ben McLaughlin, passing it to Tulley.

Tulley raised the spyglass to his right eye. "Yup. I can even see Tampa all the way up at the end of the bay. Oh, and I see the lighthouse down at Egmont Key."

"Martha, you've got the best location on the whole bay. Congratulations," Darby said to his sister-in-law.

"It's lovely," Martha responded flatly.

A large rowboat from a Tampa Bay Pilots Association boat rested on the muddy western shore of Walker's Key. The pilot boat itself rode calmly at a mooring in deeper water, just outside the Walker's Key channel, where two large pelicans were diving for fish. The sun was approaching its highest position in the sky.

Captain Walker, Tulley, Martha, Darby, and Ben McLaughlin stood atop the highest hill on Walker's Key, forty feet above sea level. The party had come to Walker's Key to take stock of what Tulley had purchased and discuss details relating to the new home of Tulley and Martha.

Tulley wore a light blue baseball cap on his head, backwards. Wearing a cap backwards sort of defeated the point of wearing a cap, Darby mused, but he had largely given up trying to understand the workings of his brother's mind years earlier.

A substantial assemblage of lumber, bricks, and hardware rested down near the beach. Earlier that day, a barge had brought this material from a Tampa lumber yard. The construction of Tulley and Martha Walker's house would begin within a few days, just as soon as the contractor from Tampa could send a team of carpenters down to the island.

Darby knew that Martha was unhappy about moving to Walker's Key. He knew that she had not wanted to move to Florida at all, and if she *had* wanted to move to Florida, she certainly wouldn't have chosen this remote location for her home. She was, after all, a city girl. On a recent night in Tampa, Darby had overheard Martha talking with Tulley. She had asked him if they really had to go through with the plan. Tulley had told her that it was far too late to back out now, and that he and his father had worked very hard so that he and Martha could have this opportunity. The view over the bay from the heights of Walker's Key could do little to mitigate the misery Martha must have been expecting for herself here. Her husband might revel in the isolation, but it would be a struggle for her, Darby knew.

"We are standing where the lighthouse will stand," said Ben. "Down on that lower hill is the house site." He pointed down to a spot about a dozen yards from where they stood. "Even from that lower point, you will have wonderful views in almost all directions."

Darby ran his thumb and forefinger through his beard. "Are we sure that if the house goes there it will be clear of the easement for access to the lighthouse?"

Tulley had with him a large, rolled-up surveyor's plan, which he unrolled and studied for a moment. "Yup. The easement is further to the south. And it won't matter anyway. I'm the only one who will ever need to get to the lighthouse," he said.

As McLaughlin and the Walkers were discussing the details, an old, battered canoe entered the Walker's Key channel and drew up to the island. Conversation stopped as the group watched a very tall, lean man in his late twenties step out of the canoe and pull it through the muck to a point where it would not float away. The man's long hair was pulled back and tied into a ponytail. He made his way up the hill to McLaughlin and the Walkers.

He extended his hand to the captain, clearly the most senior and most authoritative member of the group. "Greetings, sir," he said, "I'm John Powell."

"Kenelm Walker," said the captain, shaking John's hand. "And these are my sons, Tulley and Darby, and Tulley's wife, Martha. And this is Ben McLaughlin," he added, gesturing to Ben.

"John and I have met before, Captain," said Ben.

"It looks like you are fixing to build a house up here," said John, addressing the group, but focusing primarily on the captain.

"Yes, that's correct. My son and daughter-in-law will be living here. A lighthouse will be constructed right about where we are standing now, and Tulley will be in charge. It will be a huge benefit to mariners on the bay."

"I imagine it would be," said John. "So you're planning on living right here on this island?" John asked, looking directly at Tulley.

"Yup," said Tulley.

"Well, then, I'm sorry to have to tell you that you can't live here. Nor can you build anything here. Not a lighthouse. Not a house. Not even an outhouse."

"Now look here," said the captain, "I don't know who you think you are, but my son just purchased this island from the State of Florida. The deed is valid, and his title is good. By my reckoning, he has every right to build here."

"Your people may say that you own this place," said John, "but still you can't build here. And you can't live here."

"What right, sir, do you have to tell my son what he can and can't do with his property?" asked the captain, his voice remaining calm despite the rising tension. "Who exactly are you?"

"Captain," Ben interjected. "John is ..."

"Thank you, Ben, but I can make my own introductions," John said. "As I said, I am John Powell. My great-grandfather was Osceola, chief of the Seminoles. I was born just a few miles from here, on land occupied by my ancestors for generations. The State of Florida never owned this island. This island belongs to my people. It will always belong to my people."

"Mr. Powell," said the captain, "if you believe that you have a legal claim to this island, you have a right to file a petition with the Hillsborough County Court up in Tampa, and your claim will be fully and fairly considered. However, unless and until the court issues a ruling indicating that my son's title is somehow defective, then this island is his property and he is free to do with it whatever he chooses."

"Mr. Walker, my friend, I do not dispute your statement about what your court and your law may say about this island. But it was stolen from my people and it doesn't matter what your court and your law may say about it."

"If that is all that you have to say to us, Mr. Powell," said the captain, "then I believe that your business with us here is concluded and I will wish you good day."

"There is more that you should know, Mr. Walker," John continued. "This island was created by the native people. For a thousand years it was the feasting place, a ceremonial gathering place of a great nation. The ground on which you are now standing is made up of shells of oysters and clams and the bones of other fishes that my people consumed right here. Were it not for these people, the spot where you are now standing would be underwater."

"We are aware of these facts, Mr. Powell, and they change nothing," said the captain.

"I am not quite done speaking, my friend," John continued. "This island is also composed of the bones of hundreds of my people, my ancestors. Their remains have been buried here so their spirits would be together through eternity. What you are actually standing upon is, to use the words of your people, a cemetery. If I were to build a house on top of the graves of your ancestors, how would you feel about that, Mr. Walker?"

Darby was shocked to hear this claim about the island being a burial ground, and he was sure that his father was just as shocked. Darby had known the island was an Indian shell mound. Everybody knew that. This fact was obvious to anyone who set foot on the place — white shells covered the ground everywhere you looked, and if you dug your toe down beneath wherever it was planted, you would find only more shells. However, nobody had ever said anything to the Walkers about bodies being buried among the shells. Darby had never heard of humans being buried in an Indian shell mound, but then, before relocating to Florida he had never heard much of anything about Indian shell mounds except the one in Grandfather Walker's story about rescuing the slaves from Pensacola.

A light suddenly flared in Darby's mind. My goodness! Darby thought. This shell mound is the same shell mound on which Grandfather Walker and the runaway slaves took refuge fifty years earlier while getting away from the bounty hunters! It had to be! Grandfather Walker had said that there was only one such mound right on the eastern edge of the bay, and this island fit the description in his grandfather's story perfectly. While sailing up and down the bay with his father in recent years, Darby had observed this hill many times before, but he had not realized until recently that the hill was an island, or that it was a shell mound, and now he was sure that it was the very shell mound that saved his grandfather's life when a storm swept up the bay fifty years earlier.

Captain Walker closed his eyes and pressed his hands together for a moment before responding to John Powell about his last claim.

"Captain Walker ..." Ben started to say, but the captain motioned for him to wait.

"Mr. Powell, friend, I respect you, and I respect your ancestors. I pledge right here and now, on behalf of my son and my family, that if any human remains are discovered or disturbed in the process of any activities undertaken on this island, we will restore the disturbed remains to their original state and mark their location."

John looked into the captain's eyes. "Mr. Walker, I believe that you are an honest man with good intentions. I recognize that you believe that you are doing the right thing. I must warn you, however, that your pledge is not enough. This island is a burial ground. There are human remains all through the is-land. I am powerless to prevent you from doing whatever you will do, but must inform you that the spirits of my ancestors will not tolerate anyone living or building structures upon their graves."

John closed his eyes and looked up at the sky, as if in prayer. When the captain started to say something, John put up his hand, signaling the captain must stop speaking. The captain complied.

When John opened his eyes a moment later, he looked again at the captain. "I must warn you that if you proceed with your plans, if you build a house here or if anyone lives here, then after the earth travels ten times around the sun, you and your sons will die. Good day, my friends."

With that, John turned around, walked down the hill to his canoe, dragged the canoe out into the water, stepped into it and paddled off. The Walkers and McLaughlin watched John's departure, speechless.

Nobody said a word until John's canoe had exited the Walker's Key channel and turned south behind a mangrove island and out of view. After John's canoe was no longer visi-ble, Darby turned to his father and asked, "What do you make of all that?"

Before the captain could answer, Ben stepped in. "Gentle-men, you should know who John Powell really is. He's a for-tune-hunter who goes up and down the shores of Tampa Bay in his canoe digging here and there in hopes of finding buried pirate treasure that doesn't actually exist. He makes money by plundering parts from wrecked boats and selling Indian relics and bird plumes to tourists from the North, or to gift shops that cater to them. He has no regular home, pitching his tent wherever he stops. I doubt there is a single drop of Indian blood flowing in his veins, although I don't know for sure. I don't believe for a second that there are any human remains on this island. Even if there are, they aren't from John's ancestors. The Seminoles came to Florida from other areas only in the last couple of centuries. They weren't the ones who made the shell mounds around here. Earlier tribes not connected to the Seminoles built the shell mounds in this area. These tribes were wiped out by disease when the Spanish explorers came through in the 1500s. I think you can put everything John just told you out of mind for good."

The Captain quickly responded. "Well thank you for clearing that up. I didn't believe what we were hearing about human remains, but it's good to have your confirmation. I think we're done here for today, so I suggest we head off. Ben, we'll drop you back at Gulf City. Your help here has been invaluable."

"Right, Captain. You know, I'll just say one other thing about our phony Indian friend. If I didn't know any better, I would say he looks much more like Tulley's brother than Darby does. And they are just about the same height and build. One might even think Tulley and John were twins."

"Well, now that you mention it, there is a resemblance. Anyway, that's just more evidence that John is no Indian."

During the discussion with John Powell, Darby had observed something other than the resemblance between John Powell and Tulley. Darby had seen that Martha was sizing John up with eager intention, in a way that in other circumstances might have led to an intimate encounter. She'd been undressing John with her eyes. Darby noticed it when Martha stood a little straighter, pulled in her stomach, and, as discreetly as one could, raised her hand to her head and felt about her hair to confirm it was in its proper place. He also saw her face take on a bit of a glow and her eyes brighten. Darby thought this was odd, inappropriate, and more than a little bit troubling. Darby felt sure he was the only one who noticed all of this, with the exception of John, who couldn't have missed it.

Ben and the Walkers walked down the hill to the rowboat, then rowed out to the pilot boat. Shortly thereafter, the rowboat was hanging from the pilot boat's davits and the pilot boat was sailing north towards Gulf City.

A great blue heron had been watching the party of humans unnoticed from behind a Key Thatch Palm at the southern point of Walker's Key. After the pilot boat sailed away from the Walker's Key channel, the heron spread its large wings, took off, and flew in a large arc over Walker's Key before disappearing south. No further human activity was visible that day from Walker's Key.

Later that evening, when Darby and the captain were alone, Darby turned to his father. "Dad, am I mistaken, or is there something familiar about Tulley's island?"

The captain smiled broadly. "Yes, of course. I'm glad to know that at least one of my sons paid attention to my father's story. If my father had not spent the night on the island all those years ago, you and I might not even exist."

Egmont Key

Spring, 1898

Captain Walker's home was on Egmont Key a narrow, low-lying barrier island at the mouth of Tampa Bay, nearly two miles long and about three quarters of a mile wide at its widest point. Owned by the federal government since the United States gained possession of Florida in 1821, Egmont Key had served many functions over the years. In the 1830s, it had been a detention facility for Seminole Indians being transported to the Oklahoma territory after the conclusion of the Seminole Wars. A lighthouse was built at the island's northern end in 1848. After being destroyed in a hurricane, a new one was built in 1858. During the Civil War, the Union Navy occupied Egmont Key. They built a hospital on the island to treat Union soldiers suffering from yellow fever. Many confederate prisoners were held on Egmont Key during the Civil War, and escaped slaves and Union sympathizers also stayed there. Egmont Key had also served as a quarantine station during the yellow fever epidemic of the 1880s.

In 1888, two Tampa Bay captains had banded together and established the Tampa Bay Pilots Association, which had since then been guiding ships hailing from other ports up and down the twenty-four mile stretch of water between Egmont Key and Tampa. They set up a pilot's station near the southern tip of the island, including a fifty-foot lookout tower from which to see the incoming ships and a long wooden pier for visiting vessels and for their pilot boats, which were used to take the pilots out to greet the incoming vessels.

Shortly after Captain Walker had joined the Pilots Association as the third pilot, he had built a house for himself just inside the northern edge of the pilots' five-acre compound. Like the other pilot residences, the captain's house was a simple two-story structure. It had four bedrooms on the second floor. The first floor contained a kitchen, a pantry, a dining room and a large parlor. A wide covered porch stretched across the front of the house.

The first several years of Captain Walker's time on Egmont Key were very peaceful, pleasant and largely uneventful. Then, in April 1898, not long after the sinking of the U.S.S. Maine in Havana Harbor, the Spanish-American War broke out over the issue of whether Cuba should gain independence from Spain. In order to be able to prevent a possible Spanish invasion, the U.S. Government quickly began building a military base, Fort Dade, on Egmont Key. Construction commenced on a new hospital, barracks, officers' quarters, a mess hall, an administration building, a guard house, a boat house, a wharf, and various ancillary structures.

One of many shipments of construction materials and hardware arrived at Egmont Key one afternoon in late May. Included in the shipment was a wooden box containing dozens of locksets manufactured by Superior Lock Company. Each lockset came in its own cardboard box with its own six keys pre-cut to fit that particular lock. Upon arrival, the locksets were sent to the quartermaster's shed for safekeeping.

It was late in the afternoon. The young officer in charge of the quartermaster's inventory had had a very long day and was unusually fatigued when the wooden box of locksets was finally plopped down in front of him. He was about to close up the shed for the day and was annoyed at receiving this last-minute arrival to inventory and put away properly.

After counting the locksets and logging them in, the officer was carrying the wooden box to a corner of the shed when he banged into an end of one of the supply shelves. The impact caused the wooden box to fall from his arms and crash down, dumping its contents of locksets onto the dimly lit floor. "Oh, fuck it all!" cried the officer. Only two of the many cardboard boxes broke open, fortunately, but the six keys from each of those two boxes ended up all together in one jumbled mass.

The officer picked up all of the intact cardboard lockset boxes and stacked them neatly on the supply shelf. Then he knelt down and contemplated the two boxes that had broken open and spilled their contents. He knew that there were six keys for each lock and that they were pre-cut to fit just that one lock. He realized that before putting these sets away he would have to sit down and try each of the twelve keys in the two locks so that all of the keys would end up with the correct lock. But he was just too exhausted to deal with it right then, so he scooped up the spilled contents into the now empty wooden box and dumped them out on his desk. Something to finish first thing in the morning.

The next morning, the quartermaster was the first one to arrive at the shed. He immediately noticed the officer's desk and the contents of two lockset boxes dumped in a mess on top of it. This was not acceptable. The base commander was coming for an inspection and would arrive any minute. Everything had to be perfect. The quartermaster hurriedly made two identical piles of the lockset components, including six keys in each pile, and then he dropped one of the two piles into each of the two cardboard boxes on the desk, took the boxes back to the corner where the locksets belonged, and then placed them on the supply shelf. There was now essentially no chance that all of the keys in these two boxes would fit the locks.

Adrift

October 4, 1898

"Oh, hell's blazes!" yelled Captain Walker as his sailboat, which had been knocked onto its side by a rogue and unusually forceful gust of wind, tossed him into the warm water of Tampa Bay. He was a quarter mile off an uninhabited stretch of shoreline south of Tampa and north of St. Petersburg. It was Friday morning, and the captain was making his weekly return trip from Tampa to Egmont Key on the boat he'd playfully named *Pequod* when he'd acquired it ten years earlier.

The *Pequod* was a sturdy sixteen-foot sailboat that was perfect for sailing up and down Tampa Bay. The captain had been a third of the way down the bay when the *Pequod,* caught by the wind gust, pitched him overboard.

The captain had Wednesdays, Thursdays, and Fridays off. Unless the weather was too foul, he would sail the *Pequod* from Egmont Key up to Tampa Wednesday morning and then sail it back to Egmont Key on Friday.

On Wednesday evenings, the captain joined a weekly pinochle game with several captains with whom he was close friends. He spent Wednesday nights at his favorite hotel, the Hotel Arno on Tampa Street. He had all of Thursday to knock around town, take care of business, and visit with friends. Thursday evenings and nights he spent with his special lady friend. She had a standing reservation at Henry B. Plant's Tampa Bay Hotel, the finest hotel in town.

The captain's Thursday appointment was never a disappointment. His paramour was an incredibly wonderful woman for whom he cared deeply, but he understood she would never marry him. At her request and for her own reasons, the affair was kept secret. The captain told nobody other than his lawyer about this weekly engagement. He always booked his room at the Arno House for Wednesday and Thursday night even though he never spent Thursdays there. Early on Friday morning, he would slip back into his room at the Arno House to grab another hour or two of sleep before checking out and starting his return trip to Egmont Key.

On this Friday morning, the captain had, as was his custom, set sail from Tampa on the *Pequod* on his return trip to Egmont Key. He had noticed that the wind was a bit erratic but did not feel the least bit concerned about it. Now fifty-five years old, he had been sailing all kinds of boats for nearly five decades. His sailboat was just a toy compared with the steamships he'd commanded. He knew that if the weather suddenly turned on him, he could always head straight to the shore, from which he was never far, and wait it out. Storms in the area were usually short-lived, but if the bad weather endured, it would not be an impossibly long trek to a house on the peninsula, where somebody would provide shelter.

When the gust struck, the captain was thrown into the water head-first. He tumbled down and dropped below the surface. It happened so fast that he didn't have time to think, and seawater entered his mouth as he went down, choking him. For what seemed an eternity, the world was spinning and going black. The captain knew then what it felt like to die.

Suddenly, the captain's head popped out above the water, but he found himself in a world where everything above him was white. There was no wind. All was perfectly quiet except the gentle sounds of water caressing his dead body. A whitish light was even and muted. "I am on my way to heaven," thought the captain. He coughed a couple of times and the seawater he had swallowed left his mouth.

The white shroud above the captain began lowering itself onto the captain's head, and then actually pushing down on him. The truth of the situation became clear. "No, goddamnit! I am NOT at the gates of heaven!" screamed the captain. He recalled one of his father's favorite expressions: "Appearances are often deceiving."

The shroud pressing down on the captain was the *Pequod's* sail. The mast and the sail were starting their way down through the water as the hull of the *Pequod* rolled over. The descending sail would drown the captain if he did nothing. He used his right foot to pry off his left shoe, then his left foot to pry off his right shoe. He angled his head so that his mouth was fully above the water, took in a deep breath, and dropped down below the surface of the water again. He kicked and swam as hard as he could in a straight line. The direction he took was impossible to determine, but it did not matter as long as he got out from underneath the sail.

Looking up from under the water, the captain finally saw the edge of the sail and a greater brightness beyond. With another strong kick, he was beyond the descending sail. He fought his way back to the surface, gasping for air as he broke free of the water. After taking several deep breaths, the captain got his bearings and swam around the mast and sail to the hull of the *Pequod*. Looking up at the sideways hull, the captain perceived a serious problem.

"Confound it!" The captain could probably have righted the sailboat if he had been able to climb on top of the centerboard just after the boat flipped onto its side. His weight on the centerboard would have pushed the centerboard down into the water and forced the boat back upright. But the centerboard had retracted into its housing. Without the centerboard to climb onto, righting the boat was impossible.

The captain knew earlier that morning that the centerboard wasn't locked in place quite as it should have been. A clevis pin, a sort of bolt with a large head on one end, went through holes in the centerboard and its housing, locking in the centerboard. The clevis pin could slip out of place if not held by a cotter pin, which was little more than a loop of wire twisting through a hole at the end of the clevis pin. That morning, as the captain was rigging the boat, the cotter pin, worn from years of use, had broken into pieces. Nothing was preventing the clevis pin from sliding out of its holes and, in turn, releasing the centerboard from a locked position. The clevis pin probably would have stayed in place if the boat had remained upright, but as the boat capsized, the clevis pin had slid out of place and the centerboard had become free to fall into its housing in the hull. "For want of a cotter pin, the kingdom was lost," he thought to himself. "This is no way to run a ship."

The only thing he could do was let the boat complete its slow roll, then climb onto the bottom of the hull and either wait until somebody came along and provided assistance or the confounded boat floated to the shore.

The captain held onto the rudder of the *Pequod* as the mast and the sail slowly but inexorably pushed their way downward through the water. As the capsizing process neared completion, he regarded the black stenciling on the transom with an unhappy scowl. The higher line, now the lower, said "*Pequod.*" The lower line, now the higher, said "Egmont Key." The stenciling was upside down and reversed. The name of the sailboat would be perfectly legible to a seagull flying upside down, the captain angrily mused. He was filled with self-contempt for getting himself into such a ridiculous and humiliating situation.

Unknown to the captain, the contents of his jacket pocket, including his wallet and the key to his room back on Egmont Key, had slipped out into the water during his head-first ejection from his perch on the starboard side of the sailboat. Everything was on its way to the sandy bottom below.

A large, blue crab, scrabbling along the sand at the bottom of the bay, watched a strange, shiny object as it dropped through the water toward the sand — Walker's key. It landed with an all-but-inaudible "pfff" less than a foot away from the crab. The crab crawled forward to the key, grabbed it with one of its large claws, and thrust it in its mouth. After less than a second, the blue crab spat the key out of its mouth, turned around, and scrabbled away.

"Hell's blazes!" the captain yelled again, treading water as he regarded his fully overturned boat and grabbed onto the bottom of the inverted transom, which was now on top. "I haven't capsized a blasted sailboat since I was seven," he soliloquized. "Here I am supposed to be the best goddamned ship captain in Tampa Bay, and I can't even sail a tiny sailboat! Hang it all!"

Climbing on top of the *Pequod's* inverted hull proved a challenging proposition for a well-nourished fifty-five-year-old man. He had not had any recent occasion to climb up onto an inverted boat hull and was unaccustomed to regular physical exertion, with some limited exceptions. The only feature to try to grab ahold of was the slot through which the centerboard had retracted, but that slot was too far away from the water. The lowest point of the hull was the stern. The captain made several attempts to kick his way up the hull directly adjacent to the stern, but these efforts proved unprofitable. Each time he got his bulky frame part of the way up to the crest of the hull, he slipped right down and plopped back into the water.

The captain even tried to employ the *Pequod's* rudder, which was rising impotently into the air instead of down into the water. However, the rudder was uncooperative. Every time he kicked himself partway up the transom, hanging tightly onto a section of the rudder in an effort not to slip back, the rudder would swing, causing him to lose his grip. Back in the water he went.

Finally, the captain came up with a better idea. He swam to the bow of the *Pequod*. Once there he reached underwater and felt for the bowline, which he untied. He swam back to the stern with the bowline and tied one end to the starboard stern cleat, which was just underwater, then threw the line over the hull. He pulled the line taut through the port stern cleat, and tied it firmly. With the rope tied across the hull serving as something to grab onto, he was finally able to pull himself fully out of the water and onto the overturned hull.

The captain was exhausted. He was also thirsty. Though surrounded by water, there was not a drop to drink. He draped himself over the center of the bottom of the hull in the most stable position he could achieve, his head closest to the bow and his unshod feet closest to the stern, then collapsed. His clothes were soaked and his energy drained. "Hell's blazes," he muttered again.

The captain lay motionless on top of the bottom of the hull for several minutes before he lifted his head and slowly pulled himself up to a seated position above the slot into which the centerboard had retreated. He looked around. He was too far from shore to swim and there were no other vessels in sight. The current was gently propelling the *Pequod* in an easterly direction to the center of Tampa Bay.

Sailboats turned turtle were not designed to be ridden on, the captain mused. In order to avoid slipping off into the water, he had to have one leg dangling off to the port and one leg dangling off to the starboard. Meanwhile, his bottom was astride the keel, a ridge not anywhere near as subtle as one might have thought. Fortunately, though a thin layer of clouds had dimmed the sun, there was no threat of a storm, and it was a warm day. The captain's clothes would dry in short order, as long as he stayed on top.

"Emily," the captain said to the sky, "if I have time, I'm going to design a boat hull that affords an old, broken-down, capsized sailor a comfortable place to rest until his rescuers arrive, or the Lord comes to take him. There will be a flat place to sit, and there will be a board which can be raised up to place behind the sailor's back. And there will be a compartment built into the hull into which a jug of water and bread and chocolate can be placed through an access panel on the inside of the boat and then removed through another access panel on the bottom of the hull. Oh, Emily, I'm becoming a tired old man."

The captain realized the idea of designing a small sailboat to be comfortable for a sailor sitting on its underside was completely absurd. A simpler and better idea would be to have a replacement cotter pin at the ready so centerboards would not retract unexpectedly, and small sailboats could be righted after they capsized.

After stabilizing himself astride the overturned hull, the captain was certain he would be spotted by another vessel within a short time, and that he would not have to wait too long to be rescued. He hoped the rescuing party would have no connection to the area so that reports of his embarrassing failure would not be recounted at local gatherings for the rest of his life. After an hour, he realized his rescue might be further off than he had thought. Another half hour later, he saw a steamship steaming down the bay. "Rescued, at last!" he thought, and he began waving his arms.

But the steamship was probably a mile away when it passed south of his latitude, and it did not slow or change course. Nobody onboard had seen the captain or the inverted hull of the *Pequod*.

In the next two hours, the same thing happened several times. Nobody aboard any of the vessels heading up or down the bay saw the hull of the *Pequod*, let alone the captain. "And another thing, Emily, when I get home, I'm going to paint this hull the brightest yellow I can find. Why are boat bottoms painted dark? They can't be seen against the dark water!"

Five hours into the captain's ordeal, his entire body ached from the hard, wooden hull pushing against him and from the awkward positions he had to maintain to avoid slipping off it. He was parched and overheated. The capsized *Pequod* had floated to the center of the bay and was slowly traveling south toward its mouth. The captain, a man rarely afraid of anything, began to consider the possibility that he would not be rescued, and that he would float into the Gulf of Mexico. There, the chances of any rescue would diminish considerably. He began to consider that this might be the end of his days on earth. "Emily, by my reckoning I may soon be fish food like Jonah, only I probably won't ever see the shores of Nineveh."

Another hour passed. The mouth of the bay was closer. "Please, Lord, I am not ready to go," said the captain, looking up at the sky. "I have had a truly wonderful life and have been loved as much as any man was ever loved. I know I have no claims on any more time here than I have already been given, but I have more I need to do. My sons need me. Tulley's little boy Christopher needs me. Please let me see my grandchild graduate from high school and set sail on his adult voyage. Take me then, if you must, but please not now."

Though never a particularly religious man, the captain recited a prayer he'd learned as a child back in Harwich Port more than fifty years earlier. Despite that effort, the *Pequod* continued its uncertain journey. Nobody came to his rescue.

Eventually, he gave up trying to sit up and resumed his prone position astride the *Pequod's* keel, his right arm and right leg dangling toward the starboard, his left arm and left leg dangling to port.

The captain continued to reflect upon his life and his family. He thought of his father's Florida experience with the runaway slaves, of the discovery of the capsized boat that had enabled three slaves to escape to freedom. He thought of the capsized boat that dumped out his two young sons when

Tulley had disobeyed the captain and sailed out of Salt Water Pond nearly thirty years earlier. He and Emily had nearly lost a son, a loss that would have been unbearable. And now, here was the captain on his own capsized boat, the third in a sequence. This one might mean the end of his life.

He resigned himself to the fact that he was unlikely to ever again walk on *terra firma*. It seemed unfair, but he also recalled what a fulfilling life he'd had, a series of adventures enabling him to love some precious souls. He thought of dear Emily, and how painful it had been to lose her. But then he was thankful he'd been given a rare second chance to be in love with another woman, and how meaningful that unexpected bond had become.

He loved each of his sons. And his grandson. He had some very dear friends, including Andrew Beaumont, one of the kindest, most generous people he had ever met.

Reflecting upon all of this, the captain experienced a sense of calm. He was so tired that he fell asleep, the upside-down *Pequod* gently rocking him as it drifted in large, lazy circles around Tampa Bay, progressing toward the Gulf.

Late in the afternoon, more than nine hours after the captain had left Tampa, he was awakened when the capsized *Pequod* shuddered and then stopped moving. It had come to rest on the eastern end of Mullet Key, south of Pinellas Point.

The captain could barely believe his good fortune.

It was not long before a couple of men came running up the beach. In another hour, the captain was back at home on Egmont Key. The *Pequod*, suffering no actual damage from the ordeal she had endured, would be bailed out, righted, and sailed back to Egmont Key later that evening.

The captain shared his home with three lodgers who had various employment on the island, and with a woman, Molly, who cooked and cleaned. One of the lodgers, a Norwegian man named Olsen, greeted the captain as he walked up the front porch steps.

The captain related to Olsen a short version of his unplanned and unpleasant tour around Tampa Bay. It was then that the captain reached into his coat pocket and discovered that he possessed neither his wallet nor the key to his room, a room that he always kept locked when away.

"Olsen, I need your help," said the captain. "Would you please fetch a ladder from the quartermaster's shed, then climb up onto the roof of the front porch, break one of the windows to my room, climb in and unlock my door so that I can get in? I fear my key is at the bottom of the bay."

Olsen obliged. Soon enough, the captain, having bathed and having enjoyed a hearty supper prepared by Molly, was asleep in his warm bed. He did not emerge from his bed until late the next morning.

Olsen arranged for a carpenter to come by the next afternoon. The carpenter replaced the broken pane of glass and installed a new lock in the door to the captain's room. The carpenter told the captain that he was in luck because this lock was the highest quality lock available. The Fort Dade base commander had specially ordered several of these special locks for the new buildings then under construction.

The commander was happy to give one of the new locks to the captain. "The commander tells me that only a professional locksmith could open this lock without one of these keys," said the carpenter.

The new lock came in a box with six keys. The head of each key was stamped "Superior Lock Co." As soon as the new lock was installed, the captain tested one of the six keys in the lock. It worked just as it should, and he placed it into his pocket for his own daily use. He tested a second key, which also worked. Clearly there was no need to test the rest of the keys. The captain thought about where the five extra keys would go so the right people could gain access to his room when necessary.

The captain decided he would hide one of the extra keys on the island, just in case he lost his own key ever again. He would give each of his sons a key, and he would give his lawyer a key, figuring that it might be his lawyer who would first need access to his room. That left one more key, and he knew who would get that one, providing she would accept it.

He went down to the pantry, took one of Molly's Mason jars from a cupboard, and placed the first "extra" key into the jar, having decided where he would bury it. There were two pairs of leaning palm trees not far from the shore at the eastern edge of the Tampa Bay Pilots Association property on Egmont Key. When viewed from the water, they made a giant "W."

Early the next morning, just before the sun came up over the eastern shore of Tampa Bay, the captain, armed with a shovel, trudged over to the "W." Sure that nobody was up and about, he dug a hole in front of the giant "W," placed the sealed Mason jar containing his spare key into the hole, then refilled it and smoothed out the sand so that it appeared undisturbed. He chuckled to himself as he did this, marveling at his cleverness.

All the while, hidden in the darkness of nearby overhanging mangroves, a man with a ponytail sat motionless in his canoe, watching. Shortly after the captain finished his task and left the beach, the canoe slipped out from under the mangroves and started across the shipping channel toward Pinellas Point. The sky above Tampa Bay brightened with the rising sun.

The Meeting of the Minds

Monday, July 9, 1900

Two days had passed since the body of Captain Walker had been found in his locked room on Egmont Key, a bullet hole through his head and his dead hand still grasping his revolver. Hetty Howes entered the law office of Andrew Beaumont at ten o'clock. She spoke briefly to the assistant at the front desk, and then the assistant showed her in to see Andrew. Hetty did not have an appointment, but unless Andrew was exceptionally busy or in a meeting, nobody ever needed an appointment to see him.

Andrew stood as Hetty entered the room, extending his hand to her with a warm smile. "Good morning, dear lady."

"Good morning, Andrew." Hetty had a serious look on her face. "I'm afraid I'm not here for a social call today. We have a problem to resolve."

"Yes, Hetty, we do indeed. But first, are you here in your capacity as journalist or are we off the record?"

"Off the record, of course."

After the two took seats, the lawyer said, "All right, then. Tell me how you perceive our problem."

"The captain did not take his own life. When I first heard the report of suicide, I tried to find a way for it to make sense in my mind. But it just doesn't. I know people can sometimes act out of character and do completely unexpected things, but it simply isn't possible the captain took his life."

"No, I agree. You don't need to convince me. But if you want an actual investigation into the captain's death, you would need to convince the sheriff. How would you do that?"

"Oh, Lord, Andrew. It's all so obvious. Where should I begin?"

"Why don't you give me five points to support your claim?"

"Okay." Hetty paused briefly. "One. The captain had absolutely no reason to kill himself. He was happy and well-loved by his friends and family. He enjoyed his work. He had plenty of money. He had things he was looking forward to."

"I agree with all that, but Sheriff Kimball would say it's entirely possible there was something going on in his life that we didn't know about. He could have had an illness he didn't share with anyone, or a financial reversal, or mental anguish. He could have been suffering from severe depression."

"Andrew, the captain and I see the same doctor. I just came from the doctor's office. He confirmed that the captain was in excellent physical health and that there were no signs of any melancholy. And you were the captain's lawyer. Wouldn't you know if he was experiencing financial problems?"

"I probably would. There weren't any financial problems, or at least none I was aware of." Andrew frowned. "I haven't yet had a formal meeting with the boys. I went to see Darby at his house yesterday to express my condolences. I am planning to go to Walker's Key to see Tulley as soon as possible. I'm going to Egmont Key this afternoon on the one o'clock boat to start sorting through the captain's papers. I'll probably sail the *Pequod* back here to St. Petersburg. If there is a financial problem I don't know about yet, I soon will. But, as for me and the doctor knowing everything that might have been going on in the captain's life, you have to admit that it's possible — unlikely, but possible — that the captain was hiding something from us. What's your second point?"

"No suicide note. The captain would have left a note for someone if he had decided to take his life."

"I agree with you on that. The captain would have left a note, but people commit suicide all the time without leaving notes. A lack of a suicide note does not prove that a death was not a suicide, and in this case it obviously wasn't enough to convince the sheriff to investigate."

"I suppose that's true, Andrew, but anyone who knew the captain knew he always kept everything in his life shipshape: his house, records, business affairs, and the vessels he commanded. Everything was in perfect order. He wouldn't have ended his life without providing a thorough and logical explanation. He wouldn't have wanted his children to wonder what had gone wrong. Am I right?"

"You're right, Hetty, but none of that would sway someone who did not know the captain. Anyway, it isn't enough to convince the sheriff to investigate, which seems to be what you want to happen. Third point?"

"It would have been completely out of the captain's character to take his own life. He was one of the calmest, strongest, most confident, and most even-tempered people I ever met."

"Hetty, people do things that are contrary to their established character all the time. You, being a journalist, know that as well as I do. In fact you just said you knew it. What's your fourth point?"

Hetty sat up straighter. "Okay. Let's suppose, for the sake of argument, that for some unknown reason the captain wanted to kill himself. I think we can agree that even if that were somehow true, and if somehow he hadn't told you or me or the doctor, which is impossible to imagine, he would not have wanted to hurt his children. He wouldn't have wanted them to think he had suffered. It wasn't that long ago that his boat overturned in the bay and he drifted for nine hours, clinging to the hull. Wouldn't that have been the perfect time to let go and slip under the waves? Or couldn't he have staged some other accident?"

"Yes. I, too, thought of his recent ordeal on the boat. That would have been a perfect time to give up, I agree. But the sheriff knows all about that episode. Everyone knows about it. It wasn't enough to cause the sheriff to doubt the conclusion of suicide."

Andrew fell silent for a moment.

"Do you have a fifth point, Hetty?"

Hetty looked across the table at Andrew for several seconds, clearly not sure whether or not to say what she was thinking. Finally, she said, "Andrew, I believe you know all about me and the captain."

"Yes, I do. He told me. I knew what he was to you, and you to him. I knew that you and he spent every Thursday night together in Tampa. And of course I remember meeting your husband back in Jacksonville all those years ago. Humphrey Loomis was his name, if I remember correctly. And I know that you took back your maiden name, Howes, after you and he decided to separate. If I am correctly informed, your husband suffered a debilitating stroke quite some time ago and ever since then has been under the full-time care of nurses back in Vermont."

"Exactly so. Well, there is something you don't know, because I had asked the captain not to say anything about it yet, not even to you. My husband died two months ago. I went to Burlington for his funeral. His affairs are being handled by his lawyer there. When I returned to Florida, the captain proposed marriage to me, and I accepted. We were going to be married in September."

Andrew took in this new information, considering it carefully. "Oh, Hetty, my dear friend, I am so deeply sorry. I had no idea about these developments." Another brief silence. "Is this something that you plan to share with Sheriff Kimball, and with the world?"

"No, it isn't. Other than you, nobody knew about the captain and me, and I'm not going to reveal it now."

"I understand, Hetty. It wouldn't change the sheriff's mind anyway. There just isn't any significant evidence that undermines the conclusion of suicide, at least in the eyes of a man who didn't know the captain. And I'm sure you've considered the bigger problem, haven't you, Hetty?"

"The bigger problem? What do you mean?"

"If we were to succeed in getting the sheriff to investigate the captain's death as a possible murder, consider who his first suspects would be. Kimball would first look for motive. Who stands to gain from the captain's death? His sons, of course. Could there be anyone else? Next question is means. Who had access to the captain's room, which, of course, was locked with the captain and his key inside. Hetty, I believe you had a key, didn't you?"

With reluctance, Hetty said, "I did. I do."

"Did you tell the sheriff you had a key?"

"No, I didn't. He didn't ask and I didn't tell him. Not much of an investigation, was it?"

"I can't argue with that. Do you know of anyone else who had a key?"

"No, I don't." There was a pause. "Wait a minute. Do *you* know of anyone else who had a key?"

"I do, Hetty. The captain told me that Tulley and Darby had keys. This is problematic, don't you think?"

Hetty nodded.

"And that's not the end of our problem, is it?" asked Andrew. "One of the main reasons for the sheriff's decision not to investigate the death as a possible murder is that both sons accepted his conclusion of suicide. Why would they so readily agree with that conclusion when we know it can't be right?"

"You're right to wonder. I spoke with Darby and with Tulley late Saturday at Egmont Key, both for my own sake and for the sake of the news report. I didn't expect Tulley to tell me anything since he never tells anyone anything. But Darby didn't say much to me either, which was pretty strange. Well, I suppose they could have been concerned that they would be the prime suspects, especially if it was discovered that they had keys."

"That's right, Hetty. Or perhaps one of them actually killed the captain."

"Darby certainly didn't kill his father."

"I agree. I don't believe that Darby killed his father. What about Tulley?"

"Oh, heavens, Andrew." A moment passed. "I just don't know!"

"I don't know, either, Hetty." Andrew paused. "And I don't know why Darby hasn't pushed for an investigation. Certainly, Darby must be sure, as we are, that his father did not kill himself. He knows, of course, that *he* didn't kill his father. I'm sure that he wouldn't even consider *you* as a possible suspect. I imagine that he didn't even know you had a key to the captain's room. That just leaves Tulley. If Tulley took his father's life, something in him must have really snapped, in which case there's no telling what he might do." Andrew gathered his thoughts. "It's hard to believe Darby would have protected his brother from an investigation if Darby believed his brother had killed their father."

"Well, as you say, Darby was probably concerned that if he gave the sheriff the idea that the captain's death wasn't a suicide, then Darby himself would be a suspect."

"I suppose that's it. Darby couldn't possibly have an alibi. He lives alone and I don't think he has overnight guests, if you know what I mean, at least not here in St. Petersburg. It would have been easy for him to pop down to Egmont Key sometime in the middle of the night."

"What if we could establish an alibi for Darby, then encourage Darby to demand that the sheriff investigate the captain's death?"

"How could we possibly establish an alibi for Darby?"

"I haven't thought about this before now, but what if I told the sheriff that Darby and I were both in Tampa together on Friday night?"

"A lie that could get you into deep trouble. Darby had no reason to be with you in Tampa on Friday night. And Darby wasn't with you in Tampa on Friday night. It's likely that someone saw him in town, and if he was here in town, he could have easily traveled to Egmont Key during the night where he could have killed the captain. Although you and I don't believe he did any such thing, there is probably nobody who could swear that he could not have done it."

"Oh, Andrew. You're right, of course. But if the sheriff isn't going to investigate what happened, then you and I need to investigate."

"Yes, we do. And I think we need to keep a close eye on Darby, for his own safety."

"That won't be easy, will it?"

"No, it won't. Darby will say that he's quite capable of defending himself, and that's even assuming he agrees that he's in danger. Here's an idea. Would you mind if Darby spent the nights at your house for the next couple of weeks?"

"Do you want me to keep an eye on him?"

"Yes, sort of. But I also think that, alone in his own house, he may be in danger."

"I see, Andrew. All right. I would be delighted to have Darby stay at my house, but how are we going to get him to do that?"

"Hetty, would it be okay with you if I told Darby about you and his father?"

Hetty pondered the question. "I suppose that's all right. There isn't any reason for Darby not to know about us now, and I know he wouldn't tell anyone."

"Right. What if I tell Darby you are distraught over the captain's death, and ..."

Hetty interrupted. "I *am* distraught over the captain's death, Andrew. It's just about the worst thing that has ever happened to me! I loved the man deeply." Hetty's eyes moistened and her lips quivered.

"I know that. I'm sorry. I'm just thinking of how to get Darby to stay at your house. Is it all right with you if I tell

Darby you are so upset that you can't sleep at night and you need someone to be in your house with you?"

"Sure, Andrew. That's not even far from the truth. You have my permission."

"All right. I'm going to go look for Darby now. Would it be all right with you if he agreed to start spending the nights at your house tonight?"

"Of course. I'll make sure the guest room is ready."

Six Keys to Egmont

Andrew left his office and walked the short distance east on Central Avenue to First Street and the St. Petersburg waterfront. It was about twenty minutes before 1:00. The steamer from Tampa had not yet arrived at the Rail Pier. A dozen people were waiting for the steamer on the benches near the steamer's empty landing spot.

Looking over at the Electric Pier to the north, Andrew saw Darby sitting on a bench aboard the *Shooting Star*. He looked at the clock at the end of the Rail Pier and scanned the horizon for any sign of the 1:00 steamer. Then he turned and left the Rail Pier, walked the short distance north to the Electric Pier, and headed out towards the *Shooting Star*.

As he approached the *Shooting Star*, Darby didn't even look up. "Hello, Darby!" Andrew called from the dock.

Slowly, Darby raised his head. "Oh, hello" came his muted response.

"Darby, my boy, are you all right?" asked Andrew.

"Oh, sure. I'm fine. Fine." Darby was aware of the despair in his own voice.

"Permission to come aboard, Captain?" asked Andrew.

"Oh, yes, of course." Darby rose from the bench and extended his hand to Andrew's hand, helping him step down from the gangplank onto the *Shooting Star*'s gunwale boarding mat.

"I see you're not working today, Darby. That's probably a good decision. You need to take time away from everything."

"Yes, well, that's what I figured too," said Darby. "I put a sign up on my shed, as you see, saying the *Shooting Star* would not be going out at all this week. Thankfully, this is the slowest time of the year for my business. Anyway, I can't shuttle passengers around while I'm in this state of mind. I'm a bit unstrung right now, to tell you the truth. I'm at a loss about what I'm supposed to do. I just got back from a ride to nowhere on my dear *Shooting Star*. Venturing out on the open bay usually improves my mood, but not today."

"Darby, I'm so sorry." He hugged Darby.

After a moment, Darby removed himself from Andrew's embrace. "Andrew, my mother always said she was sure I would never be lost at sea. But lost at sea is exactly how I feel."

"I understand, Darby. Losing a parent, especially a parent who has always been so much a part of one's life as your father was, is tremendously difficult, one of the hardest things in life. It's just going to take time for you to regain your balance, but you will survive this."

Darby considered the statement. "I imagine you're right."

Andrew paused. "Look, I'd like to speak with you about someone who needs your help, but I'm planning to catch the 1:00 steamer to Egmont Key to start dealing with your father's papers. I should probably also sail your father's boat back here, where you and I can keep an eye on it. May I stop by your house when I get back?"

"Oh, sure, Andrew." Darby's thumb and forefinger made their habitual way through his beard. "But why don't I just take you to Egmont Key myself? The steam is still up in the boiler. It would be something for me to do instead of just sitting around feeling sorry for myself. I could save you quite a lot of time by towing the *Pequod* back here to town instead of you having to sail it all the way back. You would just have to ride in her and hold the tiller."

Andrew agreed. After her lines were cast off, the *Shooting Star* began her journey south to Egmont Key. As they passed by the end of the Rail Pier, Darby looked up at the people waiting for the steamer from Tampa and waved. Nearly all of the people on the pier waved back at him.

As the *Shooting Star* moved away from the shore and out into the bay, Darby pushed the regulator lever forward, causing the boat to accelerate. A moderate wind stirred up the water enough to create some non-threatening waves. The *Shooting Star* easily flattened the waves as she steamed ahead. Andrew took a seat next to Darby on the bench in the wheelhouse. There, the noise from the waves and the wind was muted enough to allow conversation.

When the pier and the boat traffic associated with St. Petersburg's waterfront were well behind them, Darby turned to Andrew. "Who could possibly need my help right now, Andrew?" Darby asked, before returning his gaze to the view in front of the boat.

"Well, Darby, I must tell you something that may come as a shock."

"Nothing could shock me at this point, I assure you."

"All right, Darby. You see, you and your brother aren't the only ones who are devastated by your father's death."

"I'm sure that's true. Everyone who really knew my father loved him."

"Yes, but that's not what I'm getting at. Someone else loved your father in a special way, and this someone else is suffering right now probably almost as much, or perhaps just as much, as you and your brother."

"You're talking about Hetty Howes, aren't you?"

"What? Do you mean to say that you knew about your father and Hetty?"

"Then you're confirming it." Darby glanced at Andrew, who nodded. "I didn't exactly know, but I strongly suspected it. I knew Dad was in Tampa every Wednesday and Thursday night. At some point I realized Hetty's house was dark every Thursday night. Then I began to think about how unusually kind Hetty has been to me ever since she arrived in St. Petersburg, and the pieces just seemed to fit. Hetty's a beautiful and intelligent lady, and it's not surprising that Hetty and Dad would have been drawn to each other."

"But you never discussed it with your father?"

"No. It seemed to me that if Dad had wanted me to know about his relationship with Hetty, then he would have told me. He's always been exceptionally good about respecting other people's privacy, and taught me to be the same way."

"Yes, you're right about your father. Do you think your brother also figured out that your father was romantically involved with Hetty?"

"I doubt it. It's hard for him to figure out people, at least without a deliberate effort."

"Right. Anyway, poor Hetty hasn't been able to sleep a wink since your father died. She asked me if I would spend my nights in the guest room at her house until she starts to feel more like herself, but I pointed out that such an arrangement would be scandalous if anyone discovered it. You are the best person we could think of to stay over at Hetty's without creating any kind of problem. People know that you're like a son to Hetty. Do you think you could stay at Hetty's awhile?"

"Of course. I can do that. When does she want me to come?"

"If you could go over tonight, that would be great. No later than sunset would be best. It's when the sun sets that Hetty starts getting anxious. She will feel a lot better, I've no doubt, having you in the house for the next couple of weeks or so."

"Then it's settled. Say, were you really going to sail Dad's boat up from Egmont Key?"

"Yes. Why wouldn't I?"

"No reason not to, I guess. It's just that in the nearly ten years you've been here I've never seen you sail a boat. I didn't know you knew how to sail."

"There is much about me that nobody knows, and I rather like it that way." Andrew chuckled, and Darby smiled back at him.

"Did your parents teach you how to sail when you were a kid?"

"No, they surely did not."

"You went to college in Pennsylvania, right?"

"Yes, I did. Haverford College, a Quaker school not too far from Philadelphia."

"Did they teach sailing at Haverford?"

"No, but one of my teachers had a small boat at Philadelphia, and sometimes he would take his students sailing on the Delaware."

"So that's where your days as a sailor began?"

"No, not exactly."

"Then you studied law at Harvard. You learned to sail when you were a student there. Is that it?"

"No, I can't say that I did." A few seconds passed. "You've asked too many questions."

"I'm sorry. I just wondered where you learned to sail."

"And I'm not going to tell you." Andrew gazed at Darby. Darby nodded.

The men were silent for the remainder of the trip, each lost in thought.

Half an hour later, the *Shooting Star* pulled up to the Tampa Bay Pilots Association pier near the southern end of Egmont Key. The schooner *Belle*, a pilot boat, was tied up to the pier, as were a couple of smaller vessels, including Captain Walker's *Pequod*.

As Andrew prepared to disembark from the *Shooting Star*, Darby asked: "Do you want me to come up to the house with you, or shall I wait here while you do what you came to do?"

"Come along with me. I'm just going to collect your father's important papers and his latest bills and such. I'll sort through them back at the office. Perhaps I'll start making a mental note of what needs to happen with the things in his house, but of course that will depend upon what you and your brother are interested in keeping. Sheriff Kimball, as you know, has completed his investigation. He stopped by to see me late yesterday on his way back to Tampa and gave me permission to access your father's room."

When Darby and Andrew reached Captain Walker's house, they found Molly, Captain Walker's housekeeper, at work washing the kitchen floor. Andrew told Darby he needed to have a private conversation with Molly about the future of the captain's house and its residents and about a specific provision the captain had made for her in his will. Darby happily went out and took a seat on the front porch.

A few minutes later, after Andrew had concluded his business with Molly, Andrew and Darby went upstairs to the captain's locked room. Andrew reached into his pocket and withdrew the key given to him by the captain. "Superior Lock

Co." was stamped into the head of the key. Attached to the key by a string was a cardboard tag on which it was written, in the captain's neat handwriting, "Egmont. For Andrew."

Andrew inserted the key into the lock and tried to turn it, but it wouldn't turn. Mystified, Andrew removed the key and tried again, but to no avail. He jiggled it and increased the pressure while turning the key, but the key would not open the lock. Andrew looked at Darby, who traded places with Andrew and tried to open the lock. It wouldn't open for him either.

"I don't get it," said Darby. "Isn't this Dad's key? Didn't it work when Dad had it?"

"No, Darby. This is the copy your dad gave me after he capsized on the bay, lost his key, and had a new lock installed. Sheriff Kimball took your dad's key with him when he left Egmont Key last night, and the Sheriff and I weren't thinking of keys when he left, so he still has it. I have no idea why my key won't open the lock."

"Wait a minute," said Darby. "Let me run and get my key. It's on the *Shooting Star*. I knew that if I ever needed to use it, I'd be coming here on my boat."

Darby returned less than five minutes later, and handed Andrew his key. Handwritten on the tag attached to the key was "Egmont. For Darby." But like Andrew's key, despite valiant efforts on the part of the two men, this key would not open the lock.

"Andrew, did my father tell you how many keys he had to his room?"

"There were six. He had his original key, which we know worked. He said that he buried a key somewhere on the island just in case he locked himself out, but he didn't tell anyone where that was. He gave out the other four: one to me, one to Hetty, one to you, and one to your brother."

Andrew and Darby returned to the kitchen, where Andrew asked Molly if she knew anything about keys to the captain's room. Molly explained that Sheriff Kimball had asked her the same question, and she had told him that, as far as she knew, Captain Walker's key was the only one in existence.

They returned to the Pilots' pier. They had been unable to unlock the captain's room, but there was no urgency to gaining access to it, and they didn't want to break the door, or a window, to get in. They tied the bowline of the *Pequod* to the *Shooting Star*, and steamed away from Egmont Key at a reduced speed. Andrew rode in the *Pequod* and held the tiller so she'd stay in line behind the larger boat.

On the trip back to St. Petersburg, Darby periodically checked to make sure the *Pequod* was under control directly behind the *Shooting Star*. As the sailboat was towed behind, her bow rode high above the water, and Darby could see on the underside the brightest yellow paint ever painted on any boat hull before or since. It made him think of his beloved father, of the day they'd spent together a year earlier "painting the hell out of that blasted hull," as the captain had described it then. Each time Darby looked back, Andrew gave him a thumbs up sign.

When they landed at St. Petersburg, Darby secured the *Pequod* to the pier in a spot just behind the *Shooting Star,* and then Andrew climbed out of the sailboat and up an adjacent ladder, He stood on the pier, where Darby joined him.

"Andrew, aren't you glad you didn't have to sail this boat all the way up here on your own?"

"Yes, I am."

"It's been a very, very long time since you last sailed a boat, hasn't it?" Darby knew that he was going too far now. Normally he would have dropped the issue as soon as Andrew's discomfort had become apparent, but nothing in Darby's world was normal anymore.

"Thank you for your help, Darby," said Andrew. He gave him a wink and a half-smile as he turned and headed back into town.

After Andrew left the pier, Darby made sure that the *Shooting Star* and the *Pequod* were properly put to bed, checking lines, putting away loose gear and tidying everything up.

Back on Egmont Key, a large gopher tortoise was crawling near the shoreline in front of four palm trees that from a distance appeared to form a giant "W." The tortoise stepped down into a new and unnatural depression in the sand directly in front of the four palm trees, a depression which the gopher tortoise had never before encountered.

The Big Sleepover

Andrew made his way to back to his office building and went upstairs to the office of the *St. Petersburg Post.* Four massive wooden desks stood in different areas within the large, open space. A conference table stood in the center of the room. There was a typewriter on each desk. The surfaces of three of the desks were neat and tidy, but the surface of the fourth desk was submerged under an angry sea of papers. Beside each desk was a wire basket. All of the baskets were empty except for the one adjacent to the messy desk. This one was overflowing with trash. Hetty was at the back of the room placing a folder into a filing cabinet when she saw Andrew enter the room.

"Hello, newswoman," said Andrew, entering the premises.

"Hello, counselor," Hetty answered. "I was just getting ready to call it a day. How'd it go with Darby?"

As Andrew looked around the room, Hetty said, "Don't worry, everyone else has already left. Come have a seat at my desk."

Andrew nodded and joined Hetty at the messy desk. "Darby will be at your house before sunset this evening."

"Good. I will enjoy having Darby at my house."

"I hope so. There is another thing I should tell you. Darby figured out on his own that you and the captain were in a relationship."

"That doesn't surprise me. Darby is a perceptive young man. I'm relieved to know that he knows."

"The captain said Darby had always been observant, ever since he was a little boy. Listen, Hetty, I'm wondering if I could borrow your key to the captain's room at Egmont. Neither my key nor Darby's key work in his lock. There must have been some mix-up with the keys somewhere along the line. Anyway, I'd like to try your key. And while I'm at it, there is one more key I'll want to try."

"Of course. I have my key somewhere here in my desk." After a few moments of shuffling through a thoroughly disordered collection of pens, pencils, office tools, and random objects in the middle drawer of her desk, Hetty pulled out her key to the captain's room, and handed it to Andrew. The key was tied to a tag that said "Egmont. For Hetty." On the head of the key was stamped "Superior Lock Co.", just like the others.

"How do you propose to get the other key you want to try? I assume we're talking about Tulley's key."

"I thought I'd just ask him for it," Andrew responded.

"Andrew, if Tulley had anything to do with his father's death, do you really think he's just going to hand over his key to his father's room? He probably doesn't even know the rest of us were given keys, and he may not even admit he has one."

"You have a point."

"Why don't I ask Darby to take me over to Walker's Key when we know that Tulley won't be there? I'll tell Darby I need to speak with his brother privately, and I'll go into Tulley's house and see if I can find the key."

"How can you plan it so Tulley won't be there?"

"Tulley goes up to Tampa the second Friday of every month to sell oysters and stock up on supplies — or at least he always used to. He and the captain would sometimes meet for breakfast at the Hotel Arno when Tulley came up. If I can get Darby to take me, I could go this Friday."

"I guess it's worth a try, Hetty."

Later that evening, just after the sun had gone down, Darby arrived at Hetty's house, a massive two-story Victorian with a three-story turret at its southeast corner. One of the grandest houses in St. Petersburg, its First Avenue lot afforded a commanding view across Tampa Bay. Hetty was sitting in her spacious front parlor, watching the last hints of daylight fade from the waterfront. Darby brought with him a bag of clothes and sundries.

"Darby! I can't thank you enough for agreeing to stay with me during this difficult time. You are such a dear boy."

"It's my pleasure. I don't really feel much like being alone right now either. I want you to know that I'm sorry for your loss, now that I officially know what you and my father meant to each other."

Hetty and Darby embraced warmly, sharing their profound grief. Darby really was glad to be at Hetty's house. Over the last several years he had grown to care deeply for her, and he knew the feeling was mutual.

"Darby, you can take the room at the top of the stairs. It's all ready for you. Why don't you go up, drop your things, and then join me in the parlor. I have some biscuits and tea ready for us."

Darby headed upstairs while Hetty went through the rooms on the first floor, methodically closing all of the blinds.

Andrew, meanwhile, had been watching for Darby's arrival at Hetty's house from down the street. When he saw Darby go inside with his bag, he set off to Darby's house back on Second Avenue North. Darby had long ago asked Andrew to hold a key to his house, in case there was ever an occasion when Andrew had to get in. Andrew reasoned this was such an occasion, even though he and Darby had not discussed it.

Though nobody else knew this, though he would never receive any payment for doing it, and though the job had never actually been given to him, Andrew Beaumont had decided it was his job to catch Captain Walker's killer. It was also his job to protect Darby Walker. He wasn't sure at this point if it could still be his job to protect Tulley Walker too, but he had saved Tulley once already by keeping him out of jail back in Boston.

At Darby's house, Andrew let himself inside and made a complete tour of the place, unlocking the back door in the process. He had carried a bedroll with him and a bag which contained a few personal items and some food. If anyone showed up at Darby's house for the purpose of harming Darby, Andrew would be there and Darby would not be.

Andrew pulled the sofa in the front room a short distance out from the wall against which it was positioned, and spread his bedroll between the wall and sofa. He could sleep there, unseen by anyone who might enter the house. Sleeping on the floor wouldn't bother him. He had slept in far more uncomfortable places in the early part of his life.

Hetty Investigates

Friday, July 13, 1900

On Monday, when Darby first stayed at Hetty's house, Hetty had asked Darby if he'd take her to see Tulley at Walker's Key so she could have a private talk with Tulley about her relationship with the captain. When Hetty suggested they go on Friday, Darby had agreed, though he wasn't sure Tulley would be home. If Tulley was sticking with his usual routine, he'd probably be up at Tampa. But Darby would enjoy the trip with Hetty either way.

Shortly after ten o'clock in the morning, Darby and Hetty set out for Walker's Key on the *Shooting Star*. When they arrived at the tiny island, Darby saw immediately that Tulley's boat was not at the landing. Darby said it didn't appear Tulley was home, but Hetty said that she wanted go on up to the house and check. That was fine with Darby. He had nothing else planned for the day.

Darby waited aboard the *Shooting Star* as Hetty went up and knocked on the front door. When there was no answer, she turned the knob and let herself in.

Hetty found what she'd come for without a lot of effort. In the kitchen, just to the right of the back door, three keys hung from hooks. The key on the right looked familiar. Its cardboard tag said, "Egmont. For Tulley."

Hetty grabbed the key and placed it into the pocket of her billowy dress. Then she went into the bedroom and carefully searched through the drawers of the two dressers she found there. Finally, she opened the bedroom closet. She looked on the floor under the hanging clothes, she plunged her right hand into the pockets of the coats in the closet, and then she felt around on the shelf high up in the back. Her hand came into contact with something hard and cold. Removing Tulley's revolver, she slid it into the pocket of her dress alongside Tulley's key.

Just as Hetty was emerging from the bedroom, Darby entered the front door. "Is everything all right?" he asked. "You've been in here so long. Obviously Tulley isn't home."

Hetty was caught off guard by Darby's unexpected entrance. For one second, her eyes flashed the terrorized look of a bank robber caught with her hands in a cash drawer. She quickly regained her composure. "Oh, I just wanted to be certain he wasn't here. And you know, I've never had a chance to really see this place, so ... You probably didn't know I was such an awful snoop, did you, Darby?"

"Hetty, you're a journalist. Of course, you're a snoop! Now are you ready to go back to St. Petersburg? We'll look for Tulley another time."

"Yes, let's go."

On the return trip to St. Petersburg, Hetty asked Darby about his childhood back in Harwich Port, and particularly about his early relationship with Tulley.

"Well, if you really must know, Hetty," Darby said, "when we were kids, I always wanted to be friends with Tulley, but Tulley seems to have hated me since I was born."

"Is that so?"

"Yes. I think Tulley resented my very existence, like I'd displaced him as the center of our parents' universe." Hetty watched as Darby raised his hand to his beard and subconsciously traced the lines of his jaw, his trademark gesture. "When we were kids, Tulley once tried to kill me."

"Seriously, Darby?"

"We were just kids. In the years since, I've come to believe that it wasn't anything he'd really thought about. It was an impulsive act by a young child."

"What did Tulley do?"

Darby recounted the long ago boating incident on Nantucket Sound. "Now I can't say with total certainty that Tulley tried to drown me, and perhaps he would have been devastated if I had actually died, but it's fair to say he deliberately put my life at risk. I would have died if that fisherman hadn't been on the beach. Ever since that happened, I never really trusted him again."

"Wait a minute ..." Hetty tried to interject.

"Hetty, all I ever wanted was to be my brother's friend. He's always disliked me, as I said, and he's done some rotten things to me over the years. But even with all of that, I don't hate him. Still, after my experience that day on the sailboat, I knew that I had to be careful around him. As I say, I could never trust him."

"Darby, I clearly remember your father telling me the same story, only it was completely different."

"I'm not following you."

"Your father wasn't there when the sailboat capsized, but he arrived home shortly after. He raced to the beach as soon as your parents noticed that your boat had left the salt pond. He spoke with everyone involved, including the fisherman at the beach and another man who had joined him when they found you."

"Of course, Hetty. I'm sure my father got the full report."

"Darby, you're not the one who almost drowned. That was Tulley!"

"What are you talking about? Of course I'm the one who almost drowned."

"No, Darby. When the boat capsized, it was Tulley, not you, who hit his head on the boom. Tulley was unconscious. You swam to the beach. You ran up the beach and got the fisherman. You saved Tulley's life!"

"Oh, Hetty. No. No."

"Yes, Darby. Your father had to carry Tulley back up around the pond to the house. Tulley was put into bed for the rest of the day. Your father said you were perfectly fine, and that you were the hero that day!"

"Oh, Hetty, I don't know," said Darby. But fragments of the distant, broken memory of that day shifted around inside Darby's head, attempting to find their proper connections.

"Darby, our brains can go haywire when we are under extreme emotional stress. Isn't it possible that you were in such a state of extreme fear, perhaps even shock, when all this happened?"

"Oh, Hetty, I don't know about that," said Darby, and there was no more talk of it.

Darby didn't know if his father had somehow gotten the Nantucket Sound story wrong or if Hetty misremembered his father's telling of it. Either way, Darby had a very hard time imagining that Hetty's version could possibly be correct.

For the next couple of days, Darby puzzled over what his next steps would be. Darby was sure Tulley had killed their father. Nobody else had the means, the motive, and the opportunity. Sheriff Kimball wasn't going to investigate, which was actually good because there was apparently no evidence connecting Tulley to the crime, and Darby would be under suspicion just as much as Tulley. If anybody did any digging, Darby's regular trips to New York would be uncovered, and that would be a disaster. If they learned his big secret, a jury would probably be happy to convict Darby of a crime which he did not commit.

What was Darby to do? If Darby didn't deal with Tulley, who might Tulley murder next?

The Reckoning

Monday, July 16, 1900

The *Shooting Star*, Darby Walker at the helm, cruised slowly to the boat landing at Walker's Key. Darby pulled out his pocket watch. Nine fifteen. Darby was about to confront his older brother. This event had been looming most of Darby's life, even as the one thing in life Darby couldn't stand was conflict. This shortcoming had caused him to put off this day far too long.

The morning was bright. A warm breeze blew gently from the east.

Darby secured the *Shooting Star* to the pilings at the end of the boat landing and began his walk up the path to Tulley's house high on the shell mound. In the large pocket of his jacket was the Smith & Wesson Model 3 revolver Grandfather Walker had given him, with the full approval of the captain, the summer Darby turned eighteen. Grandfather Walker had given Tulley a similar weapon shortly after Tulley's eighteenth birthday.

When Grandfather Walker had made the presentation of the revolver to Darby, he had sat Darby down and told him that the world was a dangerous place and that Darby needed to know how to defend himself against evil people. Grandfather Walker made sure that Darby knew how to fire and maintain the gun. Before today, Darby had never had occasion to use it, but today was different. At this moment, each of the revolver's six chambers contained a bullet.

Upon reaching the front door of Tulley's house, Darby paused to gather his strength.

Tulley surely must have seen his arrival. Darby thought it strange Tulley had not rushed to the door to greet him or to send him on his way.

Darby knocked. No answer. Again. No answer. Opening the door, he walked in.

Motionless, Tulley sat in a chair by the front window of the parlor, surveying the magnificent view, including, of course, the *Shooting Star* at the boat landing.

"Hello, Tulley."

Darby pulled out his revolver, pointing it at his older brother. Darby felt like a nervous, quivering, trembling blob of jelly, but did his best not to show it. His arm felt like it was going to shake itself off the rest of his body, but he was pretty sure it did not appear that way to Tulley. He was struggling with an internal conflict on a scale he had never before experienced. His body reflected the struggle quite clearly even if his mind didn't fully recognize it. Darby could not tolerate conflict. He had never tolerated it. Could he kill his brother? Even at that moment, Darby didn't know.

"Welcome to Walker's Key, Darby. I see that you have come to kill me."

Darby could hardly believe he was pointing a loaded revolver at his brother's head. He could not count the number of times he had thought of killing Tulley. He remembered the time he'd gone to the barn and fetched the cranberry scoop. He was going to ram the scoop's hard, wooden teeth through Tulley's soft neck while Tulley lay sleeping, but he'd chickened out.

Now he was about to really kill Tulley. Finally. But it felt wrong. Darby stood where he was, staring at his brother, feeling like his own head was on the verge of exploding into a thousand pieces. Still, the gun was pointed at his brother.

"It's probably a good idea to kill me," said Tulley. "That's what I'd do if I were in your shoes."

Darby said nothing.

"But let me help you out, Darby. Shoot me with *your* revolver, and it will be clear that you did it. You will be convicted of murder. The thing to do would be to get *my* revolver, shoot me with that, then arrange it to make it look like I'd done it myself. That would be much better for you. My revolver is on the shelf in the back of my closet. It's loaded. You're welcome to it."

"Tell me why you did it," said Darby.

"Darby, I'm sure you can come up with a convincing reason without my help. Dad never loved me. You were the apple of his eye. I was the black sheep. That's how Dad saw it."

"Dad loved us both!" Darby protested.

"He never loved me the way he loved you. And can you blame him? You were the perfect son. You're kind, thoughtful, responsible. You're truthful, handsome, athletic. You succeed at everything you do, everyone likes you, and you always did everything Dad asked. I, on the other hand, never did anything right, never did what Dad wanted me to do, have no likeable qualities, and have never had friends. I don't understand people, and they don't understand me. I nearly killed you when we were kids. I stole your ninth-grade school report and said that I had written it. I wrecked Dad's schooner on Passage Key bar and tried to blame you. I told Dad about your unusual dalliance, expecting that you'd be thrown out of the family. I filed a false claim relating to the loss of great-grandfather Walker's first vessel, and for that I would have been sent to prison for a long time if Dad hadn't used his connections to save me. Dad thought I was worthless. It turns out he was right.

"One thing, Darby, before you kill me. I know you won't believe this, but I really am sorry for all the things I've done to you. That poisonous envy was never about you. It was about what I lacked."

Darby was shocked. This was a dramatic change in position for Tulley. It was also a tremendous revelation to Darby that Tulley had *not* been unaware of all the rotten things he had done over the last thirty years.

"You killed Dad because you thought he didn't love you? There must be more to it. Something else happened between you and Dad."

"Just shoot me, Darby. It's not worth the effort explaining. My life is over. I have no wife anymore. My son is gone. I have no family, actually. End it for me."

"Tell me what happened. You had some sort of fight, didn't you?"

"As a matter of fact, we did. It was late in the day on Friday, July 6—yes, the day before his body was found. I went to Egmont Key and asked Dad to give me ten thousand dollars. He said no. He got angry with me. The whole thing got very ugly. One of his lodgers was there when I left—the Norwegian guy, the tall one. He saw me storm out of the house, so it's probably only a matter of time before I'm charged and convicted of Dad's murder."

"Sheriff Kimball isn't investigating. He's certain that Dad killed himself. Nobody's being charged with anything."

"That's true right now, but as soon as the Norwegian goes to the sheriff, I'll be charged with murder. The trial and the publicity will bring shame to the family. I'll be sentenced to death. It's better for everyone if you kill me. I'll help you stage it so nobody will suspect you. Just like they will say I staged Dad's death to look a suicide, except that you will actually get away with this."

"Wait a minute. Why did you ask Dad for money? You couldn't possibly need ten thousand dollars."

"Martha left me in June. She took Christopher with her. They left when I was away for the day fishing, and I don't know where they went. They may have gone back to her parents in Maine. I'm not sure.

"Before she left, Martha told me she wanted a divorce. She couldn't stand being with me anymore. I'm all but certain she had a lover, though I don't know how she managed it or who it was. I'm even wondering if Christopher is my son.

"Anyway, Martha said that if I gave her ten thousand dollars, we could make everything easy and I'd even get to keep Christopher. If she didn't get the money, she said she would accuse me of abusing her and Christopher. She said I'd be locked away.

"You probably have no idea how dangerous Martha is. I had no idea of this when I met her. Nobody has any idea. She's very intelligent and nearly always gets her way. The entire French Spoliation scheme involving great-grandfather's schooner was her concoction, as you probably remember.

"For a while, I thought Martha and Christopher would come back, but by the end of June I realized they weren't coming back. I went to Egmont that Friday and told Dad what was happening. I figured he'd come up with the ten thousand dollars. Instead, he said no, this was a problem I had to solve myself. He became angrier than I've seen him in years."

"Then you killed Dad to get your inheritance and pay off Martha?"

"That's what the state prosecutor will say, and I will have no way to disprove it. I had the means, the motive, and opportunity, didn't I? As for means, you know Dad gave me a key to his room at the same time he gave you one. As for motive, I needed money. Molly, the housekeeper, had already left for her usual night off in Tampa, but that Norwegian guy was in the house, or at least he was there when I finally left. He was in the kitchen with his back turned when I stormed out, so I'm not completely sure it was him. Anyway, whoever it was can testify that I was there and left in a huff. As for opportunity, I knew Dad's schedule. I knew that Molly was off on Friday nights and that Dad was often the only one at the house then. I imagine that only a few people knew this. Not only was I seen at Dad's house shortly before his body was found, no living person saw me later Friday night or early Saturday morning. I have no alibi for that later period. Case closed. Just kill me. I didn't kill Dad, but my life is over anyway."

"What do you mean you didn't kill Dad?"

"I have done many things I regret, but I'm not a killer. You, Darby, know how to read people. Surely you see that I'm no killer. It's not in me to do such a thing."

"But didn't you try to kill me when you capsized the sailboat when we were kids?"

"Of course not. I was foolish, but I never wanted to harm you. I just wanted to scare you."

"But I nearly drowned! If it hadn't been for the fisherman who swam out and saved me, I would have died!"

"You're not remembering this right. *I* was the one who nearly drowned. You tumbled out feet first, head above the water, just as you have tumbled out of predicaments all your life. I doubt that your hair even got wet. You floated to the beach uninjured and no worse for the wear, just as one would expect of you. Meanwhile, the boom hit me in the head and knocked me unconscious. You ran up the beach and got the fisherman who swam out and dragged me back to the shore—unconscious, but alive. I can't believe you don't remember this."

This was the way Grandma Nick had remembered the event, and it was the way Darby's father had described the event to Hetty. The pieces of Darby's broken memory suddenly clicked into their proper places. His memory of nearly drowning was false. Tulley had been the one who nearly lost his life, not Darby.

Darby placed his revolver on a table and took a seat in a chair a few feet away from his brother. He felt profound relief. Darby knew his brother was not a killer. He was also relieved to learn that he, Darby, was not going to have to kill his brother.

Darby would not have been able to do it! He could not have killed his brother even to avenge their father's murder! Darby was not able to kill anybody. It wasn't in him.

Darby's right hand went up to his beard. He pulled his forefinger and thumb through it a couple of times. He looked at the floor for another moment, then up at Tulley.

"Tulley, all this time I thought you'd tried to kill me when were kids. After that day, I wanted to trust you but couldn't. I wanted to be your friend. That's all I ever wanted, actually. But I couldn't do it. All this time ..."

Tulley looked over at his brother. "Yup."

Darby was nearly overwhelmed with emotion, but he had to focus on the problem at hand. "Tulley, if you didn't kill Dad, who did?"

"I don't know. Dad had no enemies. I can't think of anybody who benefits as the result of his death, other than you and me, of course."

"Well, doesn't Martha stand to benefit, indirectly, when you get your share of Dad's estate?"

"I suppose that after I get my share of the inheritance from Dad, Martha will proceed with a divorce. And there will be lots of money for her to get her hands on. But I don't see how Martha could have killed Dad. I'm not saying she wouldn't have done it if she had the opportunity. I've recently gained a new understanding of how evil she is. But how would she have gotten into Dad's room?"

"Did she know where you keep your key to Dad's room?"

"Yes, I guess she did. I never hid it."

"Where do you keep the key, Tulley?"

"To the right of the kitchen door."

"Is the key there now?"

Both men stood and walked the few steps to the kitchen at the back of the house. To the right of the door was a piece of wood with three hooks. There were keys hanging from two hooks.

Tulley stopped in front of the hooks and his hands shot up to his face.

The third hook held no key.

"Oh, Lord! The key to Dad's room is gone! What does this mean? Do you think Martha killed Dad?"

"It appears that either Martha killed Dad or perhaps she gave the key to someone who killed Dad."

Tulley slumped onto the kitchen floor and put his hands on his head. His face registered extreme dismay and his eyes were welling up with tears, reactions Darby had never before witnessed in his brother.

For the first time in Darby's life, Darby felt deep empathy for his brother. He had often considered the idea that his brother had been dealt a rotten hand and that his brother, accordingly, was living a difficult life, but that had been a purely rational thought. He had never felt as he did now. For the first time, Darby felt real compassion for his star-crossed, misfit brother. Despite the unpardonable things his brother had done, Tulley was a fragile soul. Though Tulley almost never displayed most of them, he possessed all the same emotions as everyone else.

Darby saw his brother's humanity. He sat down on the floor next to Tulley and put his left arm around Tulley's shoulders.

"I've been framed!" Tulley exclaimed. "I knew things looked really bad, but I hadn't considered the possibility that someone was setting me up."

Darby thought about the situation, caressing his beard.

"Tulley, I'm not sure you've been framed. Whoever murdered Dad wanted the murder to look like a suicide, and it does look like a suicide. There's a legal principle called the 'Slayer Rule,' that says that a murderer cannot profit from his crime by inheriting from the person he killed. I have a friend in New York, a lawyer, and he told me about this several years ago. The rule says that if a person is convicted of murdering someone, then, for the purposes of that person's estate, the murderer is treated as having already died."

"I see, Darby. And if I'm considered already dead, what happens to Dad's estate?"

"Dad never updated the will he wrote before you were married. If you're dead, then under Dad's will everything goes to me."

"Okay, so maybe I haven't been framed. But shouldn't I be worried that I'm about to be killed by whoever killed Dad so that all of my inheritance will go to Martha?"

"I don't think you need to worry about that until fifteen days after the date of Dad's death."

"What are you talking about, Darby?"

"Didn't Dad give you a copy of his will?"

"Yes. I have it, but I've never read it."

"Has Martha?"

"I don't know. She probably did read it. It's in my desk with my important papers. I knew of no reason to hide it. What are you driving at?"

Darby answered: "When he had it prepared, Dad explained his will to me. On the advice of his lawyer, he put in a provision stating that if either one of us failed to survive him by fifteen days, that person would be treated as if he had died before Dad died and would therefore get nothing. The reason for the provision was to make things as easy as possible if one of us died within a short time of Dad's death, or perhaps in the same tragedy. Such a thing wasn't so very unlikely, given that both of us spent so much time with Dad at sea.

"In that case, instead of Dad's assets passing through two estates, Dad's and the estate of the deceased son, they would only pass through Dad's estate. It would also do away with the problem of figuring out who died first, the son or Dad, in case both bodies were found at the same time."

"But how would it have been fair if Dad had died and I had died and then nothing went from Dad's estate to my wife or son?" Tulley asked.

"Dad told me his lawyer suggested that he get rid of the provision after you got married, but Dad felt that if you and he died around the same time, I would have done the right thing and managed your part of the inheritance for your family."

"Of course you would have, Darby. But what you seem to be suggesting is that after this Saturday, my life really will be in danger, right? Unless Dad died a day later, in which case I'm safe through Sunday, too, as if that makes any difference."

"That seems right. If you are alive through Saturday, or possibly through Sunday, then the fifteen days will be up. Your half of Dad's estate would go to you and then, if you are killed later, it would pass through your estate to Martha. Your murder could be made to look like a second suicide. The story would appear to make sense. Your wife leaves you and takes your son away from you. Then your father commits suicide. Then you are alone on your island. After all that, any man might become suicidal."

"I may have only a few days left to live," said Tulley. "Lucky me."

"Tulley, if we're right about Dad's murderer, you are in no danger through the end of the day on Saturday. After that, you can't stay here. You will have to come to St. Petersburg and stay at my house. Perhaps we'll even get Andrew Beaumont to stay too, for added protection. Will you do that?"

"Yup," said Tulley, his face still reflecting anguish. "Darby, what happens with Dad's estate if *both of us* fail to live for fifteen days after Dad's death?"

"Good question. Dad explained that if you and I both fail to survive for at least fifteen days, then what we would have inherited goes instead to those who inherit his estate under the intestacy law—the law that says what happens when there's no will at all. In Dad's case, without a will and with both of us dead, your son, Christopher would inherit. Martha would be the one controlling that inheritance until Christopher reached the age of eighteen. It certainly wouldn't be what Dad would want."

"No, it wouldn't," said Tulley.

"Listen, a bit earlier you told me that when you and Dad had that dispute at Dad's house that Dad's lodger, the Norwegian one, Olsen, saw you leave the house. Is that right?"

"That's right. It must have been Olsen, though I couldn't swear to it. All I know is that it wasn't the other two lodgers, who are much shorter. I don't know how long he had been there, but I'm sure the guy saw me storm out of the house. He was in the kitchen with his back to me when I went out the front door. He was wearing a large straw hat."

"Don't you suppose Sheriff Kimball would have interviewed Olsen as soon as he had the chance? Wouldn't Kimball have made it a point to interview all of Dad's lodgers before reaching any conclusions?"

"Yes, of course. I think I see where you're going with this."

"If Olsen didn't say anything to Sheriff Kimball about seeing you at the house that day, then he's protecting you. But he shouldn't have any legitimate reason to do that, should he? Olsen had every reason to be in the kitchen when you were there—he lived in the house after all. But if Olsen didn't tell the sheriff that he saw you there too, and if that omission were later discovered, it could be a problem for him.

"But if Olsen is the one who has been having an affair with Martha, and if Olsen killed Dad, Olsen would want to protect you, at least for now. He needed Dad's death to appear to be a suicide, just as it appears to be. You don't get your inheritance if you are convicted of killing Dad, and if you don't get your inheritance, Martha doesn't get anything when she divorces you. Then Olsen doesn't get anything from Martha."

"Then Olsen's our guy! He's the one who was having an affair with Martha! And he's the one who killed Dad!"

"Let's not jump the gun on this. Appearances are often deceiving, as Dad said. But I would say Olsen is our prime suspect at this point."

"Shouldn't we tell all of this to Sheriff Kimball right away?"

"No. Think about it. Did you tell Sheriff Kimball that just before Dad's body was found you were at Egmont Key, and that, while there, you had a big argument with Dad because he refused to give you ten thousand dollars?"

"Of course I didn't say a word to the sheriff about any of that. I may be a lot of things, but stupid isn't one of them."

"Right. I know that. But what evidence do we have right now that we can share? Consider what happens if you go back to the sheriff and say, 'Um, Sheriff Kimball, there's something important I forgot to tell you. I had just had a big fight with my father because he wouldn't give me ten thousand dollars so that I could pay off my wife who has taken my son from me and wants to divorce me. Mr. Olsen saw me leave the house and didn't say anything to you about it, which means he must be the murderer and now you should go arrest him.' How would that play out?"

"I follow your drift, Darby. What can I do?"

"Let me think about this, Tulley. We still have a few days to come up with a plan. Dad's gone. We can't bring him back, but we're going to get through this."

Before Darby left, Darby and Tulley hugged each other, something they had never done previously.

Darby Investigates

Tuesday, July 17, 1900

The sun shone down on the calm, warm waters of Tampa Bay as the *Shooting Star* passed south of Pinellas Point, proceeding west to Egmont Key. Passing by Mullet Key, Darby spotted a pod of dolphins swimming between his boat and the shore. Dolphins always looked happy, Darby thought. People should be more like dolphins.

Just as he'd done eight days earlier, Darby pulled the *Shooting Star* alongside an empty section of the Pilots' pier near the island's southern end. The *Belle* was out making a connection with an incoming steamer, but Darby knew where her usual place at the pier was and he secured his boat elsewhere.

Darby left the pier, pausing when he reached the beach. The water was a gorgeous shade of blue-green, palm trees swayed in the breeze, and a pelican was diving for fish just north of the pier.

Darby missed his father more than words could express. As he took in the extraordinary sights and colors, however, he drew comfort from the knowledge that for the past ten years his father had lived in one of the most beautiful places on earth. He was also grateful that his father had found a second true love.

At the front door of his father's house, he knocked. It felt odd to be knocking, now that Darby was an owner of the house, or would be. Nevertheless, Darby was the epitome of propriety, and this house was still home to others.

Molly soon opened the door. The housekeeper hugged Darby, ushering him inside. Just like his father, Darby treated Molly more like a family member than a paid housekeeper. The captain had taught him that everyone should be treated with respect and kindness.

Molly and Darby went into the kitchen, taking seats at the kitchen table. Molly offered Darby tea and a biscuit, which he gratefully accepted.

"Molly, have you thought about your plans?"

"Yes, I have. The Pilots Association has already found a captain to step into your father's position. He's from Charleston. I met him when he was here for his interview, and he seems a very nice gentleman. I guess the Pilots Association has the right to buy your father's house back from your father's estate. They'll do that, then rent the house to the new captain until everyone is sure that he and Egmont Key are a good fit. After that, he'll be given the option to purchase the house. Anyway, the new captain has asked me to stay on, and I'm more than happy to do that. I love living here."

"I'm so glad to hear that, Molly." Darby let a moment pass. "Has Attorney Beaumont told you what you need to know about Dad's will?"

"Yes, he did that when you were both here recently. Mr. Beaumont told me that your dad left me an annuity. That was unexpected, and very generous of him."

"My father loved you and said that you were always exceptionally kind, though he blamed your talent in the kitchen for his large belly."

Molly chuckled.

Darby continued. "Molly, I was hoping to see Hans Olsen. Is he home?"

"Oh, dear, Darby. I'm afraid you won't be able to see Hans."

"Why not?"

"Hans left Egmont some time ago."

"You mean he left for good?"

"Yes, I'm sorry to say that he has."

"Do you remember how long ago that was?"

"Let me think now." Molly's eyes looked up for a second as she pondered the question. "It was the middle of June."

Darby was astonished, though he did his best not to show it.

"Yes, he boarded a steamer bound for Europe. Signed on as a deckhand. He told me that he wanted to go back to Norway. He had enjoyed his time here, but he really couldn't understand why anybody from Norway would choose to stay in the United States for more than a short time. He said that people here were duped by tales of streets paved in gold, and that life was better in Norway."

"Hold on," said Darby. "Are you sure about the timing—the middle of June?"

"It was June 14, actually. I remember because the day he left happened to be my birthday. He gave me a book of photographs of the world that he'd found in Tampa, and he also gave me a birthday kiss." Molly blushed.

Darby thought back to what Tulley had told him, that he had seen Olsen in the house after arguing with the captain on July 6. Darby's world seemed to turn upside down as he contemplated the implication of Olsen's earlier departure from Egmont Key.

Thanking Molly for a pleasant visit, Darby returned to the *Shooting Star*. He untied his beloved boat from the Pilots' pier, climbed aboard, and steamed away from Egmont Key, heading back toward St. Petersburg.

His brother had lied to him the previous day and he'd believed it! Tulley really did kill their father!

Holy Mackerel! How did he miss the fact that Tulley had been lying? His method of convincing Darby of his innocence was so convoluted and clever! Tulley must have charted the whole thing long before Darby had showed up at Walker's Key. Should he have expected anything less from a master chess player? If Olsen hadn't decided to return to Norway, Darby would still be thinking Olsen was the killer and Tulley was innocent.

Now what was he going to do? He didn't have any real evidence to provide to Sheriff Kimball that proved Tulley killed their dad. Nobody had been present when Tulley went to Egmont Key to do the deed. No witnesses. Perhaps Tulley had even already concocted a story in which Darby appeared to be their father's murderer. Perhaps he laid a trap for Darby!

As the *Shooting Star* rounded Pinellas Point, Darby remained absorbed in his thoughts. If Tulley was so mentally unstable that he could kill the captain, why wouldn't he kill Darby too? Even better, why not arrange it so Darby gets sent away for their dad's murder? Either way, Tulley gets all of the estate.

Darby thought back to his time with Freeman Scott. What had Freeman said about killing? He'd said that to stop evil in its tracks, sometimes killing was necessary.

Darby thought back to Manuel Silva saying Tulley would end up killing someone. Manuel had been right: Captain Walker was dead. Who might be next?

Oh, Lord help him! He had to do it! Darby had no choice. But was he able to do it? Was he strong enough?

Darby remembered another thing Freeman Scott had told him: "Sometimes, when you have no choice, you find that you are able to do things you thought you could never do."

Okay. But Grandma Nick had said: "People who dance have to pay the fiddler." Was Darby ready to be sent away for life, or perhaps hanged? Another memory found its way into Darby's thoughts, something Manuel had said: "You could make it look like a suicide."

A plan was forming in Darby's mind. Darby was going to kill Tulley. It would look like a suicide. As horrific as it was to contemplate, Darby had no choice.

Steaming back to St. Petersburg on this warm, sunny day, Darby shuddered, suddenly cold.

Andrew Investigates

Wednesday, July 18, 1900

Just after sunset, Andrew Beaumont knocked on the front door of Hetty Howes's house on First Street. As on the prior evenings, Hetty greeted him and invited him in. In the large front parlor, he joined Hetty and Darby, who had been playing checkers at a card table.

"My friends," said Andrew, "I have rather important information to share."

"What is it, Andrew?" asked Hetty.

"Today I sailed on the steamer to Egmont Key. Darby, you remember that when you and I were there at the beginning of last week, we found that neither my key nor yours would unlock the door to your father's room."

"Yes, that's right," said Darby. "They didn't work."

"Well, today I tried Hetty's key and Tulley's key," Andrew said.

Darby's right hand touched his beard. "But how did you get Tulley's key, Andrew?"

Hetty answered: "Darby, when you took me to Walker's Key last Friday, I saw Tulley's key hanging on a hook in the kitchen and I grabbed it. I'm sorry for the deception, but we had to find out if Tulley's key worked in the lock at Egmont Key."

"Hmmm. You two could have let me in on the fact that you were investigating my father's death, don't you think?"

Andrew spoke up. "We didn't want to alarm you, Darby, not without having more information. Both Hetty and I wondered from the outset whether Tulley had something to do with your father's death."

"I see," said Darby. "So does that mean I'm not really staying here at Hetty's house because Hetty can't sleep? I'm really here because you think my life is in danger?"

"Yes, Darby, we do think your life may be in danger," said Hetty. "But it's also true your presence has been a comfort to me."

Darby took that in, then turned back to Andrew. "What about these keys? What did you find out?"

"Hetty's key didn't fit the lock," Andrew said. "Just like my key and your key did not, Darby." Andrew paused. "Tulley's key fit the lock."

Even though they'd been braced to hear it, both Darby and Hetty registered surprise.

"Where does that leave us?" asked Hetty. "Is it time for us to go back to Sheriff Kimball and ask him to re-open the case?"

"No, Hetty, not yet. We must not act precipitously. This is evidence, but hardly conclusive, probably not enough to convince the sheriff. It's still possible someone else has a key to the captain's room, or that someone borrowed Tulley's key without him knowing. Let me continue working on this a few more days."

"All right," said Hetty. "Darby, you must promise that you'll stay away from Walker's Key until this is sorted out. Don't put yourself in any situation where you're alone with Tulley."

"Right," said Darby. "Don't worry."

After Andrew said his goodbyes, he once again made his way to Darby's house on Second Street North. Letting himself in, he took up his position on his bedroll behind the sofa.

Like the prior nine nights at Darby's house, nothing unusual happened that night. Perhaps staking out Darby's house had been a waste of time. However, Andrew knew that if anybody wanted to kill Darby before the fifteen-day waiting period under the captain's will expired, there were still three more nights left to do it.

After sunset the next day, Thursday, July 19, he took his place on the bedroll behind the sofa. Andrew was tired and quickly fell asleep, despite the nearly full moon making everything in the house brighter than usual.

Having had an indescribably traumatic childhood, Andrew was not a heavy sleeper. He could sleep through normal noises but would be awakened by other noises that were not supposed to be there. Shortly after midnight, he heard light footsteps on the front porch. Andrew was awake before the knob of the front door slowly turned. As a man entered the house, Andrew watched from his hiding place.

The figure carefully made his way through the parlor and toward the rear of the house. Andrew could see him, but only from the side and back. The man was tall and lean, and wore a baseball cap just like Tulley's. The cap was turned backwards, like Tulley's cap always was. He carried a large knife.

Andrew remained perfectly still. Andrew had Tulley's revolver with him, Hetty having presented it to him the prior week. However, it was not Andrew's intention to confront any intruder right there at Darby's house unless necessary to defend himself. Creating a crime scene at Darby's house would just complicate everything. Better to take care of the problem somewhere else.

The man went through the kitchen and the back bedrooms, clearly searching for Darby. After a while, he reappeared in the doorway between the parlor and the kitchen. This time he was facing forward. Andrew glimpsed the intruder's face and was sure it was Tulley.

After the intruder left, Andrew remained on his bedroll several minutes, dreading what he had to do next.

Murder by Death

Friday, July 20, 1900

Thirty minutes after the sun went down, Andrew Beaumont left his modest home on Third Street South. He headed east down Central Avenue toward the waterfront. Tulley's revolver was in his coat pocket.

He turned right on First Street and continued to Hetty's house. When he knocked on her front door, Hetty swept aside a curtain. After peering out to see Andrew, she rushed to the door and invited him inside.

Hetty and Darby were working on a jigsaw puzzle. Andrew declined their invitation to join them for part of the evening, saying that he'd had a long day.

Instead of going either to his own house or to Darby's house, Andrew headed up First Street to the Electric Pier. The *Pequod* was secured to the pilings just beyond the *Shooting Star*, just where he and Darby had left her.

Andrew carefully climbed down a ladder from the pier and stepped into the cockpit of the sailboat. Then he sat down on the bench seat nearest the pier. He was hoping that sailing a sailboat was one of those skills that you learn once and never forget. He was also hoping that hoisting the sails would involve no complications beyond what he'd encountered on the last sailboat he had sailed, which had also been the *only* sailboat he'd ever sailed.

Andrew had been taught to sail when he was nine years old, back in 1839. That was when he and five other slaves on the Beaumont Plantation outside of Pensacola decided to run away. They'd had the good fortune to meet a kindhearted sailor from Cape Cod who had a sailboat and offered them passage to the Bahama Islands. The sailor had been Nathaniel Walker, father of Captain Kenelm Walker, grandfather of Tulley and Darby.

Three of the slaves, including Andrew, had left Nathaniel behind on a beach west of Key Largo, and then sailed east across miles of open water towards the Bahama Islands. When they were within sight of one of islands, a British ship picked them up and took them to Nassau, where they officially gained their freedom. After being rescued from slavery by Nathaniel Walker, Andrew felt eternal gratitude to him.

Since 1839, Andrew had had no occasion to sail a boat, but his memory of the trip from Pensacola to the Bahama Islands sixty-one years earlier was as clear as if it had happened the prior week. He was able to judge the direction of the wind, which was out of the north, and he was able to determine that the boat was already positioned such that the sails could be raised without anything crashing into the pier. He was able to figure out how to unfurl the mainsail and hoist it up. The jib also worked as he remembered. It took some time, but he was able to identify the necessary moving parts, including the centerboard, rudder, and the sheets used to pull in or let out the sails.

Before too long, the *Pequod* was sailing east toward the far shore of Tampa Bay, Andrew at the tiller. The wind was moderate, and from a favorable direction. No tacking back and forth was necessary. It was as if the conditions on the bay that evening had been created just for Andrew's benefit.

His destination could not possibly have been better marked. He headed straight for the lighthouse at the top of Walker's Key. The beam from the lighthouse flashed in Andrew's direction every ten seconds, impossible to miss. The moon was nearly full.

As the *Pequod* sailed east through the gentle night, Andrew thought about the unlikely path that had brought him to this point. He had met Captain Kenelm Walker in 1884, when seated next to him at dinner at Carleton House in Jacksonville. When Andrew learned that the captain was Nathaniel Walker's son, he was nearly speechless, the chances of such an encounter being impossibly tiny. However, instead of divulging that he'd been rescued from slavery by the captain's father, Andrew allowed no outward showing of his delight in having closed this circle, and he said nothing about it.

Andrew knew that Nathaniel Walker had since died, and he was sure that when he had reconnected with Nathaniel in Harwich many years earlier he had identified himself only as "Dee," which was a shortening of "Drew" and was what he had always been called on the plantation. There appeared to be very little chance that Kenelm Walker would make the connection between Andrew and Kenelm's father if Andrew didn't want him to make it.

Andrew had always felt that it was the best course to say nothing of his real connection to the Walkers. He reasoned that the family might conclude that any kindness he showed them had arisen out of a sense of obligation, probably not recognizing how good it made him feel to repay his debt to Nathaniel. Accordingly, Andrew had never told anyone why he maintained close ties with the captain from the day he met him or why he moved to Tampa Bay when he did, which had been shortly after learning the Walkers would be moving there. In fact, Andrew had been careful throughout his adult life to say nothing to anyone about his true origins. It was nobody's business anyway.

Just as Andrew had never told Hetty what his real connection to the Walkers was, he did not tell her that evening that he was on his way to Walker's Key. Having concluded that Tulley had murdered Captain Walker and was planning to murder Darby as well, Andrew's mission was to stop Tulley. Exactly how to do this remained to be seen.

Andrew's experience as a slave for the first nine years of his life had taught him that there was no limit to how cruel people could be under certain circumstances. The experience had also taught him that it was sometimes necessary to take the most extreme measures to prevail over such cruelty and evil, including taking the life of another. He had personally known a fellow slave who had taken the life of a white man who'd been beating him nearly to death on a regular basis. And of course, he knew of plenty of people who'd taken the lives of those who would have otherwise killed *them* during the Civil War.

As incredibly painful as it would be to do, Andrew was prepared to take Tulley's life if he determined it was the only way to ensure Darby's safety. He had the advantage of possessing Tulley's revolver, loaded with bullets in all of the six chambers, and Andrew didn't think Tulley owned another firearm.

After about an hour and a half, the *Pequod* closed in on the eastern shore. Andrew recalled the time sixty-one years earlier when he, five fellow slaves, and Nathaniel Walker had found refuge from bounty hunters on the tiny island that was now Tulley's home. Perhaps Walker's Key had saved Andrew's life as much as Nathaniel Walker had. Now there was a chance that Tulley, or possibly Andrew, was going to die on the island.

Shortly before entering the channel, Andrew lowered the jib and let out the mainsail. The *Pequod* slowly and noiselessly glided into the channel and up to the boat landing. Nathaniel Walker would have been favorably impressed by Andrew's sailing skills, evidently undiminished by the passage of time.

After securing the *Pequod* not far from Tulley's boat, Andrew stood on the landing's wooden planks, assessing the situation. It was after ten o'clock. No lights were burning inside Tulley's house nor was there any indication that Andrew's arrival had been observed. A bright moon lit up the island, making its white shells glow as the lighthouse cast its rotating beam high above.

Andrew made his way to the beach. Again, he stopped. Still no movement. No noise or indication that he had been observed.

He took Tulley's revolver out of his pocket and walked slowly and quietly up the hill to the house. Rather than further delay the inevitable, Andrew grasped the knob to the front door, only to discover that the door was locked. He stood in front of the door for a full minute, listening for any sound from the house. Eventually, he moved to the window to the left of the front door, trying to open it. That, too, was locked. He stepped off the porch as quietly as he could to try the other windows.

At the kitchen window he pushed up on the lower sash. It responded favorably, sliding upwards. Andrew raised the sash as high as it would go. He put his head in through the window and listened. Nothing.

Though it was darker in the house than outside, there was still plenty of moonlight coming through the windows. Andrew's eyes adjusted to the darkness in the kitchen. Tulley wasn't in the kitchen.

Andrew climbed through the kitchen window. Once inside, he moved toward the front of the house, his right hand gripping Tulley's revolver. Confirming Tulley was not in the parlor, he assumed Tulley was in the main bedroom. Andrew crept to the bedroom door. When a board creaked under his right shoe, Andrew stopped and waited several moments. No response came.

Finally, Andrew reached the bedroom door. With Tulley's revolver pointed forward in his right hand, he quickly opened the door with his left hand.

Andrew saw Tulley Walker's body sitting upright in the chair next to his bed. There was a hole in his forehead. Bits of brain tissue and spots of blood were splashed across the wall behind the chair. The stock of a shotgun was resting on the floor near Tulley's feet, and Tulley's lifeless right hand was still grasping the trigger.

For a moment, Andrew was paralyzed by shock. He sat in a chair by the far wall of the bedroom as his eyes welled with tears. He had feared Tulley's life would come to a premature and unpleasant end, and not necessarily through any fault of Tulley's own. Tulley had been dealt a lousy deck. Many people learn to adapt and overcome the tremendous obstacles which life puts in front of them. Tulley was not one of those people.

Andrew was sure that a breakdown had led Tulley to kill his father. It had led him to try to kill Darby. Unable to find Darby, and being in an insane rage, Tulley must have returned to his island and killed himself.

Andrew sat there in the chair several minutes, considering how to proceed. He finally concluded that he could not report his discovery of Tulley's body. He didn't even want Hetty to know that he'd gone to Walker's Key in the middle of the night to confront Tulley and, potentially, take his life. He felt that it would be too shocking for her to learn that he was contemplating killing someone, even if that someone was a murderer.

If anyone found out that Andrew was at Walker's Key at this point in time, Andrew would surely be charged with Tulley's murder. He thought about how the situation would appear, and whether or not the truth would work as a defense. He'd never heard of the "already dead" defense to a murder charge. "I did go to kill him, but I discovered he was already dead." No.

Andrew thought of an expression he had so often heard the captain say: "Appearances are often deceiving." Well, this was one situation where the appearance could deceive. Based entirely on being at the wrong place at the wrong time, Andrew could hang for a murder he did not commit. Andrew also knew very well that his skin color would be a huge liability in any courtroom in which he was a defendant.

Andrew now had no reason to formally question the conclusion that Captain Walker had taken his own life. Nothing good would come of it. Captain Walker's death was best left alone, with the authorities believing it a suicide. And now that Tulley was dead, Andrew was no longer concerned about Darby's safety.

There was nothing more Andrew could do. He returned to the *Pequod* and sailed back to St. Petersburg.

Back at the Beginning

⊲ ST. PETERSBURG POST ⊳
Double Tragedy Unfolds on Monday
Suicide & Boiler Explosion
Take Lives of Brothers

WEDNESDAY, JULY 25, 1900. Alone, in his modest house at Walker's Key, three miles south of the Little Manatee River, Tulley Walker, keeper of the lighthouse there, pressed the muzzle of his shotgun to his forehead and took his own life.

The body, still erect in a chair, remained undiscovered until Monday, when a party of residents of Gulf City, headed by Deputy Sheriff Ben Mc-Laughlin, found it. The body was in a state of advanced decomposition, indicating that Walker had been dead for several days when found.

Walker was in the government service as the keeper of the lighthouse. He was from Harwich

Port, Massachusetts but had moved with his family to his island ten years ago. Walker was 38 years old.

Walker's family, consisting of his wife and young son, is now in New England where they have been visiting relatives for some time. During their absence, the lightkeeper was alone at his home at Walker's Key.

The light at Walker's Key is of a patent that keeps burning eight days without attention. The residents of Gulf City, which is the nearest settlement to the light, noticed that it had gone out Sunday night. They surmised that Walker had fallen ill, and went to Walker's Key Monday morning to investigate.

Walker had been dead at least three days. Nothing about the house had been disturbed. No one had wandered that way since the tragedy occurred. Deputy Sheriff McLaughlin went to Tampa at once and reported the facts to Sheriff Kimball.

DARBY WALKER KILLED
IN BOILER EXPLOSION

Meanwhile, as the search party from Gulf City was on its way to Walker's Key, Tulley Walker's only brother, Darby Walker, was on his way from St. Petersburg on his steam-powered vessel, the *Shooting Star*, also to investigate why his brother's lighthouse had gone dark.

Shortly before the *Shooting Star* reached Walker's Key, its boiler exploded, instantly killing Darby Walker and destroying the boat. Darby Walker's body has not been recovered. The St. Petersburg Post has learned that Mr. Walker was recently in Tampa for the purpose of acquiring a new pressure release valve for the boiler on his vessel, but he had not yet been able to install it. The new valve was found later in the day in his home.

Darby Walker was also originally from Harwich Port, Massachusetts, and had relocated to St. Petersburg ten years ago. He was the sole proprietor of Walker's Ferry Service, based here in St. Petersburg at the Electric Pier.

Darby Walker was 35 years of age and left no family.

Tulley Walker and Darby Walker were sons of Captain Kenelm Walker, the Tampa Bay ship pilot who took his own life earlier this month at his home on Egmont Key.

The community is in shock as a result of this string of tragedies and is grieving over the loss of the father and his two sons.

Nature's Eldest Law

Six days earlier.
Thursday, July 19, 1900

Lying in the bed in the guest room of Hetty Howes's comfortable home on First Avenue, Darby was wide awake. He had fallen asleep when he had gone to bed, but now he was staring at the ceiling and his mind would not stop racing. The nearly full moon allowed enough light into the room for Darby to see the time on the clock sitting on the dresser. It was shortly before midnight.

Darby had decided that he had no choice. He really did have to kill his deranged and dangerous brother. He had also come up with a plan to make sure that he would never be charged with the crime. Darby had gone to Tampa the prior day to begin to build a foundation for his plan.

Darby's plan meant giving up everyone and everything he knew in St. Petersburg and never coming back. It meant he would not put his business affairs in order, nor tell a single soul where he was going, nor even say goodbye.

He would bring with him nothing more than a small bag with a single change of clothes. He would not be able to withdraw any money from his bank account, though he felt confident he would eventually have access to it. Fortunately, he kept a couple of hundred dollars in cash hidden away for emergencies. There was nothing to like about this plan, especially the part about killing his brother, but Darby had no choice.

He was resolved to kill his brother the next morning, then disappear forever. This would be his last night in St. Petersburg.

After several minutes of lying in his bed, Darby concluded that he wasn't going to fall asleep anytime soon. The nearly full moon certainly wasn't helping. Instead of just staring at the ceiling in the darkness, Darby decided he would go and see his beloved *Shooting Star*. He opened his bedroom door and saw that Hetty's bedroom door was closed. No lights were burning anywhere in the house. Darby dressed, closed the door to his bedroom, and left the house as quietly as he possibly could.

Darby made his way up First Avenue to the Electric Pier and then out the pier to the *Shooting Star*. He walked down the ramp, boarded his beloved vessel, and took a seat on the port bench near the stern. He could look out from the boat and see everything south of the pier. It was an incredibly beautiful night. The air was warm beneath the cloudless sky and there was a pleasant breeze. The nearly full moon was halfway up the eastern sky and its light bounced off the rippling water in a wide swath all the way across the bay. Every ten seconds, the beam from the lighthouse at Walker's Key swept across, briefly illuminating even further the shore at St. Petersburg.

Darby was overcome by sadness as he contemplated the magical, perfect scene and realized that after tomorrow morning he'd never see it again. He'd never again see Hetty, nor Andrew, nor any of his dear friends at Tampa Bay.

Through tears, Darby was gazing at the shoreline between the Rail Pier, to the south, and the Electric Pier. He was absorbed in his mournful reflections as the beam from the Walker's Key lighthouse swept up the shoreline. Gentle waves licked the beach, creating a soft, familiar rhythm.

Suddenly Darby thought he noticed movement, something coming out from under the Rail Pier. The beam illuminated something briefly, then left it in relative darkness. Darby waited a few seconds for the beam to sweep by again, focusing on the spot where something seemed to have moved.

The beam of light swept up the shore. Yes, he saw it again! It was a man in a canoe, paddling toward the shore. Suddenly free from the moon shadows cast by the Rail Pier, the man and the canoe could be seen even without the lighthouse beam.

Darby wondered what in heaven's name anybody would be doing at the waterfront at this hour in a canoe. He continued watching as the canoe reached the shore. The man got out and started pulling the canoe onto the beach. The lighthouse beam was sweeping up the shore. When it illuminated the man this time, Darby saw it was a tall, lean man. In the low light, the man looked like Tulley. He wore a baseball cap, on his head backwards.

The man removed the baseball cap for a moment, shook it out, and placed it back on his head, still backwards but with the bill pointing down a bit lower than it had. During the moment when the hat was in the man's hand, Darby saw the man's long hair tied up into a ponytail at the back of his head. It wasn't Tulley! It was John Powell, that odd, peripatetic, faux Indian of Tampa Bay. But what was John doing in St. Petersburg at this hour? Darby decided he had to find out. He dried his face with a shirtsleeve.

As John pulled his canoe to a spot further up the beach, Darby left the *Shooting Star* and sprinted, light on his toes, to the beginning of the Electric Pier, careful to make sure John was not looking his way. Darby stopped when he reached the shore, crouching to the ground.

John began walking up the beach to the foot of Central Avenue. He crossed First Street then continued walking west on Central Avenue.

Where was he going? Darby followed at a safe distance, pausing and crouching every so often to make doubly sure that John was not looking in his direction.

When John reached the end of the first block of Central Avenue, he turned right on Second Street North. Darby was not far behind, hugging the buildings on the north side of Central Avenue and hiding in the moon shadows.

Darby sprinted to the building at the northeast corner of the intersection of Central Avenue and Second Street North, the building housing the offices of Andrew Beaumont, Esquire, and the office of the *St. Petersburg Post*. As he reached the corner of the building, Darby peered around and saw John on Second Street North, approaching First Avenue North. Darby rounded the corner and continued his pursuit.

Darby, still a safe distance behind John and unnoticed, watched as John passed the Floronton Hotel, a huge wooden structure. He continued walking north on Second Street North.

Darby shortened the distance between them. John Powell had stopped in front of Darby's house.

Darby was aghast. He wasn't sure what John was up to, but something was wrong. Darby advanced until he stood directly in front of the northern end of the Floronton Hotel's front porch, his body closely pressed against the building.

Darby could see John clearly in the moonlight as he lingered in front of Darby's porch. John reached into a jacket pocket and removed a large knife. Moonlight glinted off the blade as John turned it in his hand.

John went up the steps to the porch. Opening the front door, John walked into Darby's house. As soon as John was inside the house, Darby sprinted to his property and found a hiding place behind a large bougainvillea in front of the porch.

It was obvious John had come with the intention of killing Darby. At that moment, it also became clear to Darby that John had killed Captain Walker. Darby realized that Tulley had seen John Powell, not Hans Olsen, inside the captain's house just after Tulley had argued with the captain, just before the captain was murdered.

Darby's mind raced, and then the pieces of the puzzle snapped together. John was having an affair with Tulley's wife.

Darby thought back to the day ten years earlier when John showed up at Walker's Key with the crazy story that if Tulley built his house there, all the Walkers would die. He remembered Martha eyeing John with intense desire. It may well be that Christopher wasn't Tulley's son, just as Tulley feared.

The implications were huge. Darby was overjoyed to realize his brother had not killed their father, and relieved to learn that his brother wasn't trying to kill him.

But, of course, there was John Powell to deal with. John had murdered Darby's father and was inside his house intent on murder again.

Within Darby surged an inner strength new to him, a strength borne of self-preservation and a level of anger Darby had never before felt. Darby was not going to shy away from the task ahead. John Powell was not going to kill Darby. Darby was going to kill John Powell.

John would emerge from the house without having accomplished his mission. Darby waited in his hiding place behind the bougainvillea for several minutes. Then, as expected, Darby heard footsteps on the front porch. John walked down the front steps and turned south on Second Street North.

Darby darted to the garden at the back of his house. He picked up an old, heavy, iron shovel, then returned to the street. Shovel in hand, Darby followed John at a safe distance as John retraced his steps back to the waterfront.

In a few minutes John was back at the shore, bending down at the stern of his canoe preparing to drag it back into the water. Just then, Darby's voice called out softly from behind him.

"Hey, Osceola!" the voice said.

John started to rise as the heavy iron shovel crashed down. "This is for my father," said Darby, just before the blade of the shovel slammed into the back of John's head with a sickening thud, instantly snapping his spine. Those were the last words John ever heard.

Darby felt suddenly unburdened. It was as if a layer of himself, a heavy, disabling layer of impotence and suppressed rage, had fallen away from him forever as he had lowered the shovel. He knew he would never be quite the same person he had been before this moment.

Darby looked down at John's crumpled body and let the shovel fall from his grip. He knelt down beside John's body and felt for a pulse under the jaw. There was none. Darby stood. His hands shot up to his forehead. What have I just done? As soon as he asked the question, the answer came to him. His action had not been one of vengeance. It had been one of self-defense, "nature's eldest law" in the words of John Dryden. He had taken the life of the man who had just tried to kill him, who would surely have tried again, and who would then probably try to kill Tulley. He had done this in order to save himself and his brother. Darby had never thought himself capable of killing another person, even in self-defense. He had underestimated himself. It was just as Freeman had said to him all those years before, "sometimes, when you have no choice, you find that you are able to do things you never thought possible."

Darby realized something else. Andrew and Hetty had saved Darby's life! They had made sure that Darby was staying over at Hetty's house, out of harm's way. Had they not intervened as they did, John Powell's knife would be protruding from Darby's own dead body at this very moment.

But what now? Darby couldn't go to the authorities. He had been the only one watching as John had gone into his house, knife drawn. While there was no doubt about what John had been up to, Darby would be unable to provide any evidence beyond his own account of what he had seen. That would not be enough to prevent him from being convicted of murder.

Darby knew he had to do something with John's body, and fast. After satisfying himself that nobody was around, he dragged John's canoe into the water. Then he dragged John's body to the canoe and hoisted it onto the canoe's gunwale. Next he stepped into the canoe and pulled the body into it. As he stood in the canoe, he saw an old spyglass under the seat at the stern. It looked familiar, so he picked it up and studied it. Just as he thought, it was his grandfather's spyglass. "N W," for Nathaniel Walker, was painted on it. He had last seen the spyglass on a bookshelf in his father's room, which is where his father had always kept it. Darby knew that his father had treasured it more than any other object he possessed, and had decided that he wanted to hang onto it and pass it down in the family, which meant not taking it out on the water. The discovery of the spyglass in John's canoe was independent confirmation that John had been inside his father's room and had been the one who killed him.

Darby paddled the canoe out to the *Shooting Star*, which floated calmly at its place alongside the Electric Pier. Again he made sure that nobody was about. He pulled John's body aboard his boat, and then he pulled John's canoe aboard too. He sat for a few moments thinking about what he would have to do next.

One hour later, Tulley was awakened in his house on Walker's Key by the familiar chugging of the steam engine of the *Shooting Star* as the boat pulled up to his boat landing. He looked out a front window, and in the moonlight Darby stepped off the boat.

Tulley lit a lantern and opened his front door as Darby made his way up the path.

"What the devil are you doing here at this hour? I hope you haven't come to kill me again."

"I need to come in and sit down," said Darby, not acknowledging Tulley's attempt at levity. Tulley beckoned him in, and they took seats in adjacent chairs in the front parlor.

"You don't look like yourself," said Tulley. "What's going on?"

"You're not going to believe what I'm about to tell you," said Darby.

"Okay."

"I have an old, beat-up canoe and a dead body on the *Shooting Star*."

"Good God! Have you gone completely mad?"

"No, Tulley. John Powell is on my boat. He's dead. I killed him. And I have his canoe on the boat too."

"Darby, you're talking nonsense."

Darby understood Tulley's disbelief. After all, Tulley had spent much of his life treating Darby contemptibly without any reciprocation by Darby. Of course Tulley wouldn't believe that Darby could hurt anyone, let alone kill. But over the next few minutes, Darby told Tulley what he had witnessed that evening and what he had done.

"I found this in John's coat after I hit him over the head." Darby pulled a folded piece of paper out of his pocket, handing it to Tulley. An address in Portland, Maine, was written on the paper, along with the words "You must come only between midnight and 4 a.m."

Tulley confirmed the handwriting was Martha's.

"I also found Grandpa Walker's old spyglass in John's canoe. You know, the one that Dad kept on the bookshelf in his room. John must have stolen it from Dad's room when he killed him."

"Right. Dad would certainly never have given that spyglass to anyone outside the family."

Darby had had the whole ride over from St. Petersburg to devise a plan. "Tulley, I think I know what we need to do."

"Okay."

"We know from Martha's note that she and John were conspiring to get Dad's money. John killed Dad, and then he tried to kill me. There is evidence that you were Dad's killer. For one thing, you had the only key that worked in the lock to Dad's room, besides Dad's key which was found in his pocket."

"Hang on. How could anyone possibly know that?"

"It's a long story, but both Hetty and Andrew do know that. Apparently Dad had also hidden a spare key somewhere, but nobody knows where that one is or whether or not it fit the lock. Anyway, Hetty and Andrew are at least partially convinced that you lost your mind and murdered Dad. I imagine that Martha was planning to threaten to accuse you of Dad's murder, after I was dead, unless you turned over your inheritance to her. I'm guessing that she and John carefully planted some other evidence that would implicate you further if it were pointed out to the sheriff. If her effort to blackmail you failed, she could always file for divorce and get at least half of the inheritance that way."

"I see. All that makes sense."

"As long as you and I are still alive, we remain the primary suspects in Dad's murder. We are the ones who stand to inherit his estate. Nobody saw what I saw tonight — John coming to my house to kill me. I don't think either of us can take the chance that we can successfully prove our innocence, or prove that Martha and John are guilty."

"No, I agree."

"In addition to that, even with John out of the picture, we know that Martha is a very dangerous woman. She had John kill Dad. She tried to have me killed. Who knows what she might do if she finds out that John is dead."

"She could just decide to kill me and make my death look like a suicide, like Dad's."

"Right, Tulley. We need Martha to think you're dead."

"Yup," said Tulley.

"As for me, my position will be even more precarious if you're out of the picture. Think of how it would look. Dad's dead. You're dead. I'm still alive and I've inherited all of Dad's money, other than some incidental bequests. If I'm still alive, somebody is going to wonder about all of this, and pretty soon I'll be on trial for murder. Once my own secret is exposed, there's no way a jury would acquit me."

"Yes, you're quite right. So what do we do?"

"I propose we put John's dead body in your house and make him look like you. This death, like Dad's, will appear to be a suicide. We'll do the best we can to make it look that way, anyway."

"Okay," said Tulley.

"We might miss some detail in this deception, but if everyone thinks I'm dead too," Darby continued, "nobody will even consider the possibility I killed anybody or that your *apparent* death was not a suicide. Or if they do briefly wonder if your death was actually a murder, who could they identify as having had any motive to kill you?"

"Nobody other than you would have any motive to kill me," said Tulley. "Not even Martha, since I haven't yet lived long enough to inherit my share of Dad's estate. But, Darby, *you* must appear to die *after* the fifteen-day waiting period in Dad's will or else Dad's entire estate goes to Christopher, which would work out just fine for Martha."

"Yes, that's right," said Darby. "And with Dad gone and you gone, I don't really want to stick around here anymore anyway. I love Florida and I love St. Petersburg, but for a long time I've been thinking it's not really the best place for me."

"I understand, little brother," said Tulley. He had never before called Darby "little brother."

"Do you?"

"I do."

Darby and Tulley looked at each other and Darby knew that Tulley really did understand. "So how are you going to stage *your* death?" Tulley asked.

After Darby explained how he would fake his own death, and after agreeing what they had to do that night and as to the rest of the plan, Darby and Tulley stood and embraced. Tears streamed down Darby's face. Darby loved his brother. He always had, even when he had thought of killing him. And Tulley loved Darby, always had. The distance between them had always been unpleasant for both.

"Now, Tulley, remember, when we're done staging your suicide, you're going to have to say goodbye to Walker's Key. You can't take anything with you. I'm going to leave you in Tampa. You must go directly to the train station and take the first train heading north. Until you reach the destination, speak to nobody other than railway agents, and then only if absolutely necessary."

"Yup," said Tulley.

Darby gave Tulley a note on which he had written the address where Tulley should go. He gave him a second note, which he was to give to Darby's friend at that address. He also gave him a hundred dollars to cover costs.

Tulley located the scissors Martha had always used to cut hair. Darby and Tulley positioned John Powell's head over the stern of the *Shooting Star* and Darby cut John's long hair so it resembled Tulley's. Then the brothers carried John's body up the hill and into the house. They removed John's clothes, which Darby would dispose of in St. Petersburg, replacing them with clothes from Tulley's closet. They positioned John's body in a chair in Tulley's bedroom. Darby placed the barrel of Tulley's rifle beneath John's jaw and pulled the trigger, blowing John's brains out against the wall behind the chair.

Then Darby and Tulley returned to the kitchen, where, with Darby's input, Tulley wrote the following note:

> July 19, 1900. I pray that I may be forgiven for my sudden departure. After my father's suicide, I cannot go on with this life. I will see you again, dear Martha. God bless everyone, especially my dear Christopher.
>
> Tulley Walker

They left the note on the kitchen table. Then, in the bushes on a barrier island south of Walker's Key, they hid John's canoe, a Mason jar containing another hundred dollars, and their grandfather's spyglass.

Tulley made sure there was only enough fuel in the fuel tank serving the Walker's Key light to keep it burning for another two and a half days. That would be enough time to get safely beyond the fifteen-day waiting period under Captain Walker's will, at which point Darby could steam across the bay to check on his brother and appear to die in an explosion of the *Shooting Star*. Tulley locked the doors to his house and exited through the kitchen window, pulling the lower sash closed behind him.

After completing everything they had to do at Walker's Key, Darby and Tulley boarded the *Shooting Star* and steamed up the bay toward Tampa.

"Tulley, there's something I want to tell you," Darby said as the *Shooting Star* headed north through the darkness.

"Okay," said Tulley.

"I almost killed you once when we were kids."

"I know. You got Grandpa's cranberry scoop from the barn, you brought it into my room while I was laying on my bed, and you were thinking of jamming it through my neck."

"How did you know that?!"

"I watched you."

"You mean you weren't asleep?"

"Not asleep, just pretending. A trick I learned from old Freeman Scott. He startled me once when I was trying to steal doughnuts from him on his front porch."

"Right, of course! But then why didn't you jump out of bed and stop me?"

"I knew you wouldn't be able to go through with it. Not then. I wanted to see how far you'd get. You see, Darby, I know a lot more than you think I know. I may not have as much intuition, but I study things."

"Oh! I suppose you do! Well, anyway, I wanted to say I'm sorry for wanting to kill you."

"I know. I forgive you. I'm sorry about everything I did too."

"And I forgive you, Tulley." Darby paused. "I miss Dad so much! And Mother, too." Tears welled up in Darby's eyes. "You're the only family I've got left."

"I know. I miss Mother and Dad too. Life will never be the same."

The *Shooting Star* continued her journey. After a few more minutes, Tulley said, "You know, Darby, it wouldn't have worked."

"What wouldn't have worked?"

"The cranberry scoop. You couldn't have killed me with it."

"What?"

"The teeth aren't sharp enough. A young boy couldn't possibly jam it through another boy's neck. Maybe if you'd got me to fall onto the teeth of the cranberry scoop from a great height, that might have worked."

Darby and Tulley laughed.

"Tulley, I have a question for you."

"Go ahead."

"Andrew Beaumont has always said that he grew up in Philadelphia. I have sometimes wondered if that's the truth. What do you think?"

Tulley looked at Darby. "Andrew isn't from Philadelphia. I thought you must have figured that one out."

"He's from a plantation in Pensacola, isn't he?"

"Yes."

"He was one of the slaves Grandpa rescued all those years ago."

"Yes."

"I wondered if that was true. How did you figure that out, Tulley?"

"Well, it's like this. I'm in Tampa a couple of years ago to sell my oysters. It was an unusually good take that day, so I decide to pick up a newspaper and a sandwich and have a leisurely lunch in the park by City Hall before returning home. I'm sitting against a tree, reading my paper and eating my sandwich, when two men come along and sit on a bench only a few yards away on the other side of the tree. They don't see me, and I don't turn to look at them, but there is no mistaking Andrew's voice. It quickly becomes clear that Andrew and this other fellow, who was perhaps a little older, are talking about their days back on the plantation in Pensacola, and about the time they spent together when they reached the Bahama Islands after Grandpa rescued them. At first I don't believe it, but then I realize it has to be true. And it explains why Andrew has been so eager to save us from disaster, as he has on several occasions."

"My God, Tulley! Why on earth didn't you tell me this when you found it out?"

"Two reasons. For one, I really thought you must have already known. For the other, if you didn't know, I didn't feel that it was my place to reveal Andrew's secret. The last time I tried to expose someone else's secret, as I'm sure you recall, Dad made me understand that I was way out of line."

Darby was extremely surprised, not by the fact that Andrew had been one of the slaves his grandfather had helped
rescue, which he had already suspected, but by the fact that
Tulley had turned into a much more decent person than Darby
had ever thought possible.

"Tulley?"

"What?"

"Once we're away from here, do you think we should let
Andrew know that we're okay? And do you think we should
tell him that his secret is out?"

"Hmmm. I suppose we should," Tulley said. "We should
also let Hetty know what's going on while we're at it. It
doesn't seem fair to keep either of them in the dark. We can
trust them both."

Before long, the *Shooting Star* was approaching Tampa.
Darby piloted the boat to an empty stretch of shoreline just
outside the city. Tulley and Darby hugged each other. Then
Tulley jumped off the bow of the *Shooting Star.*

"See you when I'm dead too," said Darby.

"Yup," said Tulley, turning away and disappearing
up the beach.

Darby was back in St. Petersburg in the bed in Hetty
Howes's guest bedroom before the sky brightened in the east.

Trusts and Estates

July 31, 1900

Central Avenue wasn't busy yet. The shopkeepers and other business people were only just beginning to get ready for the unfolding day. Hetty sat with Andrew in Andrew's office. They were having coffee. A note which had just come to the office sat on Andrew's desk.

"Andrew, I gather that Ken must have told you about the visit by John Powell to Walker's Key when they were building the lighthouse there, and John's ridiculous threat of an Indian curse on the Walkers."

"Yes, he did. He also told me about the striking resemblance between John Powell and Tulley, but I had forgotten that piece of the story. You know, my sources tell me that John Powell actually *was* a descendant of Osceola, but that the great majority of his ancestors were Scottish and John didn't care at all about his Native American heritage."

"My goodness. It's a strange and complicated world. But what about the next to the last sentence in the boys' note, the one thanking the man rescued by their sailing instructor? I assume that Ken was their sailing instructor, but I didn't know that Ken ever rescued you."

"I guess there's no need to keep this secret any longer, Hetty. I had not wanted the Walkers to know the reason for my great interest in their welfare, but it turns out that the boys had somehow figured it out, and it doesn't matter anymore in any case. Ken didn't teach his sons how to sail. It would be fair to say that Ken rescued me a few times over the years, but not in the way the boys mean in their note."

Hetty looked puzzled. "I don't understand. If Ken didn't teach them how to sail, then who did?"

"Ken's father, Nathaniel Walker, taught the boys how to sail."

"All right, but how did Nathaniel Walker ever rescue ... oh, my goodness! You were one of the slaves from Pensacola!"

"Indeed. Now you know the secret of Andrew Beaumont. I guess I'm not as good at keeping secrets as I thought I was. One day I'll tell you the whole unbelievable story, though it sounds like Ken must have shared with you what his father told you about it."

"Yes, Andrew. My word! You do know how to keep a secret, by the way. Ken never told me that you were one of the slaves rescued by his father, and I'm sure he would have told me that if he had known it. He told me you were the most brilliant lawyer he ever met, and that's why he always hired you. I

do want to hear you tell the whole Pensacola story sometime."
She paused. "Say, what happens now with the captain's estate?"

"That's a rather complicated situation. And you probably wouldn't be surprised by this, but the captain's estate is fairly substantial. He purchased several significant parcels of land around Tampa Bay, and they have turned out to be phenomenal investments."

"I'm sure that's true. The captain ran his finances the way he ran his ships, and he was not a big spender. You know, accumulating wealth was never really his goal. He gave away plenty of money to those in need. He did, however, maintain a sense of humor even about his finances. He would often say that one day he was going to be wealthier even than Hetty Howes." Hetty and Andrew chuckled. "But what are these complications, and how do you handle everything that's happened in the last week?"

"Under the captain's will, as you may recall, each son only inherits his share if he survives the captain by a full fifteen days. The earliest the captain could have died was late on the evening of July 6 and the latest he could have died was early on July 7. That means that in order to inherit, each of his sons would have to be alive either at the end of the day on July 21, at the earliest, or at the end of the day on July 22, at the latest.

"Now of course I'm talking only about appearances here. Tulley was not alive at the end of the day on July 21. The body at Walker Key was so badly decomposed when found on July 23 that it must have been dead for at least three days. There is also the note left by Tulley, which is dated July 19. I'm certain that I'll get a death certificate indicating Tulley died before the end of the day on July 21. Tulley, therefore, won't inherit anything, which is to say that Tulley's estate won't inherit anything. That means that nothing passes to his widow Martha.

"Darby, however, was alive on the morning of July 23 when he set off for Walker's Key. You and Will Dyer were witnesses to his departure. Therefore, the captain's estate, other than some incidental bequests, goes to Darby's estate. I have Darby's will. He designated me his executor."

"That makes sense. But what about the fact that Darby's body was never found? Doesn't that make him a missing person, and don't you have to wait seven years before you can get a certificate of death for him, then get Darby's will allowed in court?"

"Not exactly, Hetty. Darby could still be considered a missing person. But the law on this point is different than what most people think. The law is that after a person has been missing seven years, they're presumed to be dead. Prior to the expiration of the seven years, the person is presumed to be living, but that's a rebuttable presumption. I can file a petition in the Probate Court seeking a determination that Darby is dead right now. I'm confident I can get the Probate Court judge to issue a ruling that Darby died when the *Shooting Star* exploded. Nobody has the slightest doubt that this is exactly what happened."

"But what happens to the captain's money once it lands in Darby's estate? What does Darby's will say?"

"Darby's will leaves all his assets to a trust which a lawyer up north created for him. Darby identified that trust and the name and address of the trustee, but never gave me a copy of the document. I asked him if he wanted to tell me how his money would be handled under that trust. He told me that his trustee would have broad latitude, and everything would come out the way it should. He did say he had made generous provisions for both Tulley and Christopher. He felt it was the right thing to do."

"I see. Well who is the trustee of this trust?"

"The trustee is a lawyer in New York, a special friend of Darby's." Hetty glowed upon hearing this. Andrew continued. "His name is Michael Chamberlain. I made some inquiries after Darby gave me this information, and I'm confident that he's reputable and trustworthy. For what it's worth, he's also wealthy. I'll be sending him a letter this week to fill him in and let him know what I have to do in order to probate the captain's will and then Darby's will."

As he answered this question, Andrew glanced at the note that had just come to his office. It had come in an envelope addressed to Mrs. Henrietta Howes Loomis and Andrew Beaumont, Esquire, Central Avenue, St. Petersburg. The envelope had been furnished by Carleton House in Jacksonville, with information about the hotel printed on the outside. Both the address on the envelope and the note itself had been typed. Hetty and Andrew had already read the note carefully.

Appearances are often deceiving.

It was actually the Indian, who now rests peacefully.

His girlfriend, the forger of old letters,
had joined him in a plan.

Thanks to the kind and wonderful lady
who rescued their father

and to the kind and wonderful man
who was rescued by their sailing instructor,

the brothers are free.

As Andrew and Hetty were drinking their coffee and discussing the big news in Andrew's office, the doorbell rang at the Chamberlain home on Park Avenue in New York City. Michael happened to be passing through the foyer, so he answered it himself. When he opened the door, he was overjoyed to see Darby standing in front of him, and his face lit up. "Darby!" Michael exclaimed. "Now, finally, you are home!"

Michael stepped onto the front stoop, swept Darby off his feet and held him tight as he turned in a circle. Tears of joy streamed down their faces.

In the large drawing room of the Chamberlain house, Tulley was playing chess with a woman to whom Michael had recently introduced him.

"Oh, mercy," said the woman. "It looks like you've won again."

"Yup. Checkmate," said Tulley.

A
EPILOGUE
v
Walker Widow's Walk

THE PORTLAND PATRIOT
Widow Commits Suicide

SUNDAY, DECEMBER 9, 1900. A terrible tragedy came to light early on Saturday when the body of Martha Walker, formerly Martha Gould, was found floating in the harbor, face down. It is believed that during the night Widow Walker, 38 years of age, jumped off one of the piers into the frigid water and that death came quickly. Several months ago, around the time of the tragic death of her husband, Tulley Walker, a lighthouse keeper at Tampa Bay, Widow Walker and her young son returned to Portland to take up residence with her parents. Friends say that Widow Walker was managing well until she returned to Tampa Bay to settle her late husband's affairs. Following her return to Portland, she was acting strangely, frequently telling people "They are coming to get me."

When asked who she feared was coming to get her, she declined to provide particulars. It is understood that the extreme despair caused by the loss of her husband caused Widow Walker to become unhinged. No foul play is suspected in her death. The community is saddened by this tragic loss, and hearts go out to her son and to her parents.

CPSIA information can be obtained
at www.ICGtesting.com
Printed in the USA
FSHW010634100519
57977FS